RULE

ABBI COOK

Maddox Rule lives a life most men can only dream of.

Nothing is out of his reach, thanks to his family's wealth and power.

He wields that control with one goal—his pleasure.

But the good life he enjoys comes with strings, and if he wants to keep doing all those things he loves, he has to live up to his family's expectations.

That means taking a wife, even if he doesn't want one.

Not that I have any interest in being shackled to him either.

When the man holding the most of my father's debt, the notoriously cruel Stephen Rule, decides I'd be a perfect wife for his wayward son, I understand the true effect of my father's lifetime of mistakes.

He won't have to pay for them. I will.

Just how I'll have to do that is up to one man. Maddox Rule.

2021 Dark Vine Media LLC

Published in the United States

ISBN: 978-1-7355993-5-9

Cover design by Clarise Tan of C.T. Cover Creations

Contains themes that may upset some readers

CHAPTER ONE

*M*addox

THE MEN SITTING IN FRONT OF ME IN THE FAMILY crypt beneath the Rule estate are supposed to scare the piss out of me. With their black robes and their gold masks that cover every inch of their faces, they're supposed to make me quake in terror at their wrath.

Other people fear God or natural disasters. I'm supposed to fear these seven men.

Then again, I'm a Rule, so that whole fearing these people thing isn't really anything I have to worry about. My family has controlled this group of elite men from all walks of life for generations, so whatever they claim they're going to do to me, since my father is still in power, it won't happen.

That doesn't mean I won't have to pretend for the

sake of the family, though. Always for the family. Everything for the family.

"Maddox Rule, you've been brought here today in front of the senior members of the Order of Impuratus by command of William Pendleton, head of the ancient and great house of Pendleton. He charges that you, and by extension the Rule family, have flouted the edicts of this society and orders that you answer for this," the man at the center of the table says in a low deep voice I recognize belongs to the CEO of the First Bank of New York and a frequent visitor to my father's office.

Before I can perform the necessary formalities of answering for this flouting of the society's edicts, a voice announces his disgust with this whole proceeding. "I once again want to lodge my complaint against this entire meeting. Chair, I demand it be duly noted."

My father sounds angrier than I expected him to be over this whole thing. I guess I shouldn't be surprised. Pendleton is calling into question the very idea that the Rule family should control the Order. There's no way my father wants to give up that level of power.

"It's duly noted," the chair says in that same deep voice as when he spoke to me a minute ago, but this time, I sense a hint of deference.

I know what I'm here to answer for. It's not like this is a surprise meeting. Pendleton called for it two months ago. I just can't believe I have to stand here and answer for the fact that I, Maddox Rule, still haven't produced a child yet.

At the age of twenty-eight.

"Maddox, the charge of the Order of Impuratus is quite clear. Members are to be fruitful and multiply. Yet, here you stand in direct disobedience of that edict. What say you?"

For a moment, I stand silent, my eyes scanning every one of the seven senior members as they sit in front of me. I've heard nearly all my life about these men and what this society means to the world. My father has been the head of the Order since my birth, and his father at my father's birth. Under their control, the Order of Impuratus has grown its power to include not only leaders in business and industry but politics as well. Centuries old, it's meant to keep order in society. To keep its power, it must have new members from the right families.

Families like the Rules.

So my crime, according to the group of masked men in front of me right now, is that I haven't contributed to the growth of the Order by having a child. I have no defense to this other than to admit this is the truth. I have no children.

"I cannot deny that I have no heir as of right now, but I would argue that it's not in direct disobedience to the edict," I say, knowing those are the appropriate words I'm expected to use.

Once again, my father speaks up, still unhappy this meeting was called at all. "My son is only twenty-eight. The texts of the Order give no specific age for a member, especially a member of the family in charge, to produce an heir. I have five sons, and they will each in turn have children who will grow this group. I protest this attack on my firstborn."

Finally, the man responsible for my standing here at all tonight says, "Five sons or one, you have no more potential members to enlarge this fine and esteemed ancient society. My two sons have already produced heirs who will join this group when they are of age. I believe that gives the house of Pendleton the right to control the Order because the house of Rule has not lived up to its responsibilities."

If William Pendleton wasn't a member of the Order of Impuratus, my father would have ordered him killed a long time ago. As it is, I suspect he's struggling to keep his hands from around the old man's neck. So his two sons got their two ugly wives pregnant and now both have sons? It's not like it's difficult to do.

Well, at least the getting someone pregnant part.

"Mr. Pendleton has a point, Mr. Rule," another hooded and masked member in front of me says in a deep voice. "With no heirs, you will have to give up your control here."

I don't recognize the voice of whoever that is, but I'm sure my father does. I see him clench his fists and then relax his fingers in that way he does when he's furious but can't do anything about what's enraging him.

All of this because I haven't gotten some girl knocked up yet.

"Well, I am still in control and while I've followed the guidelines regarding calling this meeting, I can say with confidence I will not be relinquishing control of the Order any time soon. My family has been in power here for as long as any of us can remember. That will not be changing because my son will produce an heir."

The men murmur behind their masks, and of course, Pendleton has the balls to demand a timetable. A few other men join in on the demand, so I listen in surprise to hear my father actually announce a date when it will happen.

"Considering the realities and limits of biology, Maddox must be given at least a year. No less can be required. So until then, the house of Rule will control this Order of Impuratus. I call for this meeting to adjourn."

His friend the banker quickly seconds it, and that's that. I'm left standing there in the center of the room in shock.

My life as I know it is over at the age of twenty-eight.

BY THE TIME I GET UPSTAIRS, I'M FUCKING LIVID. I don't want a kid. I don't need a kid. Fucking old men and their goddamned Order.

Two of my brothers, Julian and Trace, are waiting for me in the hallway outside my room, partly curious about what I just had to deal with and partly eager to bust my ass. What else are brothers for?

"How was the visit to the Villains Club?" Trace

says with a laugh as I storm past them and into my room. "That good?"

I grunt in his direction as he and Julian follow behind me. Taking their places on the bed, they watch me as I pace back and forth, unable to control my anger.

"So what the fuck happened? You look like you could tear through steel you're so pissed," Julian says with a chuckle.

"Where's Helix? I figured he'd be here too."

"He said he had better things to do than hear about the Order. You can regale him with the details when we get to Shane's," Trace explains.

"Probably still pissed about that thing with that girl," I snap, amused for a moment that he could still be angry about that.

Trace chuckles. "You broke the bro code, Maddox. Helix was into her. I'd be sleeping with one eye open if I were you. You know how he is. I'm surprised he hasn't tried to retaliate yet."

I throw my younger brother an irritated glance and roll my eyes. "You snooze you lose. That's what he gets for that brooding bullshit he likes to pull. You want something, you take it. That's all I did. He's got nothing to complain about."

Before Trace can try to come up with another explanation about why Helix should still be pissed at me about some girl, Julian waves him off. "Yeah, yeah. Whatever. We all know how Helix is. Make sure you don't let your guard down. Now let's get to what the old guys of the Villains Club wanted," he says with a laugh.

"Mock all you want. Someday it's going to be your turn."

I know that threat is mostly hollow because the reality is they aren't firstborn sons. Nobody is going to tell them they have to start having kids before they want to. I'll just be expected to keep producing heirs.

The two of them look at one another and then back at me as I continue to pace through my rage. "Our turn for what? It's just a bunch of guys who hold parties and like to stroke their own egos," Trace says, not entirely incorrectly.

The Order's parties are definitely legendary, and if that's all my membership in that damn club was, then I'd be happy. All the booze and women a man can enjoy used to be what I thought they were about.

Until recently.

"Yeah, well now you get to hear about the ugly part of the Order of Impuratus. It seems I need to have a kid."

My brothers sit silently just starting at me, grown men left speechless with one simple sentence. I'm not the only one who can't believe I'm going to be a father soon.

"A kid? Holy fuck! Like you need to have someone give you a baby? What the fuck for?" Julian asks in amazement.

I stop in front of the bed and practically growl out my answer. "To be fruitful and multiply for the fucking Order."

While I return to pacing, they digest the bizarre news that they're going to be uncles and I'm going to be a father soon. No wonder Helix bailed on this little get-together. He probably knew already what the damn Order was going to demand. He and my father are tight like that, so he probably gave him a head's up while neglecting to clue me in to what awaited me.

Someone tell me again how being firstborn in this family does me any fucking good.

Trace leans back against the headboard and folds his arms behind him. "Well, maybe you're looking at this all the wrong way. I think you should consider this carte blanche to fuck as many gorgeous women as you want. They think you should have kids? Have fucking twenty then. If Dad thinks this is okay, let him pay for them. Think of it as a perk of the Villains Club."

As much as I want to be pissed off, his oddly sunny outlook on this might be the way to go. Those assholes want me to give this family and their stupid Order heirs? Fine. Then heirs they'll get, and in the meantime, I'm considering this a license to fuck my brains out.

"I think I'll do just that. It just pisses me off that a bunch of old men I don't even know have some sway in what I do," I say and then take a deep breath. "Remember when we started our own version of the Villains Club in high school?"

Back then, the Rule boys ran that private school our father forced us to attend. We had the choice of all the girls we wanted, to say nothing about drugs and booze.

"Those were the days," Trace says with a shit-eating grin.

"I liked our version a hell of a lot better than these fucks," I grumble, still pissed the Order gets to dictate to me when I have to reproduce.

"Maybe this won't be so bad after all, Maddox. Free reign to fuck doesn't sound so bad to me," Julian says with a chuckle.

That's exactly how I plan to look at this, just as soon as I get over being pissed off. Let the summer of fucking my brains out begin.

THE AIR HANGS HEAVY IN MY FATHER'S OFFICE, A result of his refusal to open a single window in this goddamned room. He insists on keeping it as dark as a tomb and hotter than hell so everyone who walks in feels as uncomfortable as a whore in church after a few minutes.

I know why he does this. He understands what many others don't—manipulating the circumstances of the situation always makes things better for you. The darkness and excessive temperature force people to be off their guard because they're far too focused on their comfort instead of what my father says in their negotiations. They end up signing on the dotted line not being able to read much of what they're agreeing to, but by the time that occurs, all they want to do is escape the sauna of his office to get a breath of fresh air.

He doesn't even bother trying to be subtle about it anymore. Then again, when you're Stephen Rule, you don't have to.

"Maddox, sit down. We have to talk."

I move toward the leather chair in front of his desk knowing what he really means is he has something to say and I need to listen. I understand my role in this little play we perform.

Although I suspect after the meeting of the Order last night I know what he has to say to me, I'm hoping he wants to tell me he doesn't approve of my driving the Jag after drinking or leaving the pool house a disaster after the party two nights ago. My job during one of those lectures is to nod and agree to everything he demands. No more drinking a bottle of whiskey if I want to drive. No more having parties that make him have to deal with an ugly mess.

No problem. I can just drive one of the other cars and party at the guest house. There's always a way around everything. You just have to look for technicalities. I've learned from the best. Fuck, I've seen my father order someone's death based on the tense of a goddamned verb in a contract.

I take my seat as ordered and absentmindedly run my fingers over the brass rivets that travel down over the arms. When I was a boy, those cool metal studs helped me deal with the temperature in here. I always wondered how they could remain so cold to the touch while the rest of the room felt stifling hot.

"Maddox, I think it's time we discussed your future plans," he says flatly in almost a bored tone.

Future plans. At twenty-eight, the only future plans I want to think about are which woman I'm going to have next and where I'm going to party later tonight. Why isn't he bothering one of my brothers with this bullshit? Julian loves to think about all things future. The guy is practically a walking billboard for making plans. Fuck, he'd probably join in with a goddamned spreadsheet to really get the talk rolling.

And Nick could definitely benefit from one of my father's stern talks. The last I checked he was nearly failing out of college. Trace or Helix could always benefit from this talk my father's about to launch into too. Hell, they're nearly my age, so why do I have to deal with this?

The easy answer is because I'm the oldest. Everyone likes to say there's some benefit to being the oldest of five sons, but a lot of damn good it's doing me right now.

I play along, sure my father isn't interested in my next conquest or where the next time I get blasted will be. I know what he wants to hear, even if I don't want to talk about it.

"Well, I've been looking at a biotech company that looks ready to hit it big. I think it could be a good investment, sort of like when you took over that computer giant years ago."

It's actually nothing like that, but he's nothing if not someone who loves to have his ego stroked. I might not look like I give a fuck about business or anything else my father does, but I pay attention. At least enough to bluff my way through these occasional talks he and I have.

In the dim light of the room, I see him nod. "Great, but that's not what I mean and I think you know that. I think it's time you settle down. I have someone in mind who is going to make you a perfect wife, and as you well know, that's an integral part of being a successful man and carrying on the Rule name. It will also quiet Pendleton and anyone else in the Order who's grousing about you not having an heir."

Every word after settle down hits my ears like someone's talking to me underwater. They make little sense but I understand just enough to know I hate every syllable.

Forgetting my place, I choke out, "Wife? As in some woman I'm supposed to marry? I thought the whole thing with the Order was about having a child. Nobody mentioned anything about me getting married."

It sounds far more flippant than I intend it to, but at this moment, my head is spinning from the shock of what my father's planning. I'm not even thirty. My father didn't get married until he was well into his thirties, for Christ's sake. Why does he want to chain me to someone so early in life?

My mouth feels like all the moisture that should be inside it has been sucked out, leaving my tongue like some dried out thing unable to function. I want to tell him there's no way in hell I'm marrying anyone right now. Marriage? I've never even had a girlfriend for more than a few weeks, for fuck's sake.

"Life is not all about getting drunk and sleeping with easy women, Maddox. You have responsibilities as a Rule. You will live up to them."

Nothing in that answer gives me any sense he's not one hundred percent serious about this. Since I have nothing to lose, I clear my throat and ask the only question that I have.

"Do I get any say in who's going to be this wife you insist I have?"

Even in the darkness of the room, I can see the displeasure at my question written all over his face. His eyes narrow and his mouth flattens to an angry straight line.

"As I already mentioned, I have someone in mind. She'll be the perfect wife for you. She's beautiful, and I'm sure when you see her, you'll agree."

At least there's that. Not that I'm the type of man who generally goes for more than a beautiful face and great body, but I've never before had to think of anything permanent in my choice of women.

Before I can ask anything more, he stands from behind his desk and smiles down at me, the shadows against his face making him even more grotesque than this plan of his to marry me off before my time. "Get ready. The wedding will take place at the end of the month."

And so ends our talk.

The clock is now ticking down to the end of my freedom.

illow

MY FATHER STUMBLES IN AT NEARLY MIDNIGHT, knocking over the metal coat tree in the foyer so it crashes to the floor. Our home might be larger than most, but my ears are attuned to the sound of his nightly activities after all this time.

I wait for his routine to begin. Close the door far too loudly. Foolishly tiptoe down the hallway past the stairs making far too much noise not to be heard. Pull out the kitchen chair, scratching the metal legs across the tile.

He completes each of these in the order he does every night, the final action sounding like nails on a chalkboard and ensuring I won't be able to get back to sleep any time soon tonight. Nothing out of the ordinary about that either.

And like every other night, I walk downstairs and find him sitting at the table with his head in his hands. What is it tonight? Has he gambled away the rest of our money? Or has he done some damage with his car and the police will be here at any moment? Or possibly something worse now that I see how distraught he seems as opposed to other nights?

"Can I get you anything, Daddy? How about a glass of water? That might make you feel better."

He shakes his head rapidly and waves away my suggestion but never looks up at me. "No water. I'm fine."

That's not the truth. He's not fine. He hasn't been fine for as long as I can remember. Not since my mother died before I even got the chance to get to know her. That was fifteen years ago.

No, he's anything but fine.

I consider sitting down across from him and asking what's wrong, but there's no point. He's had too much to drink. He won't make much sense and then tomorrow he'll apologize and promise never to do it again.

And then tomorrow around this same time, we'll repeat this little routine like we do every night.

"Okay, Daddy. Don't stay up too late."

I turn to leave, but he says, "Wait, Willow. I have something I need to tell you."

"Okay."

I know what he wants to say. He wants to tell me how much he loves me and how much he misses my mother. It's part of this nightly play he acts out.

When he lowers his hands, I see them shaking. What could be wrong? We've lost nearly everything there is to lose. All we have left is this house.

Oh my God! He gambled away our home.

"Daddy, please tell me you didn't do anything foolish. Please tell me you didn't lose the one thing we have that's all ours," I say as my stomach drops from utter dread.

His faded blue eyes fill with pain as he stares up at me in horror. "No, no. I would never do that, honey. This was your mother's house. I couldn't do that to her memory."

Relief washes over me for the briefest moment before the ever-present dread I live with day in and day out comes rushing back. His shaky hands could just be from drinking too much, but they could be a hint that something else is wrong.

"Then what is it, Daddy? What's happened?" I ask as I sit down next to him and take those trembling hands of his in mine.

He lets out a heavy sigh and shakes his head. "I need you to know I would never hurt you, Willow. I know I've made so many mistakes, but I never meant you any harm. You needed a mother, but I could never bring myself to even think about replacing your mother. Maybe I was wrong. I don't know. Maybe if I had gotten remarried then things would have gone differently. I don't know. So many things have gone wrong for us."

I gently squeeze those trembling old hands of his as he continues to ramble on. "What is it, Daddy? Just tell me and we can deal with it like we've dealt with everything else. Whatever it is, we'll handle it."

Another sigh is followed by a frown that etches itself into his expression and looks like it might never go away. "You deserve to have everything you've ever wanted, honey. I hope you know that. I wish I could have given you all those things."

"I never wanted things, Daddy, so don't worry about that. This is just the alcohol talking. You'll see. In the morning, you'll feel better."

As I push back the chair from the table, exhausted by another emotional night with my father, he says in a low voice, "I didn't have a choice. Please believe me. I didn't."

"Didn't have a choice with what?"

"I know you'll be able to make the best out of this, Willow. You always look on the bright side, so I know you'll do that with this too."

A thousand horrible ideas race through my mind. Is my father sick? Is he dying? What does he mean by all these cryptic statements?

"Daddy, tell me what's going on."

Grasping my hand, he holds on to me like at any minute I'll float away out of reach and he'll lose me forever. His eyes fill with tears, but in them I see he's practically begging me.

But why?

"Willow, you and I are going to be meeting with someone tomorrow. I just need you to understand that you can make this work for you. I know you can."

"Make what work for me? I already have a job, Daddy. What's this about?"

My heart slams into my ribs with each beat as I wait for him to finally explain what he means by all of this. Why won't he just say what's going on?

"Willow, please know I didn't have a choice. He's a powerful man, but they can give you things I never could. Just know that and I know you'll make this work for you."

"Make what work for me?" I scream, finally unable to stay calm any longer.

"Stephen Rule has a son. At the end of the month, you and he will be married."

His words hit me like a slap to my face. Married? I'm not going to marry anyone. I've never met this Stephen Rule person. I've never met his son. Why would he think I would marry him in less than two weeks?

"What are you talking about? I can't marry anyone. Not this month or anytime. How much did you drink tonight? You better go upstairs and get to bed. You're not making any sense."

Once again, I turn to walk away, fed up with the madness of dealing with him tonight, but he jumps up out of his chair and spins me around to face him. I stare at him in shock, stunned that my usually timid father seems so different at this moment.

"Listen to me, Willow! This is the way it has to be. I didn't have a choice. I didn't have the money to pay Rule, and he wouldn't take this house. He saw you at the store and says you'd be perfect for his son. I put him off for the past week, but I can't anymore. When we go to his house tomorrow, you'll meet his son and get to know him. It won't be so bad. He'll give you all the things a girl could want, I'm sure."

"What are you talking about? Are you saying you used me for payment for your goddamned gambling debts? Is that what you're saying? Well, I won't do it. I'm not marrying anyone. You and this man will just have to figure something else out," I say frantically, feeling my sanity slip away as the look on my father's face says he's truly serious about all of this.

"There's nothing else to figure out, honey. You'll meet him tomorrow, and then at the end of the month, the wedding will happen. I'm sorry. I didn't have a choice."

I stare at him in disbelief. There's always a choice. This can't be happening. I'm not marrying some stranger because of my father's mistakes.

A second later, everything around me begins to spin out of control and then there's nothing but blackness as I feel myself fall.

CHAPTER THREE

$\mathcal{M}$addox

MY FATHER SITS ON THE SOFA IN THE FORMAL living room we haven't used since the last time he wanted to impress someone. Whoever the girl's father is, he must be important.

Good looking and wealthy. I guess I could do worse in a wife. Not that I'm not still stunned by this whole damn thing. Stunned and disgusted, that last part courtesy of my brothers, who've spent the last week busting my balls about my impending matrimonial imprisonment every chance they get.

"Fix your tie, Maddox," my father snaps. "It looks like a goddamned clip-on."

I do as he orders and think that's because the last time I had to bother with a fucking Full Windsor knot was for my grandmother's funeral five years ago. I make it a point of not getting dressed up like a pompous ass more often than I absolutely have to.

Helix and Trace chuckle on the other side of the room. Beneath his breath, I hear Trace mumble, "Yeah, straighten your goddamned tie, Maddox."

Turning toward them, I open my mouth to ask why the hell they're here in the first place but don't get the chance before my father begins talking again.

"You're going to like her, I'm sure," he says as he brushes off a stray piece of fuzz from his black suit sleeve. "She'll do quite nicely for you."

Whatever I'm supposed to say to that, I'm not sure. I always understood that the person I ended up marrying would be chosen by my father, so it's not like I ever had any real plans to find my own wife. I just assumed I'd get to enjoy my twenties and lose my freedom when I was older, like he did.

So much for that.

"As long as she understands I don't plan to become some fucking house husband who's always around, I don't care about anything else," I say as the maid appears in the doorway.

"Your guests have arrived, Mr. Rule. Should I bring them here now?" she asks quietly in her usual nervous way, avoiding eye contact with my father.

"Yes, yes," he says with enough irritation to make me take notice. Waving his hand, he adds, "Bring them now."

"So who is this guy? Some bigwig? It's not every day you get tense before a meeting."

My father shoots me a hard glance. "Just keep

your mouth shut and don't mess this up. I fully intend on this young woman being your wife." Looking over at my two brothers, he points at them and snaps, "And one word out of either of you to embarrass this family and I swear to God you'll regret it until the day you die. Where the hell is Julian?"

They both shrug, and Helix answers, "He mentioned something about being late."

"Sometimes I wish I'd had girls," my father says, shaking his head. "Girls are so much easier."

As he complains about having the sons he supposedly always wanted, I silently wonder if my future wife's got some huge inheritance he plans on pilfering. Either that or she has something he wants. For a fleeting moment, I consider the idea that he wants her for himself, but I push that out of my mind without a second thought. If he wanted her, he'd take her for his own. There'd be no need to involve me in this marriage nonsense.

Then again, if all he's really worried about is my having a son to quell the bullshit with the Order, maybe he does plan to have her for himself once she has the wondrous child with me. I'm not sure how I feel about that. I don't want to get married, but worse, I don't want to share a wife with my father.

Suddenly, all of this feels a hundred times worse.

He stands and straightens his own tie just as the maid returns with an older man and a young woman who looks no older than eighteen. Her father doesn't seem wealthy or important, though. His brown suit is clearly cheap and old, and his black shoes are practically falling apart. His graying hair looks like he barely ran a comb through it before he left the house, and that red nose of his says he's likely a drunk. He looks like any other ordinary man who doesn't have a lot going for him.

Why the fuck would I have to marry any daughter of this person?

"Joshua, welcome. Come in and sit down. Introductions are in order," my father says in that fake way that sounds like he's wound too tightly and may snap at any moment.

What I don't understand is why he feels the need to put on a show at all for these two? Is this Joshua guy secretly some multimillionaire who doesn't care about what he looks like? Maybe he's like Howard Hughes. The image of him pissing in bottles and lining them all up along the wall of his living room flashes through my mind.

The man sits down in the chair near the window, uneasily perching himself on the edge, while his daughter remains standing just inside the door. I see my father focus his attention on her and wave her over like he can't wait to get her close to him.

Maybe he does want her for himself.

"Willow, you look as lovely as the first day I saw you a few years ago. Please come in and sit down. Let me introduce my sons Maddox, Trace, and Helix. My other son Nicholas is away in Europe for school and couldn't be here with us today, and my son Julian seems to be running a little late," he explains, practically gritting his teeth by the time he gets to the part about Julian, who is probably avoiding this whole thing since it's so ridiculous.

Everyone turns their focus to me, so I force a smile. Still unsure what's going on, I nod toward her and take my first good look at my future wife. She's beautiful in a girl next door kind of way, even if her father is some weird and eccentric millionaire. Long light brown hair and blue eyes give her a wholesome look, and a quick scan of her body beneath her pale yellow dress tells me she's thin with nice tits. Just as I thought, I could do worse if I have to marry someone.

"What do you think of our home, Willow?" my father asks, surprising me with his question.

"It's very nice," she says in a soft voice, never meeting his gaze.

"We like it, don't we, Maddox?" he continues, dragging me into this conversation that doesn't seem to be going anywhere.

"It's okay, if you like houses you can get lost in," I joke.

My attempt at lightening the mood fails spectacularly, and my father shoots me a threatening look before turning his attention back to Willow and Joshua. "I'm assuming you've explained how things will go, yes?" he asks the awkward older man who nods.

"Yes. She understands."

"Actually, I don't understand at all," she says as soon as her father finishes speaking. "Why am I supposed to marry this person?"

My brothers both laugh, which pisses me off, and

the way she refers to me like I'm some disgusting thing she despises makes me instantly dislike her. I don't give a fuck who her weird father is. No woman talks to me like that.

Before I can tell her how things are going to work between us, my father hurriedly pushes us together and toward the door. "Maddox, why don't you take Willow for a walk around the grounds while her father and I discuss things. Feel free to show her wherever you'd like. Take your time."

The last thing I want to do is spend time with her right now, but he's given me the signal he wants us to go away and I can do whatever I want with her, so I usher her out of the living room into the hall before she can protest. Closing the door behind us, I hold her by the arm and move her toward the door to go outside.

"You're hurting me. Let go of my arm," she whines.

"Stop complaining. We're just going for a walk," I say as I push her out the door onto the patio.

A second later, she takes off across the lawn like a wild animal. I chase after her, confused where she thinks she's going on a fifty acre estate manned by security and guard dogs. She's fast, though, much faster than she looks, so I break into a sprint to catch up to her. When I finally reach her, I grab her arm to stop her running and she spins around to hit me square in the jaw with her fist, stunning me for a moment.

Surprise gives way to anger that surges in me. "Feel like fighting? Okay. Two can play that game."

A second later, I take her to the ground and pin her arms above her head in the grass as I straddle her hips. She fights like a wildcat against me, but I'm much bigger so she doesn't have a chance.

"Get off me! You can't do this!" she wails, amusing me.

"No and yes I can. You know, I hadn't been interested in this whole marriage thing to you, but you're changing my mind," I say, studying her face and liking what I see, even as her blue eyes flash utter rage toward me.

"Well, I don't want to be married to you, so too bad. I'm going to tell my father this isn't happening, so let me up so I can get the hell out of here."

When I don't move because I like the feel of her fighting against my hold on her wrists, she lifts her leg, brushing her knee against my cock. "Careful, Willow. You might catch me off guard for a second, but it won't be for long, and I'll make you pay if you make that mistake."

For a second, her leg doesn't move, and then slowly she lowers it to the ground. Smart girl. If she kneed me in the balls, I couldn't say all this fun we're having now would continue.

"I don't want you. I don't care who you are or who your father is. I won't marry you."

Her eyes flash defiance like I've never seen in a woman. Who is this girl?

"Well, my father seems to want us together, and

even though I'm not really interested in having a wife, you're okay enough, so it's going to happen. Don't worry. I plan on continuing to live my life like I always have, so it's not like you'll see me much."

"Amazing you're not married already with such a charming attitude toward the institution."

"No interest in that institution. I do my job and live a good life. Why my father thinks I need a wife, especially someone like you, I don't know, but I have my marching orders and you have yours. So at the end of the month we'll be married. After that, you'll have one job."

Confused, she stares up at me with innocence in her eyes. Then a delicious idea races through my head. Is that why my father chose her? Is she a virgin? Damn. I haven't had one of those in a long time.

"What job would that be? Scrubbing your toilets?" she snaps with venom.

"No, we have staff for that. Your job is to give me children. I don't really want those either, to be honest, but it's all part of my job."

"So I'm basically just an incubator?"

I lean back away from her and smile. She does have fire in her. I have to give her that. "I promise to do my best at making them fun. How's that?"

Her hands free once more, she slaps me hard on the cheek, sending stinging waves across my skin. "Fuck you! I won't be your whore."

That's a bit too much fire for my taste, so I climb off her and yank her up off the ground. Before she can take off across the lawn again, I toss her over my shoulder and start to head back to the house as she pummels my back with her pathetic fists filled less with fury than air.

"Let me go! I'm a grown woman! You can't just take me against my will."

"That's exactly what I'm going to do if you don't stop all this bitching. We will get married, and I don't think it's going to be at the end of the month either. So buckle up, sweetheart. Today's your big day."

I listen to her alternate between protesting and begging me to let her go, but all of it falls on deaf ears. I never wanted to marry anyone, but if she's the one it has to be, we might as well get on with it. I know my part in all of this. If I want to inherit any of my father's money, then I need to play by his rules for a little while longer. I've established myself in his business as the man he turns to when he needs to convince someone to pay back what they owe him, and now because of the goddamned Order of Impuratus, he's decided it's time for me to marry and have children.

It's the long game I'm playing, and I'm not going to let the inconvenience of Willow Andrews and her insistence on being difficult derail my plans. Someday I'm going to be the owner of Rule Enterprises. If she's part of the price I have to pay to get there, so be it.

Kicking open the living room door, I see my father and Joshua turn to look at me with shock in their wide eyes. I can't imagine why either one would be surprised at how our time together ended up. Willow's father has to know what she's like, and my father has no delusions about how I am with women.

At least he shouldn't since I learned much of what I am with them from him.

"I think the wedding day should be moved up to today. Willow's in a big hurry to get married, as is evidenced by her attempt to run away, so let's get the priest here and get this done."

My declaration is met with silence from the two older men while the woman over my shoulder sobs into my back. Definitely not the way I would have imagined my wedding day, but then again, I never gave it a single thought before my father announced he intended to see me married to Willow just the other day.

Before they can say anything, I smile at my father and say, "I'm going to take my lovely bride upstairs and get her cleaned up. Let me know when Father Anthony gets here."

Willow's father jumps up from his chair and begins to babble about delays and receptions, but my father stops him after only a few seconds. "It's for the best, Joshua. We made a deal, and this is how Maddox wants it to be. I think it's time for you to go."

"But can't I even be here for the ceremony? She's my only child, Stephen."

Behind me, Willow adds to her father's pleading. "Daddy, don't let him do this to me! Stop him, please!"

Like I've seen Stephen Rule do hundreds of times before when he's decided he's done with someone or a situation, he guides a stunned and confused Joshua toward the door and past me into the hallway, all the while explaining how the last thing he wants to do is all that's available to him now. Willow sobs even louder at the sight of her father walking away as I silently congratulate myself on taking charge of the situation.

"Time to get ready, sweetheart," I say with a chuckle while I head toward the stairs.

My father catches me just as I begin to walk up toward the second floor and gives me a stern look. "Father Anthony will be here within the hour. I told him it was an emergency. He'll do it, but he's not going to approve of any of this is she's complaining the entire time. Get her settled. Understand?"

I smile and turn away to head up the stairs. I understand perfectly. Few things upset my father more than being embarrassed in front of people he admires, and while I don't give a fuck about a priest or any religion, my father does. So I have less than an hour to make Willow come around to this.

If I don't, I'll be the one to pay the price.

CHAPTER FOUR

illow

TEARS MAKE SEEING ANYTHING IMPOSSIBLE, SO when this monster who's going to be my husband sets me down on my feet, I take only two steps before I run headlong into the dresser. He laughs like anything that's happened yet is funny, cluing me into how cruel he truly is.

"Always on the move. Can't you just stay in one place for a few minutes?" he asks with a sneer in his voice.

Wiping my eyes, I clear my vision so I can see him. His black hair is pushed off his face, and as much as I hate to admit it, Maddox is stunning compared to every man I've ever met. Dark brown eyes that verge on black stare out at me like he's studying me, as if I'm some kind of specimen he's intrigued by.

My gaze drifts down his body, and although he sat on top of me not ten minutes ago, I just now notice how perfectly his clothes fit him. It's almost obscene how his white dress shirt reveals the toned muscles of his arms and chest. And even though his pants look like the simple black ones I've seen on practically every businessman who's ever come into the store, somehow on him, they look sensual the way they hug his hips and legs.

His hands grab my attention, and I silently wonder how I could have missed how big they are compared to mine. The large, expensive watch he wears only accentuates the size of them and how easily he could crush me with one hand.

My eyes move up to his face again, and I can't help but think this man is the Devil. A beautiful devil who cares nothing about me, even as we prepare to get married in an hour.

"You might not get hurt as much if you stayed put, you know."

"I wouldn't get hurt so much if you didn't throw me down on the ground and then make me cry by sending my father away when I need him most."

Maddox shrugs like my sadness bores him. "I didn't send him away. My father did."

Still, he keeps his focus trained on me. Why? And why on earth would these people want me, of all women, to marry him?

"I think you and your father have made some mistake. I don't know why you think I'm the perfect

32

wife for you, but I'm not. Clearly, you can see that, right?"

That breaks his concentration and he nods like he can't help but admit that truth, at least. "You're going to find that in this family, it's best to just go with whatever my father wants. For now, he wants us married. Soon he'll expect children. After that, my guess is he'll leave us alone, bother my brothers, and then he'll die."

"You don't sound too choked up about that. Not really a lot of love between you two?" I ask as I quickly scan the well-furnished room with things out of my price range, for sure.

"We don't run on love in this family. We run on duty. I have a duty to this family, and I do it. You'll have a duty to this family in about an hour, and you'll do it."

The way he says that sounds so final, so inexorable that my breath hitches in my chest. "And that duty will be to love, honor, and cherish you like the vows say? And give you children?"

My mention of the wedding vows makes him roll his eyes. "Love isn't really part of this, so you can forget that. And take cherish and put it where love goes. Honor and obey, Willow. Those are your duties to me. And the kids, but that falls under obey, as far as I'm concerned."

I bristle at the word obey every time it comes out of his mouth. What makes this person think I'm ever going to obey him?

"And if I don't?"

My defiance makes him narrow his brown eyes, and I instantly sense the mood between us has changed. He takes a step and stops only an inch away from me before dipping his head so we're at the same eye level, his dark eyes staring out at me angrily.

"You will or you'll understand what happens when you disobey me. For example, if you don't behave yourself and act like the doting little wife-to-be in front of the priest when he gets here to perform the ceremony, I'll have your father killed. Hell, I might even do it myself and then show you the evidence when I get home tonight before we get to making that baby you need to give me. Am I making myself clear, Willow?"

His threat against my father makes me feel like someone has my heart in a vice, and I wince at the mere thought of it. Maddox Rule is nothing but a cruel monster.

He shoots his hand out and grabs me by the throat when I don't answer quickly enough. "When you're asked a question, you answer it, Willow. Do you understand what obey means in this family, or do I need to explain it more fully?"

The feel of his fingers gently pressing against the sides of my neck frightens me, but I don't get the sense he wants to hurt me so much as just warn me. The anger in his eyes is real. However, I don't believe the threat against me is, unlike the threat against my father. If it was, he'd be squeezing the air out of me instead of merely holding me by the throat.

Then I realize what's going on. He needs me. Not

for love or happiness, but for whatever his father demands from him, including that child he keeps talking about. Nevertheless, he needs me.

So I answer as I know I must because while he might not want to hurt me, he has no problem hurting or killing my father. "I understand."

Those two simple words lead to my release, and he smiles at my willingness to tell him what he wants to hear. "Very good, Willow. By the way, that's a very pretty name. It suits you."

His ability to switch from cruelty to compliments in the span of a second or two confuses me, but I know I must play my part here or my father will suffer because of my disobedience, so I smile and demurely bow my head. "Thank you. My mother always swore if she had a girl, she'd name her Willow. I don't know anyone with my name, other than a heroine in a book I read once."

For a few moments, he doesn't say anything but finally he shakes his head and asks, "How old are you?"

The question comes out of his mouth with such sharpness that I fear whatever answer I give, truth or not, is going to make him unhappy. "Twenty-one," I say, slightly exaggerating.

Maddox doesn't respond and merely stares at me as I struggle with my little white lie. It doesn't take long feeling the intensity of his searing glare on my face before I confess the truth. "Well, almost. I'll be twenty-one in January."

Seven months from now.

"Are you a virgin? Is that why my father thinks you're so perfect that I have to marry you instead of any of the dozens of women who would kill to be my wife?"

I don't know which question levels me more, but the cumulative effect of the two of them makes me step back from him. "No, I'm not," I answer with pride, although the few men I've slept with aren't anything to boast about.

As for why his father wants him to marry me instead of all those other women he obviously would prefer, I don't bother to hazard a guess. Why Stephen Rule or his son say or do anything baffles me.

My answer seems to make him happy, and he shrugs again like all of this is just something quite usual he's gone through a million times before. "Well, get yourself ready. The wedding will happen soon."

"I don't have any way to get ready," I say as I look around the room for any new clothes to wear and find nothing. "I left my purse in my father's car, so I don't even have anything to fix my makeup, and our delightful time in the grass made my dress all dirty."

He rolls his eyes and storms past me toward the other side of the room. Flinging open a door, he steps into a closet and disappears. I consider the idea of bolting and seeing if I can escape from this house, but my run across the lawn showed me this estate is far too big for me to get very far on foot.

When Maddox reappears, he's holding a hanger with a white mini-dress hanging off it. Marching back to me, he thrusts it in front of my face. "Here you go. My first gift to you. Happy wedding day."

My mouth drops open when I see up close how little fabric there is to this dress. It's practically a scarf!

I shake my head at the mere thought of wearing that thing. "I can't wear that in front of a priest. No way."

None of this seems to bother Maddox. "Fine. Wear the dress you have on. I don't care if it's full of grass stains in the back."

Pulling my dress toward the front of me, I see he's telling the truth. Maybe the priest won't see. Anyway, what does it matter? Maddox is only wearing black pants and a white dress shirt with a tie.

I want to think that, but it does matter. I may not want to get married and I may not like the man I'm forced to get married to, but standing in front of a priest and God in a dirty dress just makes this so much worse.

With a sigh, I take the skimpy dress from his hold and put it up against my body. "This is barely going to cover my ass. I wonder how Father Anthony is going to feel about that."

"I'm going to be concerned if Father Anthony feels anything about seeing your pretty ass, to be honest," Maddox says with a smile. "Try not to make the good father want to break his vows."

He gets a scowl in response to that before I walk into the bathroom to change. The problem is there's no door to give me any privacy. I turn to see him standing in the middle of the bedroom watching my every move. Is he planning on supervising my getting dressed in this ridiculous get-up?

"Why isn't there a door on the bathroom? How am I supposed to get changed?"

Maddox gets a sheepish look. "Long story. Just take off your dress and put the other one on."

I don't know if I want to scream or cry I'm so frustrated with how difficult everything is with this man. Turning my head left and right, I look for some tiny spot in this bathroom where I can get some privacy, but I find nothing. Finally, I see the shower with its frosted glass doors.

That will have to do.

Stepping in, I quickly strip out of my lovely yellow sundress and let it fall to the grey marble tile floor at my feet. With one last disapproving glance, I look at the white dress and step into it, making sure to keep the halter tie in the front. As I pull it up my body, I'm horrified to realize I wasn't exaggerating when I said it would barely cover my ass. Even worse, the dress is cut so low in the front and is backless that I can't wear a bra with it. I remove my bra and let it fall on top of my yellow dress before clasping the halter top behind my neck.

One look down my body when the horrid thing is finally on me and I know this is the worst thing I've ever worn in my life. Who willingly bought this and wore it outside of their home?

I'm not sure I can handle knowing the answer to that right now.

I scoop up my clothes and step out of the shower

to see Maddox standing just outside the bathroom waiting for me. By the way his eyes light up, I know this is definitely not appropriate for what we're about to do.

Or maybe it is. A sham wedding ceremony doesn't deserve a decent and proper wedding gown. Why not wear something so utterly ridiculous to such an occasion?

"Move your clothes so I can see how you look," he orders.

Reluctantly, I don't force this singular issue since I'm going to have to relent anyway. Taking my sundress and bra in my hand, I hold them behind me so he can inspect this travesty of a wedding dress.

"I have to say I thought no one would ever make that dress look as good as it did on Bambi, but I stand corrected. You look incredible, Willow."

"Bambi? Please tell me the person who wore this before me wasn't a stripper named Bambi," I say as I struggle to push down the bile rising in my throat.

He throws his head back in laughter at my plea. "Stripper? No. Bambi wasn't a stripper. Now let's go. The priest is going to be here soon."

Maddox turns to walk away, and I follow him, tossing my dress and bra on the bed. "She wasn't a stripper?"

"Nope," he says without stopping as he heads for the door.

"Hooker? Oh, God. I'm wearing a hooker's dress to my first wedding. A hooker named Bambi. I think I'm going to be sick."

He looks back at me and grins like all of this amuses him. "Bambi wasn't a hooker. She was my prom date. And just for reference, the only other Willow I've ever known was a stripper who could deep throat my cock like a champ, so I'd be careful about the way you look down on other people's names."

I stop dead at the twin horrors of some teenage girl wearing this dress and him associating the name I've always loved with some cheap slut he once knew. God, I hate this and I hate him.

"Now come on, and remember to look like the loving and doting love of my life or your father will pay."

And with that, he strolls out of the bedroom like any of this is okay or normal. It isn't. Not the dress I'm wearing. Not the threatening my father if I don't do as he says and pretend for some priest as I recite the vows of marriage.

Not the fact that I'm marrying a man I just met an hour ago and already hate.

CHAPTER FIVE

*M*addox

By THE TIME MY FATHER GOT THE LICENSE FROM A judge he keeps in his pocket for much graver issues than a quickie marriage and Father Anthony arrived to perform the ceremony, the idea of being married to Willow had grown on me a bit. It's probably due more to how good she looks in that dress that barely covers anything as opposed to her personality, which changes from sulking to sniping every few minutes.

Her most recent bout of nastiness led to my threatening to kill her father even if she behaved herself from that point on. Of course, that made her tear up and look like she might break down at any moment. I can't have that if this is all going to go off smoothly.

Pulling her away from my father and the priest as

they discuss something about witnesses, I whisper, "I didn't mean that. I won't kill him if you behave, okay?"

She wipes under her eyes and looks up at me in a way that makes me regret threatening her. "You promise?"

"I promise. You do what you're supposed to, and I won't touch your father."

"What about anyone else? Promise me if I stand there in front of that priest and pretend I want to marry you that you won't hurt or kill him and you won't have anyone else hurt or kill him."

She sounds like our family's lawyer with all his contingencies and exceptions he insists on including in every contract. "I promise. No one will hurt him or kill him."

"Okay," she says softly, yielding for a brief moment I'm sure won't last for long.

"See? That wasn't so hard. Now let's go stand in front of God and get married."

And as much as I know Willow doesn't want to do that, she does, smiling for Father Anthony and not flinching a bit when I take her hand as we recite our vows in front of him, my father, and the maid standing in as a witness. She performs her part perfectly, even when the priest says I may kiss the bride and I press my lips to hers to seal the deal.

In fact, for as much trouble as she was until we had our little talk, Willow turns out to be as cooperative as I could ask. Maybe this whole marriage thing won't be a huge pain in the ass after all.

When my father and the priest walk away out into the hallway and the maid returns to her job, Willow and I are left alone in the room where we met barely two hours before. As much as I know she hates the dress she had to wear, she looks beautiful. At the same time, though, she looks lost, but I guess that's not surprising.

"You can go anywhere on the estate, Willow. If you like horses, the stables are over the hill a couple hundred yards. Feel free to have the staff help you any way you need. If you're hungry, just tell them what you want and they'll make it for you. If you want to just lay around upstairs, go right ahead. Enjoy the pool. This is your home now."

"Can I leave the estate?"

Shaking my head, I answer her question in the way I know I have to. "No, and if you try, my promise to you about your father will disappear."

Hurt fills her eyes, and she frowns. "Why? I did as you said I had to. I pretended just like you wanted me to. That priest had no idea I wasn't here under my own free will."

"Because this is your home now. If you leave the estate, it will be with me and only me. Try to leave on your own and your father will pay."

"What will you be doing? Do you get to leave this place?"

"Of course. My life will continue as it always has. I told you that. Now make yourself comfortable. This is where you live now."

I leave her standing there as I head out to get to

Shane's in time to join the party that started nearly three hours ago. This whole wedding thing put a crimp in my plans, but at least I'll have time tonight to enjoy myself.

"Wait! Maddox, wait!" Willow calls out, grabbing my arm when she finally catches up with me out in the hall.

Confused, I look down at her, not knowing what she didn't understand about what I said back there. "What? I'm in a hurry, so talk quickly."

"You said I would leave here if I was with you. Can I come along with you now?"

The question sounds so strange to my ears that I shake my head as the words amble through my brain. "No. Why would I do that?"

All the hope in her eyes begins to fade. "Well, because we just got married. It might be nice if we hung out and got to know one another. Maybe this wouldn't be so bad if we could at least be friends."

What a strange thought.

"Why should we be friends? We're married, Willow. My job is to make sure you're taken care of, which is why you have to stay here at all times, and to make it so you have children. I'll get to that later after I come back. I don't need any more friends, and I don't have to get to know you. I told you before. We both have our duties to this family. Right now, that means you obey me and do as I say or I go back on my promise and kill your father."

That hope in her eyes is replaced by tears. "And what does that mean you do now while I'm sitting here in this strange house not knowing anyone and missing the only person in my life I care about?"

"I go out and live my life, just like I said before. Now behave yourself, or you're going to find this is a very difficult life for you."

"What if I want to talk to my father?"

"When I get back, we can discuss that. Do as you're supposed to and you'll want for nothing here, Willow."

She lowers her head and in a sad voice she says, "I want to go home. I don't want to be trapped in this place alone. Don't those count?"

"No."

This time, she doesn't follow after me with more idiotic questions. Good. I don't want to answer any more of them anyway.

I GET TO SHANE'S AND JOIN THE PARTY IN TIME TO miss all the assholes I didn't want to have to deal with tonight anyway. He's sitting out near the pool already fucked up like always, so I take a seat on a chaise lounge next to him and lean back to relax just as the sun dips behind the house. The music is loud, people are having a good time, and I'm back to living my life just as I want to.

"Where the fuck were you? I told you we were getting this party started by four," he says without opening his eyes.

"I had to get married this afternoon, so that tied me

up for a few hours. Don't worry. I'll be where the rest of you fucks are in no time. A few lines and some shots and I'll be good."

For a second, he doesn't say anything, but then what I said filters through his fucked up brain and he sits bolt upright on his chaise lounge. His eyes open wide, revealing the red color from whatever he smoked all afternoon and giving him a squirrely look.

"What did you say?"

With a chuckle, I repeat myself. "I had to get married this afternoon, so that tied me up for a few hours."

"Married? As in dearly beloved, we're gathered here in front of God and way too many relatives you haven't seen in a million years to witness this man and this woman join in holy matrimony marriage?" he asks, still not believing me.

"Yeah. Married. Just like that, except there were no relatives. Just a couple witnesses, Father Anthony, and the two of us."

Shane looks around me like he expects to see my new bride somewhere nearby. Scanning the pool deck, he sees only the people who always attend his parties and then returns his focus to me.

"Married? Like there's a Mrs. Maddox Rule? Where the hell is she?"

"Back at the house. I wasn't going to bring her with me, for fuck's sake. Where's the coke?"

Shane leans forward and gets his face close to mine. "So you got married and she's back at your house and you're here?"

"Yeah. Like I was going to let her tag along? I'm not a fucking babysitter. And you didn't answer my question. Where the fuck is the coke?"

He points to a table a few feet away. "Over there, and now I'm going to need some because you've totally ruined my fucking buzz. So this wife you now have. She's back at the house. Does she have a name? What's she look like? Did we talk about this the other day, or am I totally losing my mind?"

I can't help but laugh at the way he's taking the news of my marriage. "Her name is Willow, and she's pretty nice looking. Not anyone I would have chosen to tie the knot with, but my father had other ideas, and you know how he is. Nice tits, though. I'll give her that. Enough about this whole marriage nonsense. Let's get to having a good time, okay?"

Shane throws his hands up, clearly still flummoxed by my news. "Okay. I'm just trying to process the fact that my best friend got married and never even told me before it happened. I mean, it's not like I wanted to dress up in some suit and be there, but you'd think you would have told me something about it before now."

"I couldn't. My father sprang this on me a couple nights ago, and then things sort of happened pretty fast today. She and I were supposed to get married later this month, but I pulled an executive decision and made it happen today."

"Why?"

For a moment, I'm not sure how to answer that question. Willow wasn't anyone I absolutely needed to have for my own, so it wasn't that. And it isn't that I'm madly in love with her either. That's for damn sure.

"She gave me a hard time, and I think it was mostly because she didn't want it that I made it happen today. Have I answered all of your questions to your satisfaction so now I can get fucked up, or do you have more?"

His mouth drops open, and then he finally says, "I've got about a hundred more, but I guess I'll settle for asking just one. So you married a woman you've never slept with? Am I getting that right?"

"Yep. Never fucked her. Definitely have to since good old Stephen has a permanent hard on about me giving him grandchildren to carry on the family name, but as of this moment, I haven't had sex with her."

Shane collapses against the back of the chaise lounge and shakes his head. "Well blow me over and suck my dick. Maddox Rule off the market. No more a member of the legion of bachelors. I never thought I'd see the day."

My eyes nearly bug out of my head at hearing that. "Whoa, whoa. Settle down with that bullshit. I'm not off the market in any way, and being a bachelor is no different than what I am now. I'm still going to live my life as I always have. This marriage was for my father, not me. I'm still Maddox Rule, and that means if I see something I want, I'm taking it, marriage or no fucking marriage."

"Dude, I want to be you when I grow up, man."

"Just show me to the good stuff and stop busting

my balls, okay? It's been a hell of a day already," I say as I lift myself off the chaise lounge.

Shane follows and continues with his questions, but now they have to do with the usual suspects. "By the way, no other Rules in tow today? I figured I'd get to see Helix or Trace around here somewhere."

I shrug, not sure where my brothers are. "Don't know, don't care. I haven't seen them since the lovely bride was introduced this afternoon. I'm guessing they're off hiding somewhere just in case my father decides everyone over the age of twenty-five suddenly needs to be married. You know him. He gets a bug up his ass and the next thing you know, all hell breaks loose and half the fucking family is married off."

Two snorts later and I'm ready to forget everything about my father and Willow for the rest of the night. Somebody cranks the music up as loud as it can go, and I look around for the hottest girl in the place. I've earned some from a beautiful woman tonight after all I had to deal with this afternoon.

Like a message from God, I hear a sweet voice behind me say, "Hey, Maddox. I thought you might have decided to blow us off tonight when I didn't see you earlier."

Turning around, I see Sheila Northam and silently thank the universe for giving me just what I need. Gorgeous body, a mouth sent from heaven, and easy as the day is fucking long. No muss, no fuss, no having to do much other than whip it out and let her go to town.

I deserve this and so much more, so why not?

"You look good tonight, Sheila. Feel like finding somewhere away from all these people and having a good time?"

She smiles, and I know I'm in. "Lead the way."

This is how life should be. Easy and fun. Not that bullshit my father puts on me with some marriage I don't give a damn about.

CHAPTER SIX

illow

HOURS PASS AND I DON'T SEE A SOUL I KNOW IN this place. Not that I really know anyone, but neither Maddox nor his father or either of his other sons I've met show their faces again after my newly minted husband left me standing there alone in the hallway like some sad orphan child deposited in some strange new home.

What an ass he is!

No wonder, though. Look at his father. What kind of man takes a man's daughter as payment for a debt? Only a cruel and heartless creature, for sure. So it's not surprising that his son is no less vicious.

I walk through the house and marvel at how luxurious it is. No money has been spared on the expensive furniture, rugs, and even the draperies for the enormous windows found in every room. Craning my neck, I look up at where they nearly reach the ceiling. God, they must be fifteen feet high!

This house compared to the home where my father and I live is like a palace and skid row. Correction: lived. Now he lives there and I'm stuck here being some bastard's wife no one pays any attention to.

Maybe I can use that to my advantage.

Hurrying down the hallway toward the kitchen, I see the maid who stood in as a witness at that sham marriage ceremony this afternoon. Maybe she can help me.

"Excuse me, I don't know your name. I'm so sorry. Things were are all happening very fast earlier. I'm Willow."

The woman stares at me like I'm not even there and nods her pale blond head. "Hello, Willow. I'm Emily."

"Hi, Emily. I was wondering if you could help me with something. I want to make a phone call, but I can't find a phone anywhere in this house. I'm assuming I'm just not looking in the right place because every house has a phone, right?"

I punctuate the end of my explanation with a warm smile I hope will encourage her to help me. It's not like I'm asking her to show me the secret passage off this damn estate, for God's sake. I just want to make a simple phone call.

Except for the fact that it's the damn twenty-first century and the last time I saw a landline phone I was about four. It's just that this house is so old that it has to have an old-fashioned phone somewhere.

But my gesture of kindness fails instantly. Her grey eyes look down toward the table where she was folding napkins and she says in a voice barely above a whisper, "Not this house. Mr. Rule is very strict about things like that, so I can't help you."

Mr. Rule has rules about the phone? Is she kidding?

"I don't mean you have to make the call for me. Nothing like that. Just that I want to make a call. You see, I want to tell my father I'm okay. I'm sure he's worried sick about me. He had to leave before the ceremony, but I know he must be dying to hear from me, so if I could just make a quick call, it would be so appreciated. If there isn't a home phone, do you have a cell phone I could use? It would only be a very short call."

Oh, God. I sound like calls cost extra if it's a long call. And having to lie to this woman I don't even know that my father chose to leave before the wedding instead of being forced away makes me feel foolish, but I don't care. I just need to find a way to call him.

Still, I get nowhere with her. She simply shakes her head again, this time faster so a few stray blond hairs get loose from her bun that's tightly knotted at the back of her scalp.

"Please, Emily. Just one phone call," I beg, desperate for someone to be kind here.

A heavy noise behind me in the hallway startles the two of us, and right before I turn around, I see terror fill Emily's eyes. Before I can look back, Stephen Rule's deep voice hits me like a sledgehammer to my chest.

"Come with me, Willow."

It's not an offer but a command I quickly obey, afraid if I don't that he'll tell that son of his I was bad and he'll take out his anger on my father. By the time I reach him in his office, he's already seated behind his desk.

"Sit down, Willow."

The way he says my name is what I imagine God sounds like on your final judgment day. Low and ominous, his tone terrifies me.

I do as ordered, once again, and sink into the leather chair in front of his desk. He doesn't say a word for nearly a minute, enough time for me to notice how dark this room is and how oppressively hot he keeps it in here. After a hot June day, his office has no windows open and no air conditioning, so it feels like a steam room.

"Why were you talking to the maid? Did you need something and she wasn't obliging?" he asks, instantly making me regret bothering Emily.

"No, no. Not at all. She was wonderful. She's a very nice person. I was just chatting with her because I was lonely. That's all."

"So my son has left you here by yourself, has he? Did he say when he'd be back?"

I shake my head, although I'm not certain in the dim light he can see that, so I answer, "No, he just left and said I had to stay here."

Stephen makes a grumbling noise I suspect is a signal he isn't happy with Maddox for leaving me here. Or maybe he's unhappy because we aren't busy upstairs making that baby he so desperately wants, if his son is to be believed.

"So what did you say to Emily that she refused to help you with then?"

The way he switches from topic to topic unnerves me, and I can't think of a good enough lie to offer him. Left with no choice, I decide to tell the truth.

"I wanted her help to find a phone to call my father. I'm sure he's worried sick about me, and I just wanted to call and let him know I'm okay."

My hands grip the arms of the chair as I brace myself for an explosion of anger from him. I don't understand his restrictions on using the phone, but from the way Emily responded to my request to make a call, I expect him to be angry with me.

He says nothing, and I hold my breath as I wait for the ugly response I'm sure is coming my way. The room grows more stifling as the seconds tick by, and although I know it's not possible, the walls feel like they're closing in around me.

In the dim light, I see his large hand push something black toward me. I let the air out of my lungs in a rush when I realize it's an office phone that's likely been on his desk the whole time we've been sitting here.

"You may use this phone this time. Don't ever try to use this phone unless I say you can. If you do, you'll regret it, and not because of what my son will do to you but what I will. Understand?"

I can't see his face, but I'm sure the sinister sound of his voice is reflected in his expression. My hands shaking, I reach for the phone and answer him. "I understand, Mr. Rule."

"Stephen. We're family now, Willow," he says in a slightly softer tone.

"I understand, Stephen. Thank you for letting me call my father. It means the world to me that he knows I'm okay."

My appreciation is met with silence, so I quickly dial the number and let out a sigh of relief when my father's cell begins to ring. Never before in my life have I been so happy to hear that sound. For as cruel as both Rule men have been, I wasn't sure his offer wouldn't be followed by a dead line and the sound of maniacal laughter at my disappointment filling the room.

Then I hear my father's voice and I have to force myself to not cry. "Hello?"

"Daddy, it's Willow."

"Willow? Are you okay? I didn't want to leave before…"

He doesn't finish his sentence, but I know what he means. "It's okay, Daddy. I just wanted you to know I'm safe and I'm going to be fine. You don't have to worry, okay?"

"I'm so sorry, honey. I thought we had more time. He said the end of the month. I didn't think it would happen so soon," my father says with so much regret in his voice I can barely stand it.

A quick glance over toward Stephen tells me he can hear every word my father utters, so I quickly say, "Stephen has been nice enough to let me use the phone. He's right here, and I'm so thankful he allowed me to call you to let you know it's all going to be okay, Daddy."

My father understands my meaning and changes the subject. "Do you need any clothes or anything? I can bring them over, if that's allowed."

Before I can say another word, Stephen rips the phone from my hand and hangs up the call. Crushed, I fall back onto the leather chair behind me.

"You didn't have to hang up on him. I was going to say he didn't have to come here. I understand how this works. Maddox explained everything to me. I never even got to say goodbye or tell him I love him."

"Go to your room and stay there, Willow."

I want to protest. To tell him I'm not a fucking child who needs to be in bed by eight o'clock at night. That I followed all his rules and his son's rules and still he ruined the single thing that I asked for today. I want to say all of that, but I know there's no use, so I run out of that stifling hot room and down the hall toward the stairs that will take me back to my new prison cell.

When I reach that room I already have begun to hate with a passion, I throw myself on the bed and bury my head in the pillow. This time, I can't stop the tears from flowing, and I don't want to. Let them come. Let them soak this pillow and flood this room and drown this fucking house filled with cruelty.

I don't know how long I let myself cry, but by the time I'm finished, I'm exhausted. Maybe if I sleep I can forget the nightmare my life has become.

THE BED SHIFTING BENEATH ME ROUSES ME FROM my sleep, and in the dim light of the room, I see Maddox sitting beside me. Barely awake, I smell liquor and something sweet wafting off him.

Closing my eyes, I curl my arms in tightly against my body and pretend to be asleep. I want to roll over so my back's to him, but if I do, he might notice me. I want to be invisible to him.

Invisible to every soul in this wretched place.

"I know you're awake, Willow. You're not very good at pretending."

He gets silence in response to whatever he's trying to do. I hold my breath and silently pray to God he'll just leave me alone. I don't want to even share this bed with him, but what choice do I have? Every time I even attempt to cross him, he threatens my father's life.

God, please don't make me sleep with him to save the only family I have left in the world.

"Don't worry. I don't want you tonight. I'm too fucked up. Tomorrow night maybe," he says, slurring the last few words.

Relief washes over me at hearing that, and I slowly exhale, still trying to be as silent as possible. I've spent every night for as long as I can remember dealing with a drunk man interrupting my sleep. This I can handle. Too drunk for much of anything other than some mindless chatter, he'll fall asleep in a few minutes, and then I'll be able to roll over and turn my back to him.

The first touch of his hand on me makes every inch of my body turn stiff. His palm rests against my shoulder, warming my skin. He'll drift off soon. He's too drunk to stay awake for long.

"So what did little Willow do tonight while I was out?" he asks, covering my face with his drunken breath.

Even with my eyes closed, I feel him too close to me. I lay there, playing possum for so long that I'm sure he's asleep, but when I open my eyes, I see him illuminated by the moonlight coming through the window and he's staring at me.

"You didn't answer my question, Willow. What did you do tonight while I was gone?" he asks again, but this time his tone is far more pointed.

I stare into his dark eyes and wonder what answer he's looking for. I didn't do anything wrong. All I did was lay here crying for hours before I fell asleep. I didn't even walk outside all night.

So why does he sound angry?

Unsure what to say, I remain silent and hope sleep will overtake him. That doesn't happen, though. Somehow in the few minutes that I ignored him, he's sobered up.

"How about I tell you what you did? You bothered the maid to let you call your father, and when my

59

father found out, you called from his office phone. Sound about right?"

Why would he be angry about any of that? Maybe the maid part, but why his father letting me make a phone call?

For the first time, I answer his questions, hopeful he'll understand I meant no harm. "I just wanted to let my father know I'm okay. It wasn't anything important, and your father seemed fine with it. He even invited me to his office and let me use the phone there."

Maddox grabs my hair at the top of my head, surprising me, and tears immediately fill my eyes as pain courses across my scalp. Tightening his fist, he twists the strands until I cry out in pain.

"You're hurting me!"

"What did I tell you before I left about calling your father?" he barks in my ear.

I frantically try to remember what he said, but I can't because the pain he's causing me is making even trying to think next to impossible. He definitely didn't say I could, but what exactly did he mention all those hours ago?

"Stop, please!" I sob as I try to pull his hand out of my hair. "I can't remember. Please stop hurting me, Maddox."

"I told you we'd discuss it when I came back here. Why did you deal with my father instead of waiting for me?"

"I didn't mean to. I just wanted to tell my father I

was okay. It wasn't anything. I swear. Please, Maddox!"

For whatever reason, that makes him let go of my hair. I quickly move as far away from him as I can and still be on the bed, afraid of what he'll do next.

"Where are you going, little Willow? Are you scared of me?" he asks, taunting me.

This time, I don't bother wondering what I should say and simply roll over so I don't have to look at him. If he's going to hurt me, it won't help one bit if I have to watch him do it.

But he doesn't continue to speak, thankfully, and in the silence, I begin to drift off. Just as I'm about to fall asleep, he presses his body to mine and slides his hand around my waist to hold me to him. He's naked behind me, and I feel he's hard.

"On my first night of being married, do you know what I did? I got a blowjob from one girl and fucked another. So you see, nothing new. And tomorrow night, I'll have you and whoever else I want because I can."

I want to say he can have whoever the fuck he wants and no matter what he does with me, he'll never truly have me as one of his women. I don't, though. I know better.

I've known Maddox Rule for less than twenty-four hours and I know better already.

I'm not the stupid little Willow he thinks I am.

CHAPTER SEVEN

*M*addox

SEVEN-THIRTY A.M. ISN'T THE PERFECT TIME FOR anything, despite what my father seems to think. So far this morning, I've woken up next to a woman who seems well on her way to hating my guts, if the look in her blue eyes that she wants me dead is any indication, and then been summoned angrily down to this office for some early torture to start my day.

If this is the way my married life is going to be, no wonder I never wanted to give up bachelorhood. Who could blame me?

So now I'm sitting in that leather chair in front of his desk, the one with the brass studs I can't stop running my fingers over. I've been in this sweltering hot room for over ten minutes and already understand more than ever before why people willingly sign their lives away to Stephen Rule after being subjected to this place. At this rate, if he orders me to clone angry Willow and marry her ten times over, I'll likely jump at the chance.

Anything to get the fuck out of this room.

The memory of my talking to her last night after I came home from Shane's party makes me wish I hadn't said some of those things I said. Not that I lied or anything, but maybe I could have committed the sin of omission and just not told her about those girls.

But the second that hint of guilt starts to press down on me, I push it away. Fuck that. I never wanted to marry her or anyone else. This marriage bullshit was all my father's idea. All I want to do is live my life, do my job, and have some fun after. Is that so much to fucking ask?

The man himself saunters into his office while I'm in mid-mental rage about being saddled with a wife I barely know and who might want to kill me in my sleep. Looking cool and refreshed since he hasn't spent the last fifteen minutes melting in here, he sits down behind his desk and lets out a heavy sigh.

Life must be so tough for him.

"So how did the first night of wedded bliss go?" he asks far too seriously for his choice of words.

Wedded bliss. Not exactly.

I look across the desk at him bathed in the warm light of the early morning sun and wonder how truthful I should be about last night. I could lie, but I know Stephen Rule. He'll make sure to get Willow to talk about what happened between us last night and find out the truth.

Better to just come out with it. If he doesn't like it, too bad. Maybe he should have consulted the groom before insisting on his shotgun wedding.

"Well, I'm not sure that's the right term for it. I notice you're letting some light in here this morning."

I know how much he hates when I spoon-feed him information. I'm risking him flying into a rage, but I'm not inclined to make his life easy after being forced out of bed for this meeting after only a couple hours of sleep.

He narrows his eyes to an angry squint and lets out another sigh, this one full of far more irritation. "Perhaps you didn't understand the question, Maddox. Let me rephrase it to make myself perfectly clear. Did you and your new wife have sex last night to consummate your marriage?"

Every word comes out like he's carefully deliberating on the exact one that will get his point across in the most effective way. He could have asked if I fucked her like he's asked about countless females he's heard I slept with in the past. Why he wants to make the act of sex sound so important now is beyond me.

With a chuckle at how ridiculous all of this morning interrogation is, I answer, "I got home from Shane's late and too drunk to do anything. For her part, Willow did her best impression of a dead body, so no, we did not consummate the marriage."

My father leans forward and glares at me. "Do you

think this is funny? Willow Rule is your wife, and you're legally bound to her. You have an obligation to perform your duties for her just as you have an obligation to this family. You don't have to have a dozen children. Just one son. It's all your mother had to do, although she excelled beyond what was asked of her with you and your brother, as did Helix's mother, and Julian and Nicholas's mother. It's all Willow has to do, but she can't do it alone."

The way he says that, like I'm not into having sex with women and he has to convince me to fuck someone, makes it hard not to laugh. Since I know he'll likely blow a gasket if I even show a hint of amusement right now, I solemnly nod like I know I'm supposed to and pretend that I care about all of this a fraction as much as he does.

"It was just the first night. Give her a chance," I say, happy to put off the lost opportunity of last night on her.

"I'm not worried about her. She's here and will stay here. She's not going out and getting dead drunk before coming home far too late. She's a female who will do as she must, which is sleep with you if you make an effort. So make the fucking effort or find out what happens if you don't, Maddox."

For a moment, I forget my place in Stephen Rule's world and ask, "What is it with this girl? Why are you so sure she's the one who should give the family that first male heir you insist we need? She's pretty, I guess, but there are more beautiful women out there. Trust me, I know them. And they'd give their soul for me to ask them to marry me. They wouldn't fight me on a thing. They would happily keep all our family's secrets and fit perfectly into all we do. Instead, you force me to marry Willow Andrews, who clearly isn't wealthy by any stretch of the imagination, who never wanted to marry me—hell, she didn't even know I existed on the planet until yesterday—and who wouldn't have a problem dropping the dime on all we do in a heartbeat. I just don't understand why this girl."

By the time the last word leaves my mouth, I'm sure I've just ensured myself a level of rage from my father that I've never seen in my life. I let myself get too curious, and now he'll make me pay.

I lean back in my chair, putting as much room as humanly possible between him and me to give me one or two precious seconds to react before he lets loose his anger. For his part, he seems confused at first by my questioning him about Willow, but then instead of unleashing rage on me like he's always done in the past when I forget my place, he nods once and then twice and actually answers me.

"Her name is Willow Rule. You'd do well to remember that because she's going to be your wife for the foreseeable future. Katia says you two will be very happy together, and I believe her. She also says you'll have as many children as you want."

Fucking Katia. My father's psychic who somehow has him wrapped around her little finger. That he actually believes that shit makes me wonder if he's not already well on his way to being out of his mind.

"And yes, I guess there are more beautiful women in the world I could have had you marry, but beauty has an expiration date on it that's far earlier than you expect at the age of twenty-eight. While she may not be some beauty queen, Willow is smart. You don't understand it now, but when you're sitting in this chair dealing with people as I do every day, intelligence is priceless. Someday, you'll be in charge of this family and Rule Enterprises, and while doctors can make a woman look whatever way you choose, they can never make a dumb woman smart. If I thought any of those women you like to spend your time drinking, snorting, and fucking with would have served this family better, I would have chosen one of them. Willow may seem lacking in some areas, but trust me, she's not in the areas that are important to men like us."

As usual, he's told me only as much as he thinks I need to know about why he chose her over a plethora of women I would have preferred, but I get the sense that there are other reasons he's not sharing why he believes Willow deserved to be made a Rule.

Not that he'll ever tell me. Only if it serves his purposes, which at the moment, it doesn't. So I'll have to be content with the fact that he thinks she's smart and can give me the son he believes I need to carry on the Rule name and fulfill my responsibility to the Order of Impuratus.

Except I don't give a fuck about any of it. Not her. Not having a son. Not the Rule family name. And definitely not the fucking Order.

None of it. I never have. I'm forced to pretend I do

to avoid having my life turn into one constant battle with him, but I truly don't care about any of it.

I simply had the misfortune of being the firstborn son.

"I think you might have to use a different approach with this girl. She's not the usual kind I've noticed you associate with."

"She isn't my biggest fan, Dad. She blames me for being forced to marry me, and let's just say I didn't make things any better last night."

"Well, try showing her you're not the world's biggest asshole. See how that works. I'm not saying you have to coddle her, but as with most things in this world, anything easier to deal with is going to make your life better."

"Happy wife means a happy life?" I ask, sure I'm not understanding him correctly.

My father has never been the doting husband kind. Maybe if he was my mother would still be alive. Or any of my brothers' mothers would still be around.

For one of the rare times in my life, he lets out a full laugh, the kind that comes from deep inside the belly and is genuine and real. "See? I knew you had a better sense of humor than I usually see. No, that's not what I mean, necessarily. Her happiness can't be your primary concern, but you can make it seem like it is. Understand?"

"I got it. Okay, I'll see what I can do," I say, realizing as with everything else in Stephen Rule's life, this problem can be handled not with truth or honesty but with manipulation.

He wants me to make Willow think I give a damn about her being happy to get her to behave. It's what he did with me and my brothers the whole time we were growing up, and it's what he thinks will work on her.

My father really has only one go-to play. Manipulate to get your own way, and if that doesn't work, use force. It's been the story of our relationship, and it's how he's risen to the level of power in the world that gives him billions of dollars and control over all he touches.

People do as he wants because they either think they want the same thing or they're intimidated. Those are Willow's choices now too, except she gets to deal with me.

She should consider herself lucky. Unlike my father, I haven't had any women killed because they disobeyed me.

Yet.

CHAPTER EIGHT

illow

THIS HOUSE IS A PRISON. A BEAUTIFUL, LUXURIOUS cage I'm forced to stay in. I suspect there are many women who would love to be stuck here as Maddox Rule's wife. They would appreciate the household staff who clean the rooms, make the beds, cook the meals, and wait on us hand and foot. They'd be head over heels in love with the horses and stables, gorgeous grounds and gardens, Olympic-sized swimming pool, and amenities found only at the best five-star hotels in the world.

And if I even liked the man I'm married to, I might think all of those things made being forced to stay here tolerable. But I don't like him.

Seated outside in the warm June sun, I close my eyes and try not to let my growing hate for my husband fill me. Grasping at anything to find some sense of happiness, I silently thank God it's at least nice out so I don't have to be cooped up inside.

It's been seven days since Maddox and his father shanghaied me into becoming Mrs. Maddox Rule and trapped me in this gilded cage. In that time, he's rubbed it in my face that I'm the last woman on the planet he would ever want on our wedding night, tried to sweet talk me into believing he's a nice guy on night two of our marriage, and after that didn't work, mostly ignored me while he spends his time doing whatever he does for a job during the day and partying away from this estate at night.

I've never gotten to speak to my father since that one time I was able to call him to let him know I'm okay. I imagine him shuffling around that old house of ours looking at all my belongings and wondering if I'm safe here. He knows the truth. Whatever he tells himself, he knows.

I should be angry with my father for being the reason I'm trapped here, but I can't bring myself to feel that because I know he can't help himself. Losing my mother sent his world into a tailspin, one he's never recovered from. She was his guiding light, his north star, and when he lost her, he lost his way. I don't blame him for not knowing how to keep living once she was gone. I don't even blame him for knowing that his drinking and gambling would hurt me someday. He's my father. I can't blame him for what's happened to me, even if it is his fault.

Maddox and his father, however, I can and do

blame. Both villains in this little play I'm forced to act in, they don't suffer from all my father does. Whatever happened to Maddox's mother, I have the distinct impression by the way the staff talks about her that she suffered as much as my father does and found no kindness or help from her husband or sons.

The staff also whispers about two other women, but I can't figure out who they are or what happened to them. All I've found out so far is they vanished from this house like Maddox's mother. Mostly, the staff just complains about Maddox and his brothers, something I wouldn't mind joining them in.

The fact that there are five Rule sons fills me with dread as much as wonder, to be honest. I haven't met the youngest, who I'm told is away at school. Lucky him. The others I see around the house, but they mostly look at me like I'm some kind of oddity you might see in a museum or a zoo of strange animals. On a couple occasions, Helix has popped into the dining room for dinner and given me a smile, but Julian not only says nothing to me but seems to not even notice my existence much. And Trace, well, he's not as standoffish as his brothers but it feels like any time we've talked, he's kept me at an arm's length.

Almost as if he's been told not to be nice to me.

Emily doesn't like to tell me much, but since I've made myself a nuisance by being around her so much in the past week, I have gotten her to tell me something about the family I've been forced to join. Whenever she mentions Victoria Rule, it's always with words like "the long-suffering" or "poor thing." Then her thoughts trail off, leading me to believe that the former woman of this house lived a miserable life and died young.

Of course, not until she did her duty to that wretched husband of hers and popped out the required heirs.

At first I thought she may have killed herself, something I could certainly understand if she was forced to live as I am, but something Emily mentioned about her becoming suddenly sick and then passing shortly after makes me wonder if she didn't come to her untimely end courtesy of her husband. Emily's description of how Stephen Rule took his wife's death included little more than he attended the funeral and then returned home to remove every last stitch of evidence that she'd ever resided in this house.

After knowing him for only a single week, I have a hard time not believing at the very least he didn't care for his wife and at the worst killed her. Is that my fate too now that I'm married to his oldest son? Did Victoria Rule do the one thing she had to—deliver sons so there was an heir and a handful of spares to carry on the family name—and because of that became expendable?

I open my eyes at the sound of footsteps approaching where I sit on the patio outside the living room. Dread fills me as I look around for any sign of another human being. All I want at this moment is to enjoy this beautiful late spring day. If I have to be trapped here, at least let me enjoy one tiny sliver of my existence.

But my wish goes unfulfilled when I see my father-in-law slowly making his way toward me. Unlike his sons, Stephen seems intensely interested in nearly everything I do. I sense him watching me wherever I'm in the house and even outside now. He says little to me, thankfully, but he seems to be always nearby keeping an eye on all I do. Only when he has visitors to the house is he occupied enough that I can sneak a conversation in with the maid to find out more about this place and the family I'm now a reluctant member of.

He stops in front of me, blocking out the sun. "Are you enjoying your time out here, Willow?"

I look up and wish I could squint so he wouldn't be able to see the unhappiness in my eyes. "It's very nice, yes. Normally, I'd be out enjoying a beautiful sunny day like this, but I can't, so I'll take what I can get."

Before I came to this house, I never spoke like that. Vague generalities strung together with words like nice and take what I can get aren't me. I'm someone who gets excited about fun things and lives life to the fullest. One week at this place and I already sound like a hollowed out version of my former self.

Stephen stares down at me like he's examining my face to see if my outside matches what I'm saying to him. I don't know if he doesn't trust me specifically or if he's just like this with everyone.

"I remember your mother used to love to sit out in a chair in the sun and let it warm her face. My mother used to warn her she would get a sunburn, but she didn't care."

His mention of my mother stuns me. "You knew my mother? How? When?"

Never once did she ever mention the Rule name. I'd remember that, especially after learning I'd have to marry Maddox Rule.

"Another lifetime ago. She was Catherine Shaw when I knew her. Cate Shaw. So young and full of life," he says in a faraway voice like the memory of my mother is something he enjoys.

"How old were you when you knew her? I thought she met my father when she was young, right after high school," I ask, remembering the story my father used to love to tell about how he met my mother one night at college party in Hartford.

"Just kids. By the time I left for school, we'd drifted apart. But I remember her being the sweetest person I've ever met in my life."

I stare up at him in amazement that he knew my mother. I've never heard about her life before meeting my father. The lack of any stories from her childhood always seemed conspicuous in their absence, but I attributed that to her losing her parents in a terrible car accident when she was only seven and living with foster parents until she graduated from high school.

How could someone like Stephen Rule have known my mother, a poor girl orphaned at a young age with nothing in the world to compare to all he has? I wonder if possibly the Rules haven't always been billionaires. Perhaps he wasn't born with a silver spoon in his mouth after all.

"That's how I remember her too. Sweet and kind," I say with one of the first smiles I've given anyone since I came to this house. "She was the best mother a girl could have asked for. I only wish she'd been able to be around for longer."

"Summer is always the shortest season, no matter how many days we get," Stephen says in a low voice.

Filled with sadness like I always get when I think about my mother, I ask him, "If you knew my mother so well, why did you do this to me? Why not let my father find another way to pay you back what he owes instead of making me marry your son?"

Stephen practically hardens over right in front of me, his expression turning from as kind as I've ever seen on him to stony in seconds. His answer is no less hard too, that kindness I heard when he spoke of knowing my mother absent from his voice when he answers my questions.

"I did nothing to you. Your father knew the stakes when he started betting. I told him every step of the way that you would be the price if he kept losing, yet he never stopped. If you want someone to blame for why you're here, look at him, not me."

His cruelty hits me like a slap to the face, and after a moment, I open my mouth to defend my father, but it's no use. Stephen walks away without saying another word or giving me a chance to reply. The warmth of the sun washes over me once again, the shade and coldness gone with him, but now being out here doesn't make me happy anymore.

I DON'T SEE MADDOX ALL DAY, BUT AS THE SUN SETS and I finish my dinner alone, I begin to feel a sense of dread that nighttime will bring him around. I don't want to see him any more than I want to see his father. They're both mean men who seem to delight in hurting me, so the less I have to see of both of them the better.

Emily's expression clouds over as she takes away my plate, leaving me with just a glass of red wine I had with dinner. Never much of a drinker, I'm not legally of age to drink in Connecticut yet, so it doesn't take more than a glass or two of wine to get me drunk.

Tipping the remnants of my glass into my mouth, I wonder why Emily looks so sour tonight. Terrible thoughts race through my mind. Does she know something about me that's going to happen tonight? Has she heard some plan Stephen or Maddox has regarding me? It has been a week since I arrived here. I've thought more than once that there's no way my new husband is going to tolerate me ignoring him sexually for much longer, even though he's made practically no effort to do anything with me after that first night.

I look around for the wine bottle she left when she first brought me my meal and don't see it on the table anywhere. If I'm going to have to endure something awful tonight, I at least want to have my senses dulled to the worst of it.

"Emily," I call out barely loud enough for anyone in the dining room to hear me. "Can you come here?"

She appears a second later, still looking as gloomy as before. "Yes?"

"Can you bring back the bottle of wine? I want another glass."

With a single nod, she gives me another non-verbal answer she seems to prefer and disappears. When she returns a few seconds later, she pours me a full glass and leaves the bottle on the table in front of me.

"Do you need anything else, Miss?" she asks, still refusing to call me by my name.

I answer like I always do. "No, and please call me Willow."

Unlike usual, she doesn't give me a tiny smile before she scurries away back to the kitchen. So much for any budding friendship I hoped to kindle with her. We've moved from at least smiling and acknowledging my effort to be nice to completely ignoring it.

I take a gulp of wine into my mouth and close my eyes, letting the flavors in it wash over my taste buds before I swallow it. Some kind of fruit other than grapes and something almost spicy registers in my brain. Maybe blackberries? I almost want to say that part that tasted spicy reminds me of tobacco. I imagine it's expensive like everything else in this house, although I wouldn't know the difference between fine wine and the cheap stuff.

Yet another reason I'm like a fish out of water here.

My mind drifts back to that odd conversation with

Stephen this afternoon, and once again as I have so many times in the seven days I've been here, I wonder why me. Why would he want me to marry his eldest son? He's always known I don't come from money, so I don't fit in with the world the Rule family lives in. If taking me was meant to punish my father, it seems odd that I'm given anything I want here, except my freedom of course, and married off to Maddox. Stephen's first born is cruel like his father, but other than his behavior that first night, he's been almost completely absent since.

None of it makes any more sense now than it did when I heard my father say I needed to marry Maddox Rule. If they forced me to wait on them hand and foot, I could see that as a punishment. But allowing me to bask in the sun for hours and go horseback riding for fun?

Then again, perhaps I'm simply collateral damage. Maybe my father is the one who's truly meant to pay.

But if that's the case, bringing me here and having me live in the lap of luxury doesn't make sense either.

By the time I finish my second glass of wine, I'm too buzzed to untangle the confusing mess of what's happened to me. Wishing I had someone to be with so I don't have to drink alone, I pour myself a third glass and begin to make my way upstairs to my bedroom.

My foot hits the first step and I can't help but admit that's not correct. Not my bedroom. Our bedroom.

I reach the second floor and count the doors on my way to our room. Six doors. Are they all bedrooms?

Can I simply move to another room and never have to see Maddox?

Drunken Willow likes that idea enough to giggle as she passes the last room. Which one should I choose? The one farthest away sounds best. Only if it has its own bathroom, though. Being caged up here in this fancy prison is bad enough. I don't want to have to walk down the hallway to go to the bathroom or take a shower.

Then again, they're probably all his brothers' rooms. Or maybe they live in some other part of the estate. That would make sense and explain why I rarely see them around.

All of these details ramble around in my drunken head, but for tonight, I'll go back to the room I share with my dear husband. Maybe tomorrow I can search for an open room I can claim for my own.

"Any one works, as long as I don't have to see the oh-so-fucking-charming Mr. Rule," I mumble as I try to open the bedroom door with one hand while clutching the wine bottle and glass in the other.

I take one last clumsy step into my cell and there in front of me is the last person I want to see. Maddox stands from the bed, his shirt unbuttoned and revealing a gorgeous body and tattoos on his chest and abs.

Ripped abs that look like a person could wash clothes on those things.

Oh, God. I shouldn't have had so much to drink. I always get stupid when I drink. I just assumed he'd come home late like he has every night and we could pretend I was asleep like usual.

"Celebrating something?" he asks as I struggle to force my gaze up to meet his.

"Yeah. My incarceration. Since you're one of my jailers, I'm sorry, but you can't join my reindeer games."

Maddox scrunches up his face. "What?"

Pushing past him, I walk around to my side of the bed and set down the bottle and wine glass on the nightstand before turning my back to him. "Whatever. I'm sure those of you in the upper class never watched Rudolph the Red-Nosed Reindeer at Christmastime. Too busy spooning caviar onto your crackers and ordering the staff to bring you more hot toddies."

"You're not making any sense, Willow. Maybe I should take that wine. You sound like you've had too much already."

My senses dulled, I forget who I am and that I have no real power here as I leap up from the bed and spin around to face him. Grabbing the wine bottle, I thrust it toward him and shake my head.

"No, you shouldn't, Maddox. You know what you should do? Go find whoever it is that you spend your nights with and fucking bother her! You know, the one who gave you the blowjob on our wedding night or maybe the one you slept with that night. Or one of the legions of women who think you're so incredibly wonderful. You should go find that woman and leave this one alone to drink herself into a stupor so she doesn't have to think about how utterly terrible her life is for one fucking night!"

A hundred different emotions swirl around inside me, threatening to spill out in tears that fill my eyes. But I don't want to cry. I'm sick of feeling bad, and if this son of a bitch who's the architect of my misery would just go away, I could feel at least something close to good for the first time since I got to this place.

He stares at me in shock at my outburst. Only the bed separates us, but it feels like we're a million miles apart. He doesn't understand a thing about me, and I don't give a damn to understand a thing about him. He's just a cruel asshole, and if I could make it possible to somehow disappear from this place, I'd happily never see him again.

Our standoff ends when he winces ever so slightly and then tries to force a smile. "I guess I had that coming."

His almost penitent tone throws me off, and I don't know what to say in return, so I just mumble, "Yeah, I guess you did."

Not my best retort, but between my wine buzz and his uncharacteristically humble response to all I said, it's the best I can muster. I don't know how to act toward this version of Maddox. The vicious bastard who trapped me here makes it easy to hate him, but seeing that break in his façade confuses me.

"Willow, I'm sorry for that first night. I shouldn't have said those things."

Oh, God. Now he's sorry. If I was in my right mind, I'd have something snarky to say to that, but drunk Willow can't get past those abs and tattoos and that he's apologizing for being a horrible person in that sexy voice.

I shake my head to expel all those ridiculous thoughts before they take hold in my brain. Do not give him a chance. Just because you're feeling vulnerable doesn't mean he deserves to benefit from that.

"So what, now you're going to be nice to me? Are you going to let me see my father and live like a normal person? Or is this just some act you plan to use to get me to be more compliant? Let me guess. This is all about me letting you in my pants, isn't it?"

With a shrug, he smiles, and hints of his true nature come out from behind the mask of kindness. "I don't have to do anything to get into your pants, Willow. You're my wife. I can have you whenever I want. I was just trying to show you that I felt bad about saying those things that first night."

Jabbing the wine bottle toward him, I point at him and laugh. "There. Right there is the real Maddox. Not that guy who was pretending to be nice a few minutes ago. Nope. The real Maddox just takes. So much for being sorry for telling your brand new wife about two women you had sex with on the very day you married me."

I don't know which of those words or what combination of them upsets him, but by the time I finish speaking, he's coming around the bed toward me. My reaction time is slower because of the wine, so I watch in horror until he's right in front of me reaching out for the bottle. He takes it with little effort, leaving me without the one thing that made me happy in this wretched house and my useful prop during this conversation with him.

"No more drinking for you tonight. Obviously, you can't handle your alcohol," he says with a chuckle.

His taunting feels like he's making fun of me, so I snap back, "Well, obviously you can't handle hearing the truth about what kind of dick you are. I can drink more and get better holding my alcohol, but introspection and seeing who you really are is going to be much harder for someone like you."

Again, he winces, like my words hurt him, which can't be possible since he's a heartless son of a bitch. I wait for him to say something cruel back to me in response to my nasty attack on his character, but he simply turns around and heads back toward his side of the room.

"Go to bed, Willow. Trust me. You don't want to fight with me this way."

I can't let this end like this, though, so I follow him around the bed and push as hard as I can on the middle of his back. He spins around and in his eyes I see pure rage.

Still, I don't stop.

"Why? Why don't I want to fight with you this way, Maddox?" I ask defiantly.

He steps toward me, shrinking the space between us until his bare chest is practically touching my shirt. Looking down into my eyes, he says in a low voice, "Because you're going to get hurt."

Instead of frightening me, his anger makes me bristle. Tilting my chin up, I rephrase his statement correctly. "No, Maddox. What you really mean is you'll hurt me. Not that some vague thing is going to materialize out of thin air and cause me to be hurt. No, you'll hurt me, right?"

His expression couldn't be harder when he nods and answers, "Right."

CHAPTER NINE

Maddox

I'm so not in the fucking mood for this bullshit from Willow tonight. Having to deal with my father lecturing me about how I'm messing things up for the entire family because of what I'm doing or not doing with my own fucking wife was bad enough. I don't need this too.

But here she is standing in front of me, her beautiful face tilted up so she can look at me through glassy eyes, the proof that she's far drunker than she thinks she is. Clearly, she's not a girl who's used to partying. The wine bottle is still more than half full, yet Willow is way more than buzzed.

"So what are you going to do to hurt me, Maddox? You look like a guy who hits women. Definitely can see that. So are you going to smack me around a little?

Punching me might leave marks. I doubt Daddy would approve of that. Then again, from the rumors I've heard around here, he's not exactly Prince Charming with women either, so who knows? Maybe some black and blue marks might do it for him."

"Stop before you say something that gets you into trouble you can't handle."

I'm stern enough to make it clear to even a drunk girl that I'm not fucking playing tonight, but still she doesn't back down. Jabbing her finger into my chest, she remains defiant, although she can't win whatever this is to her.

"Trouble, Maddox? What kind of trouble? Are you going to hit me? Beat me up?"

Everything in me wants to show her who she's fucking with, but I hold back. Leaning down until we're eye level, I say quietly, struggling to keep my temper in check, "Don't play with fire unless you're ready to get burned."

Willow's face twists into a sneer that would get any guy decked. "Stop speaking in clichés. Don't play with fire. You're going to get burned. Whatever. You're going to do what you want, so why do I have to watch out?"

Something snaps inside me after hearing her taunt me yet again, and I grab her by the throat, unsure of everything but that I want her to stop before I truly do hurt her. Her eyes fill with fear, thrilling me. She's not so cocky when I have my hand around her neck.

"See, I told you to stop before you get hurt, but you wouldn't listen," I say against her lips as she tries to pry my fingers away from her tender skin. "I told you this would get you in trouble, but still you wanted to push me. Still want to play, little Willow?"

"Let me go. You're hurting me," she croaks out, terror hanging off every word.

"Why should I let you go? You wanted this. You pushed me to act like this. You practically dared me to fucking hurt you, and now you don't like it when exactly what I warned you about happens?"

"I never wanted this. I never wanted any of this," she sobs.

I tighten my hold on her, pressing my fingertips into the side of her neck. A second later, I feel her knee come up toward my balls and step back from her. Now she practically hangs off the end of my hand, like some kind of unwanted doll I should throw away.

But I do want her. I've wanted her since that first night when I came back to this room and saw her in my bed. My father forced me to marry her, so why shouldn't I enjoy the one perk that comes from being tethered to her?

"Please, Maddox, you're hurting me."

Her blue eyes are watery from tears, but as I stare down at her, I swear I could get lost in them. All I'd have to do is let myself.

I release her and run my hand through my hair, desperate to get control of myself. She doesn't want to make me angry. That won't end well for her.

Still focused on those blue eyes, I don't see her pull her arm back to hit me. When her palm connects with my face, the sting rips me out of my daydreams about how I'd love to see her look at me with anything but hate in those gentle eyes of hers.

"Don't ever touch me again!" she screams before jumping onto the bed to get away from me.

Rage explodes inside me, and I lunge on top of her, taking her down onto the bed. She writhes underneath me, throwing her elbows back to jab into my chest and screaming, but she's no match for me.

Covering her mouth with my hand, I tilt my hips to press my cock against her ass in search of some way to release this energy I've got built up. "Feel that? That's how hard you get me, Willow. And now I'm going to do what I should have done days ago," I whisper raggedly in her ear.

She resists, but in a flash, I tear her pants and underwear down her legs and toss them away onto the floor. Her soft skin is tanner than I imagined it would be, sun-kissed like she's been naked outside in the sun recently. Jealousy surges in my brain at the thought that someone here saw her that way before I have.

Against my palm, Willow whimpers and shakes her head, but there's no denying me tonight. I drag my zipper down and pull out my hard cock, pressing it through her legs. She's wet, no matter how much she begs me to stop.

I feel her teeth press against my fingers and quickly move them out of her reach, sliding my hand down to encircle her neck. "If you want it rough, I'm more than happy to oblige," I warn in her ear.

Clawing at the bedsheets, she tries to get out from

under me. All that wriggling only makes me harder, and I grab her hair and pull her back against me.

"Somebody doesn't understand how little power she has," I say with a chuckle, finally enjoying at least one moment with her.

Pressing my cock to her wet pussy, I tease her for a few moments, sliding the full length of it between her lips and over her clit. She's soaking wet no matter what else she wants me to believe, and it only takes a few thrusts to make me want to have her around my cock.

I push open her legs wide and thrust one last time, burying myself balls deep in her tight cunt. She cries out and tightens her fingers in the sheets, balling them up in her fists.

My heartbeat pounding in my eardrums like a raging river makes hearing her impossible. My brain switches into the basest mode it has, and I begin fucking her in earnest. My body covers hers, and the feel of her soft skin makes me want to devour her.

Somewhere in the recesses of my mind, I realize I've never even fucking kissed her the way I want to.

Curiosity about what that would feel like overwhelms me, and I flip her over on the bed. She's stunned for a moment and stares up at me with a look of utter terror. Before she can reach out and scratch the hell out of me, I grab her hands and press them to the bed above her head.

"Don't fight and I promise to be gentle."

"And if I do?"

I lower my mouth to hers and feel her breath

coming out in pants. "Does everything have to be a battle with you?"

Willow doesn't seem to have an answer to that question, and after a few moments, I don't care to hear it. All I want is to feel her mouth on mine, kissing me like a wife should.

Just as I close my eyes, I see her staring up at me in utter confusion. I couldn't explain this even if I wanted to, which I don't. I just want something with her to feel like we aren't two warring armies trying to fight to the death all the time.

Her lips touch mine, and all I know is I've never felt anything so soft in my life. My entire body freezes in place with only my mouth moving against hers. At first, she doesn't respond, but after a few seconds, I sense the tiniest hint of a kiss coming from her.

A moan escapes from my throat into her mouth, a small hint of just how much effect she has on me. I've never been this exposed and out of control with any other woman in my life. I don't understand why Willow does this to me, but she does.

The first touch of her tongue on mine sends my body into overdrive. I stuff my hand into her hair and close my fist around those soft brown strands that smell like vanilla. Now every inch of my body wants to move.

My hips want to thrust my cock inside her.

My mouth wants to devour hers.

My hands want to pull her to me so there's no space between her body and mine.

She presses her palms to my chest, and I steady

myself for her to push me away. She should push me away. I took her from her life, no matter why I did it, and I've forced her to live in this place so strange to her.

Even if she begs, though, I won't let her go. She's mine now.

I hold my breath in anticipation of her fighting to get me off her, but instead her hands slide up over my shoulders, leaving a trail of heat that feels like I'm burning up inside. She drags her fingernails across my back, stinging my skin.

Her anger with me comes out in every touch, but I don't care why she's doing it. She can take her rage out on me. I deserve it.

"Willow, you're mine now," I groan into her ear as I push my hips forward to fill her with my cock.

With every plunge into her, I claim her as my wife. She claws at my skin, ripping her fingernails over my shoulders, while I fuck her like she possesses the very thing I need to exist. Her moans fill my ears and drown out the jackhammering of my heartbeat.

She surprises me with how willingly she responds. Maybe it's the wine. I don't know. I don't care. For the time we're together, I get a precious reprieve from being Maddox Rule, Stephen's first born, and enjoy being a man who gets to revel in the woman he's married to.

My fingers squeeze her nipple, and she whimpers into my mouth. Her teeth sink into my lower lip as I pinch harder and ram my cock into that perfect cunt.

The sound of our fucking echoes around us, a mix of lust and anger and need that fills the room.

The first moment her body tightens around my cock makes me piston into her, and then she arches her back, pressing her tits into my chest. Willow cries out as she comes, bucking against me like an animal. I pound into her, claiming every inch of her for my own, and a minute later, I come inside her until cum runs down between our legs.

Covered in sweat, I sag against her body before sliding off to the side so I don't crush her. She lays there silently, the only sound coming from her the heavy breathing that matches mine.

Willow turns to look at me and grimaces. Definitely not what a man wants to see after fucking a woman.

"Maddox, I don't do things like that," she says shyly, her cheeks turning pink.

"Have sex? You said you weren't a virgin."

"No. Have sex after saying such horrible things to someone."

She's too sweet for me not to laugh, but as soon as I let out a chuckle, her mouth turns down into a pout. "It's not funny. Don't make fun of me."

"I'm not laughing at you, Willow. You don't have to apologize for how you were. We're married. You're allowed to be as wild as you want now since I'm your husband."

She lets out a heavy sigh and shakes her head. "None of this is normal. You know that, right?"

"To fuck your wife because you wanted to?"

She doesn't answer my question probably because she understands I'm teasing her.

"Nothing is normal here. Nothing is normal in the world of the Rules. You'll get used to it."

Her mouth turns down into a frown, but she doesn't say anything. I'm not sure why, but her silence bothers me.

As much as I know I can't let her get under my skin.

CHAPTER TEN

illow

I OPEN MY EYES AND SEE I'M ALONE IN THE BED I share with Maddox. The bed I share with him. We're moving into the second week of being married, and still I can't get used to sharing anything with Maddox.

We're.

When did I begin to talk in plurals? We. Us. We're moving into the second week of us. Odd how it took so little time for me to cease just being Willow. Now we're a we instead of me being an I.

The red numbers on the alarm clock on his nightstand tell me it's a few minutes after nine in the morning. Confused, I scrub the last remnants of sleep from my head and sit up to look out the window. I never sleep this late.

Then my headache comes roaring into my

consciousness and I know why I overslept. Too much wine. I'm definitely not a drinker, for sure.

And in a flash, the memory of my time with Maddox comes rushing back and I feel my cheeks get hot from a blush. I don't know why I'm embarrassed. Isn't that what married people are supposed to do? At the very least, it's expected a husband and wife have sex.

Supposed to. Expected to. I need to stop thinking like any of this is normal because it's not. He even said so last night. After we had sex. The kind of sex I'd tell my friends about if I wasn't trapped in this fancy cage.

Then again, even if I was home safe and sound with my father again, I couldn't tell anyone I slept with Maddox. That would mean I'd have to explain that we're married, and opening up that Pandora's Box would mean I'd have to explain how it all happened and why.

No wonder they make me stay in this house. Just thinking about how I'd explain even half of what's happened in the past week makes my head spin.

Or maybe that's a hangover.

God, I don't want to think anymore. Not about what's happened and how I'm married to Maddox Rule. Not about what we did last night, even though I can't stop remembering it and wanting more.

What's wrong with me? The man forced me to marry him, keeps me prisoner in this place, and barely offered me any choice before I finally gave in last night. How could I want more of him after any of that?

It must be this place. It's seductive, for sure. The people who wait on you hand and foot, here to serve you like you're the most important person they know. The food, which borders on the incredible at every meal. The pool and grounds that offer hours of enjoyment.

All of those things I actually like. Who wouldn't? It's like living in a fairy tale. It's the loss of my freedom and my new family that I despise.

Lost in thought about Maddox's chest and abs and how they felt against me last night in this very bed, I don't hear the bedroom door open. When he appears in front of me dressed in a black suit and sapphire blue dress shirt, I'm not only surprised to see him during the day but a bit taken aback at how different he looks from how I've seen him for the past week.

And then I realize I'm naked.

Horrified, I yank the sheet up to my neck to cover me as he watches with amusement. How is he so utterly comfortable all the time around me, a near perfect stranger? It must be because he's in his own home, on his own turf. Or maybe it's because he's seen dozens, if not hundreds, of women naked in this very bed.

Before I can stop myself, I instantly feel jealous and hate this bed. I need to find another bedroom in this house today.

"Feeling shy this morning?" he asks, punctuating his question with a chuckle at my expense.

"I didn't expect anyone to walk in on me. So much for privacy. You'd think in a house this size I'd be able to find some of that," I say, avoiding meeting his gaze so I don't have to see him standing there in that suit and looking so good.

My cheeks feel like they're on fire as I sit in silence after I stop talking and he doesn't continue the conversation. My palms get sweatier by the second, which makes holding this sheet over me difficult.

Finally out of frustration, I turn to look at him and see he's smiling, like all of this is amusing to him. "Did you want something, Maddox, or did you just come back here to gawk at me?"

"After breakfast, which is waiting for you in the dining room, by the way, you're to go to the ballroom. They'll be here for ten, so time to get out of bed, sleepyhead."

"They? They who? What's happening at ten?" I ask frantically, my stomach twisting into a tight knot almost immediately. That's going to make eating anything for breakfast next to impossible, which is disappointing since I'm starving after the night I had.

He doesn't answer any of my questions but instead flashes me a far too sexy grin for first thing in the morning and turns on his heels to leave. I call after him to tell me what's going on, but he ignores me and closes the door behind him.

What's going to happen in the ballroom at ten? My mind races at the mere thought of what might be waiting for me there. Some kind of indoctrination? Why would I be required to be there and who are the they I have to meet?

A half hour and a million crazy and terrifying ideas

later, I finish my makeup and dress in the clothes Maddox brought from my house a few days after the wedding. As I have with each piece of clothing, I double check in the pockets and sleeves to see if my father slipped me a note to let me know he's okay. Like with every other item, I find nothing.

Into the silence of the room, I sigh and whisper, "I hope you're okay, Daddy."

BEING PANICKED THAT YOU'RE ABOUT TO WALK INTO a room where God only knows what's going to happen and be jumped or forced to do something painful makes eating difficult. Although Emily served me waffles with that special apricot syrup that tastes out of this world, I could barely down a single bite before my stomach felt like it would send it back up a minute later.

Thanks, Maddox. You couldn't just tell me what the hell I'm walking into, could you? Add that to the list of reasons I hate him.

"They're waiting for you in the ballroom, Miss," Emily says without a hint of emotion as she removes my plate of waffles from in front of me.

I know I'm wasting my breath, but I'm desperate to have some sense of what awaits me, so as she moves toward the dining room door, I call after her, "Who's waiting? What's going to happen?"

She doesn't answer either question, just as I expected.

Glancing up at the clock, I see it's one minute to

ten. I take one last drink of water and accept that I can't put this off anymore. Whatever my fate is, it's waiting for me in the ballroom. At least I can be relatively certain they don't intend on killing me.

Can't I?

The long walk down the dark wood paneled hallway feels like it takes forever. With every step, I talk myself out of the crazy thoughts in my head. Stephen Rule wouldn't have me killed after forcing me to marry his son. And not in a ballroom, of all places. If he wanted me dead, he could have killed me in bed while I slept, at any of the meals I've eaten in the dining room, or even out on the patio when he interrupted my time in the sun.

At least I probably won't be killed in a few moments.

But since much of this whole marrying Maddox business still seems like a mystery to me, maybe it has something to do with that. Oh, God! What if he and I will have to have sex in front of a group of Stephen's friends like kings and queens used to have to do on the wedding night in front of nobility in Europe? I saw that in a movie once. Was that ever a thing with wealthy people in this country? Jesus, is it still a thing? Until last night, we hadn't consummated our marriage, so maybe he doesn't know what happened between us and has decided to take matters into his own hands.

I see Maddox waiting for me at the end of the hall and my stomach does a backflip. He has to stop this from happening. We aren't some royalty people can watch having sex!

"You're right on time. Everyone's waiting," he says as he takes my hand and begins to guide me through the enormous doors to the ballroom.

"Please, Maddox. Whatever's about to happen, please stop this. Tell your father what happened last night so we don't have to do this. I swear I'll do anything you tell me to. Anything. Just don't let this happen."

"Let what happen?" he asks, the look on his face pure confusion.

Or maybe that's irritation. I can't tell.

As the doors open, I clutch his arm and drag my feet. "Whatever this is. Please, Maddox! I know we're not in love or anything, but I'm your wife. Doesn't that mean anything?"

My frantic pleas make him stop just before I can see what awaits me, and he turns, blocking my view to the room. Leaning down, he kisses me softly on the lips and then smiles.

"I don't know what your wild imagination has cooked up in that pretty head of yours, but nothing bad is going to happen to you. I planned a surprise for you after I got your clothes from your father's the other day. That's all."

Searching his expression for some clue to show if he's telling the truth or not, I see nothing but his dark eyes staring down at me like they always seem to be and his genuine looking smile. Could he be honestly just giving me a surprise?

"Really? Because I'm terrified that when I walk into that room that it's going to be something awful. Please don't do that to me, Maddox. I know I said some horrible things last night, but I thought we got past that."

He flashes me a sexy smile that's pure wickedness. "We did, and I had a great time. Now stop being crazy and enjoy your surprise."

When he turns away to open the door, all I want to do is believe he isn't the cruel monster I've known every moment of my time here until last night. My heart says to believe him, but my head warns trusting him or his father is a dangerous game I'm in no way equipped to play.

"Please, Maddox. Don't do this," I whisper as the bright sunlight from the ballroom streams through the open door.

"Come on, Willow. You'll like this. I promise," he says without looking back while he tugs me into the room.

Stepping aside, he reveals the surprise. Three women standing near a table covered in what looks like various fabrics of all sorts of colors. Who are these people? Why would I like this?

I look up at Maddox to see him smiling like he's thrilled to present me with whatever this is. "What's going on? Why are these people here?"

"They're here for you," he says sweetly.

"For me? Why? Are they going to take me somewhere?" I ask as my fears begin to spiral out of control once more.

Tugging me forward toward the women, he explains, "They're here to make clothes for you. You tell them what you want, and they'll make it. I've already instructed them to make a few things, so the rest is up to you."

I look over at them and then at the table. "What? Clothes? Why would I need more clothes?"

What I want to add is that I never leave this estate, so why the hell would I need anything more than the clothes I'm wearing right now. Suddenly, I feel utterly out of place as I get closer to the women. They're all dressed in expensive clothes, just like Maddox, while I'm in a cheap pair of white capris and a pink T-shirt.

They're Rodeo Drive and I'm Walmart.

I stop walking and yank my hand away from Maddox's. I don't want this. He's ashamed of me, so now I have to be made up to look like someone who doesn't embarrass him? He can go to hell if he thinks I'd be happy about that.

"Please give us a moment. My wife is feeling a bit under the weather this morning," he says in smooth voice I've never heard him use in front of me before.

Maddox turns to face me, blocking my view of them and their view of me. I expect him to be angry, but his smile remains. "Willow, I'm not sure why you think this is something nefarious, but it's just a gift from me to you."

"I think it's nefarious because I haven't had a say in a single damn thing since I was shanghaied into being your wife. All I see here are people hired to make me look like something you aren't ashamed of, although I can't imagine why since I'm not allowed to leave this place. So no, I can't see how this is a gift."

Finally, the happiness that's been present in his expression fades, and Maddox lets out a heavy sigh. "Willow, you're my wife, and that means you have to dress like you are. I have to wear these clothes when I work, and it's no different for you. It won't always be just my family in this house, and when others come here, you have to have something to wear. I'm not ashamed of you. In some ways, I envy you because you only have to wear what you don't want to once in a while. I have to do it every day. But they don't just have to make you fancy ball gowns. Whatever you want is what they'll make, so you can get whatever your heart desires."

My mind spins at the mention of ball gowns. "Why would I need ball gowns?"

I see what almost looks like hurt in his dark eyes, but it doesn't erase my suspicions about all of this. "What if I don't want new clothes? I like my old clothes."

This last question gets me another, even deeper sigh. "Does everything have to be a battle with you? I know this all began pretty abruptly, but after last night, I would have thought we'd come to some sort of truce."

"Oh, so now I'm the bad guy here? Did I take you hostage and force you to marry me? Do I keep you cloistered on this estate while I go out and have the time of my life fucking anyone I want to?"

He leans down until our gazes are level and says in

a low voice so much sharper than only a minute ago, "Do you want me to be the bad guy, Willow? I can be. It's actually my natural state, to be honest. I'm trying to do a nice thing here. You can take advantage of it and have whatever you want while I get what I want, or I can get what I want and you can get nothing that makes you happy. What's it going to be?"

Instantly, I miss the nicer version of him. This Maddox sends chills up my spine because I can sense that just under the surface, barely a fingernail's scratch deep, lurks that cruelty I've seen far too much of since I came here.

So I relent. "Okay. I'll do things your way. Whatever I want I can have?"

The sexy smile returns to light up his face. "Whatever you want. The sky's the limit. Now enjoy yourself and listen to these people. They know what they're doing."

Taking hold of my hand, he turns the two of us around to face the three women who've waited all this time for us. I feel like I should apologize, even though I don't know them, but Maddox simply guides me over to where they stand next to the table with all the fabric and introduces me to them.

"This is Sonia, Ilona, and Laney. They're sisters and the best at what they do. Trust them to make you whatever you want. Ladies, this is my wife, Willow. You are to make everything she asks for and the items I ordered. She's a beautiful woman who will look incredible in good clothes, so do your job like only you can."

I can't hide my surprise at hearing him describe me as a beautiful woman. Not that I'm not good looking in certain light and when I make the effort. But beautiful? I've never felt like that.

Maddox leans down and sweetly kisses me on the lips. "Have a good time and I'll see you later."

He leaves me standing there in shock at all of this, and when I turn around to watch him walk out of the ballroom, I can't help but admit he looks incredible in that suit. The memory of his body next to mine last night flashes in my mind as I try to convince myself I still hate him.

I should still hate him. Nothing in the past seven days has changed what happened to keep me in this house. Having a team of women to make me whatever clothes I desire won't dim my hate for him. Nothing he can do will change how I feel.

I just have to keep reminding myself of that. The problem is I was always taught to give people a second chance. But I don't want to give Maddox that.

The risk he'll do something hurtful is too great.

CHAPTER ELEVEN

illow

THE BALLROOM DOOR CLOSES WITH A LOUD THUD, and I give the three women a tepid smile as I try to be polite, even though this all feels so foreign to me. "Hi, I'm Willow," I say meekly, feeling incredibly inferior to all three of them.

"Hi! Are you ready to have some fun?" the woman named Laney asks.

She's the shortest sister by a few inches but resembles the other two with her dirty blond hair, although she's the thinnest of the three of them. I quickly scan their faces and decide she's the youngest sister with Ilona and Sonia a few years older than her. I guess they're all in their twenties. They all have a very European flair to them, and for a moment I consider where they may be from. They seem more Eastern Europe than Western, I think to myself.

Then Sonia begins to speak and I know I was right when I hear a distinctly Russian sounding accent.

"Maddox said you were beautiful, but he didn't tell us you had such a lovely figure," she says as she lets her gaze run up and down my body. "I can't wait to see you in the dresses he wants."

"How many dresses does he want?" I ask, suddenly curious about what may lie in my future that would require dressing up.

She turns to Ilona for the answer, and she says, "Five to start, but we have his permission to design as many as we like. Maddox is a man who enjoys nice things, so I don't doubt he'd be happy if we ended up with ten or fifteen."

I can't help but be shocked I might need that many formal dresses or Maddox would want them to create that many. Even more, I have the surest sense that Ilona knows the man I'm married to far better than I do.

"So let's get started!" Laney says in a bubbly voice that already makes me like her most out of the three of them.

They swarm around me with tape measures in their hands, each one wrapping hers around a different part of my body and humming while I stand stiff as a board and watch them. They mumble numbers to one another, some sounding like they're filled with disapproval and others sounding like they're impressive.

Feeling insecure when Sonia wraps her tape measure around my thigh, I mumble sheepishly, "I used to exercise a lot when I was in school, but I've sort of given it up this year."

That's a lie. Gym class doesn't really count as exercise, and saying I've given up working out this year neglects the fact that I didn't do it last year either.

Or the year before that.

Crouched down beside me, she lifts her head up and smiles. "No need to worry. You're fine."

I feel entirely not fine now that she's said that and her two sisters are moving up toward my chest. I've always wished I had bigger breasts. I'm sure they're not big enough whenever I look at other women, especially when I see them wearing low-cut shirts and dresses and compare my measly boobs to theirs.

"Maybe all the clothes could focus on a part of me that's not up here," I say as Ilona wraps her white tape measure around my breasts and hums a sound that hits my ears like utter disapproval.

"I'm afraid we can't do that. Maddox has at least three gowns that highlight your lovely décolletage. I think he likes this part of you," she says with a sparkle in her eyes.

She definitely knows Maddox better than I do. The question is how.

My focus switches from my insecurities to Ilona's long shapely legs, tiny waist, and deep green eyes, intentionally skipping over her impressive breasts that make mine look pathetic in comparison. Maddox would like a woman like her. For God's sake, any male with a pulse would like a woman like Ilona.

"I think you're mistaken about him liking this part," I say as she stands back to look at me while her sisters finish taking their measurements of my waist and upper arms.

Covering my chest, I wish these women would just be done with me so I can go outside to sit in the sun. I don't need a new wardrobe, especially ball gowns for some future social event Stephen Rule plans to hold.

"Time to get out of those clothes," Laney says in that perky voice of hers.

"What?" I ask in horror as I quickly scan the enormous room for somewhere to change.

"You need to be naked, or at the very least, in just your bra and underwear. We can't get a correct fit with you wearing those clothes," Ilona says flatly as she thumbs through the fabric on the table nearby.

"Naked? No. I don't even know you, and there are staff and other people who could walk in at any moment," I say in a panic as I look at the enormously tall windows that ring the room and could offer anyone passing by outside a show.

All three sisters stare at me like I'm some odd thing they've never encountered. Is it so strange that I don't want to undress for them or anyone else on this estate?

"Then bra and underwear, but naked would be best," Sonia says in a tone full of frustration.

I've had enough. I don't want to do this, no matter how much Maddox seems to believe I should. I can just sit upstairs in the bedroom while parties go on. In fact, I think I'd prefer that.

"Thank you, really, but I don't think this is going to work out. I'm not really in need of any new clothes, and I doubt I'll ever wear those dresses anyway, so thank you, but I'm going to leave."

The two older sisters look at each other like they can't believe I just said that, but Laney quickly rushes to my side and wraps her arm around my shoulders. "Girls, give us a second okay?"

They shrug, like all of this is of no interest to them, and she pulls me aside, directing me toward the windows that so concerned me a minute ago. "I totally understand, Willow. It's a lot to deal with when three strangers say get naked. I get it. But we need to do this because Maddox expects us to do our job, and we need your help with that."

We stop at the window and I look out, too ashamed to face her as I say, "I'm sorry. I'm not usually such a prude. It's just that this is all so new to me and everything about this house and Maddox..."

I don't finish my sentence, unsure how I'd even attempt to explain what's happened with me and him and what I'm doing here. I don't know how well these women know the Rule family. Would they even believe me if I told them all that's happened?

"You're very lucky to have such a man for a husband. He's quite the catch."

Before I can stop myself, I let my question about Ilona come out of my mouth. "Why does it seem like

ABBI COOK

your sister knows him so well? Did they date or something?"

And just like that, I feel utterly foolish. I think I'm going to throw up that tiny bite of waffle I had for breakfast.

Laney physically moves me to face her and shakes her head, smiling sweetly. "Who? Which sister?"

"Ilona."

"She wishes. Oh, she'd love it if someone like Maddox asked her out on a date, but that's all it is. Trust me. She's never been any closer to him than she was a few minutes ago. We know him because our father was friends with Mr. Rule. When he died, Maddox's father made sure to take care of us, so any time he or anyone in the Rule family needs clothing, they call us. It's because of this family that we have our successful business. But no, Ilona doesn't know Maddox any better than I do, and just in case you're wondering, I've never been with him either."

Her explanation makes me feel so stupid and small. I have no justification for being jealous. I don't even like my husband, so what does it matter that he's been with so many women that I have to wonder if he's slept with any of the sisters?

"I think she'd be a better choice for a wife for him than me, to be honest," I quietly say, hanging my head.

"Why? You're beautiful and sweet, and I can see he cares for you. It's obvious. He wouldn't bring us here and give us carte blanche to make you anything you can think of if he didn't."

I so much wish I could tell her how untrue that is.

To be able to unburden myself to another soul in this world would give me such relief, but I can't. For as kind as Laney may be, I don't know her well enough to trust her.

So I say what I can, which is my truth if not the truth of our relationship. "I have a feeling he's used to a different kind of woman. Let's just say I'm not exactly the ball gown type of girl."

Laney smiles and shakes her head. "You're exactly a ball gown type of girl because every woman is. Just wait until we get you into those gowns. You're going to feel like a princess who's ready for her big night."

Her words send a chill to my heart. "You don't happen to know when this big night might be, do you? I haven't heard anyone here mention anything about a party or an event coming up soon. Is that why Maddox brought you and your sisters here today? Is it happening this week?"

Just the thought of being paraded around for a houseful of people I don't know while I wear a ball gown makes my mouth go dry from dread.

"I don't know for certain, but he told us that he wants to put a rush on what we design and have it all ready by this weekend. So maybe they have something planned soon? Maybe next Saturday? I think I heard something about a ball then."

My knees buckle as my body goes weak at her news. Saturday? Like days from now? An actual ball? Oh, God. Why wouldn't Maddox have mentioned this? He knew he was bringing these women here to design these gowns for me after he got my clothes from my house four days ago.

"So let's get these cute capris and T-shirt off over there in the corner of the room and get down to designing some gorgeous clothes that will show everyone why Maddox married you," Laney says with a warm smile.

I let her guide me over to a secluded part of the large room, and when she leaves me to go wait with her sisters, I do what I know I must and strip out of my clothes so they can do their job and I can get some new clothes. Hopefully, no one working outside today will see what we're up to so I won't be humiliated in front of the gardener the next time I see him.

As for why Maddox married me, that's not what all these dresses are about. I don't know exactly why his father chose me, but I doubt it has anything to do with my being some beautiful woman he can show off at a ball.

Our relationship isn't a fairy tale. He isn't Prince Charming, and I'm no fairy princess. The reality is far darker than any of that.

IT'S ONLY TAKEN A LITTLE OVER A WEEK, BUT I FEEL when Maddox is around now. I don't know if it's anything supernatural or subconscious. It could just be I'm getting used to him.

My entire body cringes at that thought. Getting

used to the person who keeps me trapped here. No. I can't let that happen.

I blame my mother and father for this. Not my being held against my will here and forced to marry Maddox, although I should blame my father for that, but my tendency to want to be kind to people who don't deserve it. I wish they'd taught me to be hard. One chance and done. If someone blows it, too bad. Their loss.

Instead, I'm too soft and don't like hating. I'm definitely too soft for this place.

Maddox's footsteps up the stairs make my body go on red alert, and I turn around to watch the bedroom door for when he arrives. As always, he looks so comfortable when he strolls in, like he's in control of everything and hasn't a worry in the world.

Must be good to be him.

"How did everything go today?" he asks as he breezes by me to strip out of his suit coat and toss it on the back of the chair near the window.

"Fine. I'm sure you'll be happy with all the sisters make."

That comes out far snottier than I meant it to, I think to myself, and then stop. See? That's what I mean. The man forced me to marry him and won't let me leave this estate, and I'm worried about how ungrateful I sound when he asks about the dresses he wants made for me for some stupid ball or whatever he and that monster of a father of his have planned.

"They're sweet, aren't they? I knew you'd get

along with them," he says with a smile, either ignoring my tone or not picking up on it.

Either choice doesn't raise my estimation of him.

"Laney was nice. I don't really know about the other two. They didn't say much. Although I have to admit that Ilona seems to think she knows you pretty well."

I regret that immediately, hating how jealous I sound. Laney made it perfectly clear her sister has never been with Maddox, yet somehow the idea that she may have has wormed its way into my brain. The result is I say things like that.

His eyes light up at hearing Ilona's name, further irritating me. Why I have no idea. What the hell do I care if he's been with her? Let him be with all three sisters. I don't care if he's with dozens and dozens of Ilonas.

"Does she now? I'm not sure why she'd say that. I don't think she and I have spent ten minutes together alone in our entire lives," he says with a chuckle that makes me want to smack him.

I watch him loosen his tie so it hangs slack around his collar and think how satisfying it would be to choke him with it. Maybe I could invite Ilona to watch. That would be nice.

"You look pretty pleased at the thought that she thinks she knows you pretty well. I can see her being your type. Beautiful in a cold way would be perfect for you."

He stops fussing with the buttons on his shirt and smiles. "Willow, did something happen today with the sisters? You seem especially jealous right now, and although I have to say I'm enjoying it immensely, I am curious why this change in you has happened now."

His confidence in believing I'm jealous infuriates me. Shaking my head far too fast and knowing I don't look at all convincing, I shrug my shoulders like all of this is meaningless to me.

Why it isn't is the confusing part, but right now having to look at Maddox as he stands on the other side of the room undressing and being entirely too smug about me being jealous is muddying my ability to think clearly.

"Jealous? I don't care who you were with in the past, who you're with in the present, or who you end up with in the future. It's not like this marriage is a real thing or anything. You do you and live your life like you always have. Isn't that what you told me on our wedding day? I don't get that same courtesy since I'm trapped in this place like some kind of house pet, but I'm sure I'll find a way to live the life I've always wanted eventually."

I literally have no idea of the words that are coming out of my mouth. Every syllable just makes me sound more jealous, not less. It's like I need someone to censor me so I don't make a bigger fool of myself.

"Well, you sound jealous. You don't have to be, though. I've never been with Ilona or any of the sisters. They're more like family than women to me. If anything, I feel bad for them but nothing else."

The pity so evident in his voice, like he's so mighty and deigns to feel anything for Laney and her sisters, pisses me off. I barely know them, but I can't stop myself from defending them from his ignorant condescension.

"How nice that you feel bad for them. I'm sure that makes them happy because everyone fucking loves to be seen as a charity case. What an ass you are. Their father died and your response is to feel nothing but pity for them. You're a real charmer, Maddox."

I turn my back on him because I can't look at his smug face for another second longer. Also, I don't know why, but my emotions are all churned up and at any moment I'm going to start crying. I never even met their father and just knowing they lost him upsets me so much I can barely keep my feelings in check.

"What is this really about, Willow? How about you tell me because there's one goddamned room in this entire house I get to relax in, and you're standing in it killing any chance I have of actually enjoying a few minutes of my day. So what's your problem?"

He doesn't sound mad and his voice doesn't ever rise above slight annoyance, which only irritates me more. I spin around and see him still fussing with the buttons on his shirt and suddenly I explode.

"Fine! There are lots of other bedrooms in this house, so I'm just going to find another one and then you can have your relaxation spot all to yourself. Knock yourself out, Maddox. Have a fucking spa hour every day after work as far as I care."

I don't get two steps toward the door before he's on me, his arms wrapped around my shoulders holding me back from getting away from him. I struggle to squirm out of his hold, but he's far too strong and so much bigger than me.

"Get off me and let me go! You want to relax? Good. Just let me go stay in another room," I say, trying to pull his arms off me but getting nowhere.

"Stop trying to get away," he says in that low, threatening voice that never fails to frighten me. "You're my wife, so you'll stay in this bedroom with me."

"I don't want to! Why don't you understand that?" I scream and push toward the door with every ounce of strength I possess.

He spins me around to face him, and as he holds me by the shoulders so I can't get free, I see in his dark eyes he really doesn't understand why I want to leave. "You keep saying I'm your wife and we're married, but that's not something real to me, Maddox. You forced me to be that. You force me to stay in this house, to stay in this room with you. You force me to spend hours with those women so they can make clothes you want me to wear. None of that means anything to me because I have no say in any of it."

"No one has a say in their life, Willow. Stop acting like a spoiled child. You think I want to live the life I have? We have our roles and we play them. My role is your husband. I didn't want to get married, but here we are. I had the sisters come over today because I wanted to do something nice for you. Why do you always have to be so—"

I don't let him finish his sentence and blurt out, "Ungrateful? Am I supposed to be happy for all you've done to me? Maybe I should be grateful you don't pity me like you do Laney and her sisters."

"Not ungrateful. Difficult. Someone does something nice for you because he wants you to be happy and looks forward to the time when he can see you in a dress he had specially made for you, and all you can do is complain."

Difficult. So that's what he thinks I'm being. As if he has given me this lovely life and I just can't recognize all the goodness he's bestowed on me.

"Men always say women are difficult when they aren't acting the way they want them to. Why don't you just say what you really mean, Maddox? Tell me I'm a bitch who doesn't deserve the wonderful things you do. I bet you really think that."

His hold loosens on my shoulders, and he shakes his head. "I've been with bitchy women. Trust me. You don't even come close to them. You don't have it in you to be a bitch, Willow."

"So what am I then?" I ask, not even sure I want to know his answer but unable to stop myself from fighting with him now.

I don't know why that question sets him off, but he grabs me by the hair and pulls me hard against his body. Glaring down at me, he answers, "Maybe you should be worried about that, Willow. You don't seem to want me to act like a husband to you, so maybe I should be what other men might be in our situation. As my wife, you're here for my pleasure. I don't have to be kind or thoughtful. I can just fuck you whenever I want and get my rocks off. I think that's how I'm going to approach things from now on, starting right now."

Maddox pushes me down on the bed and a second later covers me with his body, pressing down all his weight on me. I push my palms against his chest to force him off me, but he's too strong and too big.

"Don't do this!" I cry out as he tugs my capris down my thighs.

Stuffing his hand into my hair again, he pulls hard, bringing tears to my eyes. "Don't do what, Willow? You won't accept kindness, and now you want me to show you just that?"

"You're scaring me, Maddox. Please don't do this," I say as tears begin to roll down my cheeks.

I feel his hand between my legs and then he smiles in that wicked way that's part terrifying and part sexy. "I'm the only thing in this house who can protect you, and still you want to push me away. Doesn't sound like a smart thing to me."

"No one else is hurting me right now, Maddox. The only person I need protection from at this moment is you."

"That's where you're mistaken, Willow. I can keep you safe and give you the world. You just have to accept what life is now."

"I will never accept this," I say as my tears make my vision blurry so he looks like some watery phantom hovering over me. "I will never accept you."

"Yes, you will. And when that happens, you'll see how foolish you were."

CHAPTER TWELVE

𝓜addox

THE MEN OF MY FATHER'S CREW SIT AROUND HIS office talking when I get downstairs. Instead of getting to take a shower and enjoying my night, I got to come home to more misery from Willow and then my father calling me to return to work because of some big job he needs done. Now I get to hang out with these fucks and wait in this overheated room with five other guys.

This is why I get blasted as often as I can. At least when I'm fucked up, I don't have to deal with all of this shit.

Tuck, the guy closest to my age by about a decade, nudges me in the arm with his elbow. "I hear congratulations are in order. Got yourself a little woman, huh? Good for you."

After my little go-round with Willow upstairs, it's

hard to pretend I'm the happy groom just a week into wedded bliss, but the last thing I want right now is to discuss my marital issues with any of these jackasses.

So I force a smile and say what I'm expected to.

"Thanks. You know how it is. Everyone has to settle down sometime. Guess it was my time."

Even to my ears it sounds a little too glowing, but Tuck doesn't pick up on anything in my tone and nods his understanding. "I hear ya. It's nice to have someone to come home to. I know I'd be lost without my old lady. Her cooking sucks, but the rest of her makes up for that."

Before he starts in on his true confession about how much he likes fucking his wife, a woman I've seen and wouldn't touch with a ten foot pole, my father thankfully saunters in and takes his seat so the meeting can begin.

"We've got a situation because of what happened with Delgado last month, and we need to take care of it now before it mushrooms into something that gets out of control. His people think they're going to fuck around with my shipments. They've got another thing coming."

The oldest guy in the group, a guy named Capwell who we all call Captain because the skin on his face looks like he's spent his life out on a boat, racks the slide on his pistol and grunts. "Just tell us what you want done and we'll take care of it, boss."

My father loves Captain because he says shit like that. The guy's not so much a kiss ass as he is super gung-ho about anything that involves even the possibility of killing people. I hate when I have to do a job with him because he's way too fucking eager, which gets people hurt. I'll kill someone without missing a beat, but I'm not running into places all guns a-blazing. I'm not dying for some shipment of my father's I don't get to fucking enjoy.

Smiling at his enthusiasm, he points at Jake and Tuck. "You two go with Captain. There's a meeting set up with Delgado's son who's taking over for his father for a while, I hear. He's young and green, so you'll be able to get we want out of him. Don't kill him unless you need to. I just want what they took."

My father's warning makes the smile slide from Captain's face as Jake and Tuck nod their understanding. Too bad. No chance for heroics for that ruddy-faced bastard tonight.

"Maddox, you go with Simon and Beck down to the docks and make sure this week's shipment isn't taken. And I expect this to go smoothly, unlike last time. Understand?"

I bristle at that word he always tacks onto the end of every fucking order he gives me. Understand. I always understand. I'm not a fucking moron. I understand English. I've never not understood a word that came out of his goddamned mouth.

"Got it," I mumble before I start toward the door.

"Okay, that's it. I want a full rundown on everything that happens from Captain and Maddox after both teams get done. You two meet back here when you're finished."

No understand there because Captain is included.

The men begin to file out of his office, but he stops me. "Maddox, wait. I want to talk to you for a minute."

Simon and Beck turn around and give me sheepish looks like they're sure I'm about to get reamed out for something. They pause for a moment, so I wave them off.

"I'll catch up outside. We'll take my car. I'll be right there."

My father waits until they disappear around the corner and we're alone before he says, "I haven't had a chance to ask you how things are going with your wife. Have you made any progress?"

I let that question bounce around my brain for a few moments and shrug. "If you're asking if we had sex yet, yeah."

My father's face lights up like this news thrills him. "Good! Good to hear you finally consummated the marriage. I hope to hear you two will be expecting in no time."

Since we've only had sex once, I suspect that would have to be some superstar sperm to get him what he wants. I don't tell him that, though. The last thing I want to discuss with my father is the odds of Willow getting pregnant any time soon. Better to let him rejoice in the news of the consummation, which sounds like something that should have involved a parade and fireworks.

"I'm sure it'll happen."

"Did you tell her about the ball coming up?" he

asks, far too happy about that yearly event he insists on holding.

"Not yet. I got the sisters over here today to get her fitted for a ball gown, so she'll be ready."

"Oh, the sisters always do such good work. The gown they made for that girl your brother brought last year was really a work of art. Remember? The dark red one on the girl Trace brought? Their father would be proud of them for how skilled they've become at dressmaking and designing. He always said they had a gift."

His mention of their father makes me wish I was anywhere else but standing here talking about some stupid party he forces me to attend each year. I don't even remember who Trace brought to the ball last year, but clearly, my father liked that blood red dress she wore.

"I better get going," I say, happily begging off the rest of whatever conversation he wants to have about the ball or Willow.

He waves his hand like he's dismissing me now that I've told him what he wanted to hear. "Yes, yes. Keep your eye on that shipment. I'm hoping with Captain handling Delgado's kid that there won't be any hassles. Then again, if there are, he's the man to take care of that situation. Maybe if I'm lucky, the father will be there too and I can kill two birds with one stone. Assuming there's a problem, of course."

Forcing a smile, I nod as I wonder if he's secretly made sure there will be a problem so Delgado and his kid get it. My father doesn't like being betrayed, and that son of a bitch stepped over the line with the last shipment. Serves the greedy fucker right if Captain does go at his kid. We pay him enough for his part in all of this. Any more and there'd be no profit for us.

"I'll let you know how it all goes when I get back."

"Fine. Oh, by the way, Maddox. Your brother is going to be joining us from now on."

My head snaps around, and I see him grinning, like this is the news he's waited for all his life. "Which brother?"

I know full well which brother. It's not like Trace or Julian have any interest in working for him doing what I do, and Nick isn't due home from school for months.

"Helix, of course. He's going to be starting with you guys later this week."

Fanfuckingtastic.

Without thinking, I ask the only question I ever ask when it comes to that brother. "Why?"

"Because he's a part of this family and I think he'll be an asset to the business, just as you are."

The way he says that, like Helix and I are equals on some level, practically goads me into snapping back that no matter how close he keeps him, that won't change what Helix is. My father's psychic claims he'll be the reason his empire crumbles around him, so he's bent over backwards to make my brother happy. While the rest of us have to deal with all of Stephen Rule's bullshit, Helix gets a free pass just in case Katia is right.

I don't bother saying any of that, though. It would just be a waste of breath.

"Great. I'll let you know what happens when I get back."

My father doesn't answer, already distracted by something else he's working on. All the better. I don't want to risk staying for more conversation with him and having to talk about my marriage or that fucking ball I'd give anything to not have to attend, or even worse, the prospect of having to work with the one brother I trust the least.

Simon and Beck are standing near my car when I get outside, ready to get this job going. "We got the easy part tonight, boys," I joke as we pile inside and I start the engine.

"Yeah, let Captain handle Delgado. That whole group is bullshit. Every time we go there, some kind of shit goes down, right, Simon?" Beck says from the passenger seat.

I put the car into drive and glance up at the rearview mirror to see Simon nodding behind me. "Nothing but bullshit trouble, if you ask me. Your father deserves to have better partners than that asshole. He's going to be stupid and cross him again. You watch."

The two of them continue shit-talking Delgado and his crew while I drive out the front gates of the estate. I don't know if Simon's right and that asshole will double-cross us again. If he has any sense in that head of his he won't, but that isn't saying much. He and his guys think they're all fucking John Wayne ready to shoot up the west. It wouldn't surprise me if they do it again simply because my father didn't punish them enough after the first time.

Then again, maybe that's what tonight is. If he just wanted to ensure Delgado and his men didn't disrupt anything, he wouldn't have sent the one guy with the itchy trigger finger to meet with them.

I WATCH AS THE WORKERS UNLOAD THE BOAT INTO the warehouse, just as they're supposed to. The humid summer night air feels like it's draping itself around me, and I'm ready to smack the hell out of Simon and Beck because they haven't stopped talking since we got into the goddamned car back at the house. I'm almost wishing I'd been sent with Captain to deal with that fuck Delgado.

Not that I mind the easy job. Since I'm technically working overtime today, I'm all for basically watching other people work tonight. I just wish these two next to me would stop their nonstop talking for a minute.

"Looks like this is going to be a quiet night," Beck says with a smile. "I'm good for that."

"Me too. There's a baseball game on tonight I'm hoping I can catch," Simon says with more enthusiasm than I've ever heard him talk about anything before.

"I didn't realize you're a baseball fan," I say in passing as I continue to watch the product move into the warehouse off the dock.

"Oh, yeah. Huge fan. Always have been," he answers excitedly. "I played it in high school, and ever since, I try to watch a game whenever I can. Nothing like kicking back with a few beers and watching nine innings. What about you? You like baseball?"

Shaking my head, I grimace at the thought of sitting in front of the TV watching what may be the slowest game in the world. "Nah, not a fan. I'm more of a hockey or basketball fan. A game that moves a little faster."

I instantly know I've made a mistake when Simon begins to defend his favorite sport. I wasn't looking for a discussion about the damn game. I was just making small talk, for Christ's sake.

"No, no, you see, it's really an intricate game. That's why it seems so slow moving. But it's got a lot of facets. Like for example, the whole thing with pitching. You ever—"

Before he can get another word out, a noise from the side of the building makes my head snap around, and I see two guys with guns drawn. I bark out orders for Simon and Beck to fire, but it's too late. Shots hit them both, and they drop like stones. I fire on the bastards aiming at me and think I hit one, but a second later, I feel something tear through me like a red-hot poker plunging through my skin and I collapse to the wet ground.

I SLOWLY OPEN MY EYES AND SEE NOTHING BUT darkness. I reach my hands out to my sides and feel mattress on both sides. Not a hospital room then. Too big a bed for that.

"Maddox? Are you awake?"

I recognize my father's voice instantly. I must be back at the estate then.

"Yeah. What time is it?"

"A little before three in the morning."

"What happened?"

"You, Simon, and Beck were ambushed. Delgado thought he got me once so he could do it again."

"I saw them fall before I got hit. Are they dead?"

"Yeah. But the good news is Captain got wind of the whole thing because Delgado's kid can't keep a secret. He took out him and his goddamned father. So much for them."

My father's ability to find the bright side to all of this is typical Stephen Rule. Two of our guys are dead, but we got the other guys, so it's all good.

A searing hot stabbing pain shoots through my chest, pinning me to the bed. "Holy fuck. Where'd they hit me?"

"Right shoulder near your neck. Whoever was shooting wasn't very good," he says with a chuckle.

"Well, thank God for that, I guess."

"Captain brought you back here and we had the doctor dig the bullet out before sewing you up. He says you'll be up and around in no time. I told him I'd be giving you some time off to recuperate."

The way he says that tells me the whole time off thing was to impress the doctor, not help me. He's like that. Not very paternal or even vaguely parental, but he does love to impress others and try to make them believe he's a good father.

That's why I'm confused to find him by my bedside after what happened. Maybe since everyone else on the job was taken out, he thinks he should be here. It's just odd since it's never been that way before.

"You should rest. You'll feel better tomorrow. The doctor gave you some good drugs to take the edge off. That's why you aren't screaming in pain."

He has no idea how much this fucking hurts. I might not be screaming in agony, but I'm definitely feeling some unbelievable pain in my shoulder.

"I might want to take some more then because I think it's wearing off."

"The doctor said he'll give you another shot when he gets here in the morning. It'll just be a few hours more. You can handle it, right?"

As if I have a choice.

"Yeah, I'll be fine," I croak out as another wave of pain washes over me, practically taking my breath away.

"How about I go get your wife? I'm sure she'll make you feel better just being by your side," he says, and I hear him push his chair back away from the bed.

Fuck. The last thing I need is Willow beside me right now. I don't have the energy to deal with that much anger and resentment in the state I'm in.

Before I can tell him to wait on bringing her in and to grab Trace instead, I see the door open and he walks out into the hallway. I hear the sound of voices speaking in hushed tones, but I can't understand what they're saying. I imagine she's telling him she doesn't want to play nursemaid to me, even if she is my wife.

Not that I want her to. I've been fucking shot, and I don't need to have to worry the damn woman is going to smother me with a pillow in my sleep.

The door opens with a creaking sound, and in the darkness I hear lighter footsteps than my father's. They come around the bed and stop right near where I see the outline of the chair.

"Maddox?" she says quietly and in a far sweeter voice than I've ever heard from her before.

"Yeah. Do me a favor and open the drapes. I can't stand all this darkness. I woke up and thought they'd shot my damn eyes out because all I saw was black all around me."

I hear her walk away, and a few seconds later, a tiny bit of light comes into the room, enough for me to see her clearly and not just the outline of a person in front of me. She's still dressed in those white pants and that pink T-shirt she was wearing the last time we were in this room together.

She fixes the curtains on the other three windows so I don't feel like I'm stuck in a morgue anymore. Returning to the chair at the side of the bed, she sits down and looks at me, grimacing like she's in pain.

"What's wrong?"

"I can't believe you were shot," she says softly.

"Yeah. Me neither."

"Why didn't you tell me that you do something that people shoot you for?" she asks with such innocence that I can't help but smile.

"Well, first of all, we've never talked about what I

do at all, and second of all, I wouldn't generally describe what I do as a job people shoot me for."

"Your father told me you almost died."

"My father probably said that to make this sound more important than it is. I didn't almost die. At least I don't think I did. The two guys with me did, though."

Poor Simon and Beck. No more baseball games for them.

"It seems to me getting shot is a big deal, Maddox. Are you going to be okay?"

I wince at a stabbing pain in my shoulder and then relax. "I'll be fine. I probably won't even have much of a scar to get a tattoo over."

"Is that why you have all those tattoos?"

She asks the most bizarre questions. Willow really is innocent in so many ways.

"No. I have a few covering scars, not all from getting shot, though. Mostly, I have tattoos because I like them."

She doesn't say anything else, thankfully, and the two of us sit silently for a long time as the pain ebbs and flows through me. Whatever the doctor gave me, he needs to dose me up better when he gets here in the morning.

Finally, she breaks the silence. "I'm sorry we had that fight earlier, Maddox. When your father told me you'd been shot, I felt terrible that you might die without me getting to say I'm sorry."

I look at her and see she's honestly bothered either that I was shot or that I might die before we could make up. "Well, I'm not going to die. At least I have no plans to tonight, so we're good for the next few hours."

Willow's expression fills with sadness, and her mouth turns down into a deep frown. "Don't joke about dying. It's not funny."

"I would have thought you'd be happy if I got offed, to be honest. You aren't exactly my biggest fan."

Her eyes open wide with surprise. "That's not true! I don't have to be crazy about someone to not want them dead."

"Well, it's good to know you aren't crazy about me. So were you just worried you'd have to walk around with guilt on your head for the rest of your life or were you going to miss me? I guess not the second choice since you're not crazy about me."

"Please don't be like this, Maddox. I said I was sorry," she says before hanging her head.

She's still nearly a perfect stranger to me, but there's something about the kindness that seems innate in Willow that I can't deny I like. Even after all I've done, she genuinely appears upset that I'm lying here hurt. I'm not sure I've ever known anyone as sweet as her.

"I guess we could call a truce."

For the first time, she looks at me and smiles. "I'd like that."

"Okay, then. A truce it is. At least until I'm up and around and you can hate me again," I say with chuckle.

I know that's more true than not, even as she shakes her head like she doesn't really hate me. I understand why she does. I probably would too if someone did to me what I've done to her.

It doesn't change anything between us, but for a few sweet moments, she's not unhappy. And I like that.

CHAPTER THIRTEEN

M addox

AFTER A FEW DAYS, I'M ABLE TO GET OUT OF BED and my truce with Willow makes me think we might actually be starting to like one another. Every time I need help because I'm supposed to keep my shoulder immobilized, she's right there by my side to assist. It only takes a few times before I begin to get used to her being around when I need her.

The problem is I know better than to think I should get comfortable with all of this. My past lurks in the shadows, along with my father and his interests, which always rear their ugly heads. Willow's last name may now be Rule, but she isn't one of us, and I doubt she'd like any of what this family is if she found out.

She sits on the bed next to me reading a gardening magazine she found in the library yesterday. Silently, she flips through the glossy pages, occasionally making a noise that sounds like she's happy when she sees something she likes. When she finds a picture or article she especially finds interesting, she folds down the page but doesn't actually spend any real time on the information.

Curious, I clear my throat and she turns to look at me. "Is something wrong? Do you need me to go call the doctor?"

Shaking my head, I smile at how eager she is to please. "No, I'm fine. I'm just wondering why you fold the page down when you see something you like instead of just reading the article or looking at the picture right now."

My question makes her twist her face into strange expression before she sighs. "I don't know. It's just how I've always been with catalogs and magazines. When I see something I like, I fold down the page for later."

"And then you go back at another time and read it?"

"Usually."

"Why don't you just read it right now? It's not like you have anything else you have to do."

With a shrug, she answers my question. "I don't know. It's just the way I am. I don't mind waiting."

We go back to sitting in silence while she returns to flipping through pages in the magazine. After a few minutes, she stops and turns to face me.

"I guess you think I'm weird because I do that, don't you?"

"No. I just noticed you don't stop on anything but it's obvious you're interested in the articles where you fold the pages down. Seems strange to me since I've never been patient about anything in my life."

Willow's expression softens, and she smiles sweetly at me. "It's not about being patient. I think maybe it's about putting off something good until later. That way I get to enjoy the magazine now, and then when I go back to it, I get to enjoy those articles I dog-eared. And you aren't always impatient, Maddox."

Her compliment surprises me. "Really? Name one time I waited for anything."

"You've been patient with me."

What I've been with her hasn't actually been patient. I don't want to ruin this kind moment between us, so I don't tell her the truth about how I never gave up living my life exactly as I always had before I married her. The partying never stopped. The drugs never stopped. The women never stopped. What she thinks is my being patient has simply been my being satisfied away from this place.

Away from her.

I force a smile and nod but don't say a thing. I have no problem being cruel to most people in the world.

Just not her and just not now.

"Are you feeling sleepy? The doctor said you would because of the medicine he's given you," she says and then closes the magazine.

For the past few minutes, the drugs have been slowly winding their way through my system, dulling my senses with every passing moment. "Yeah, I think so. Maybe I'll just nap for a little while."

She sets the magazine on the nightstand and gets up to leave. "Okay. I'll check back on you a little later. If you need me before then, just call my name. I'll leave the door open so I can hear you."

But I don't want her to leave.

"Stay here," I say, tugging her hand so she returns to the bed.

"Oh, okay. Do you need something?" she asks as she sits down next to me again.

"No. Just you here."

Her body presses against mine through the sheets and blanket, giving me a sense of something I don't completely understand. It can't be security. She's a tiny thing who couldn't fight off an intruder to save her own life, much less mine. I don't know what it is, but I like the feel of her next to me.

Closing my eyes, I let myself lean against her and rest my head on her arm. She's soft and easily broken, yet I feel like she's the only thing I have that's helping me stay strong.

As I drift off and the drugs take me over, I think I feel her hand brush my cheek and then my forehead. I don't know if I'm lost in the delirium of the medicine the doctor gave me or what's happening. All I know is I've never felt this happy in my life.

"MADDOX."

My name comes to me like a faraway whisper, spoken by a voice I know. Or I think I know.

Hands slowly glide over my body, from one hip to the other, fingertips trailing heat over my skin. Am I awake? Or is this the drugs fucking with my head?

I look down my body and see Willow's angelic face looking up at me. Her eyes, so often that watery blue that reminds me of the lake my father used to take us to when my brothers and I were boys, stare up into mine. They're not sad now but seductive in that way that never fails to make me wish I hadn't said those things to her on our wedding night.

My wife has a hold on me I would have never guessed could ever be possible. I don't know how she did it either. I shouldn't care about her at all.

Yet I do.

"Maddox, do you like this?"

Her mouth is so close, teasing me with what I want and what she can give me if only she'd lower her head just a few inches. The corners of her lips turn up in a shy smile, telling me she knows the effect she has on me.

"I can stop if you want me to," she says softly, her warm breath drifting over the skin between my hips and arousing me until I'm painfully hard.

Every cell in my body screams for her to keep going, and I stuff my hand into her hair, tightening my fist around the silky light brown strands. A tiny whimpering sound escapes from her throat, but still she smiles up at me.

"Don't stop."

ABBI COOK

My voice verges on panic that she will stop moving closer to my cock and deprive me of the feel of her beautiful mouth on me. Squeezing my eyes shut, I struggle to calm the need that threatens to explode inside me.

"What do you want, Maddox?"

Her voice hits my ear wrong, and I open my eyes to see not Willow but Kerry, that girl I took off Helix just because I could. She smiles up at me in that desperate way that made her an easy target for a drunken man that night.

"I know what you like, baby," she purrs as she strokes me from root to tip and back down again.

Shaking my head, I try to push her away, but I can't reach her. Unable to stop her, I watch as she takes my cock into her mouth and slides down, inch by inch until it disappears completely. I know it should feel incredible, but I feel nothing but regret. I shouldn't be doing this with her. How did she get into my room?

Our room. The room I share with Willow.

I pull myself up from the bed to push her off me, but when my hand brushes up against her head, I see my wife again. She looks up at me with hurt in her eyes.

"Maddox?"

Then I feel myself falling like the mattress isn't beneath me and there's nothing to catch me when I collapse backwards thinking I'd hit the pillows. I hear Willow say something, and after that, there's nothing but bliss.

~

"THIS PARTY IS AS MUCH A CELEBRATION OF YOUR wedding as it is our yearly ball. You and Willow will be the guests of honor."

My father puffs out his chest in pride as he talks, as if my marriage reflects positively on him more than it does on me. He's a big fan of this kind of social event stuff. To him, it's a way to exert his influence over the people in his social circle to show them the Rules still lord over the rest of them. I assume it's something from the past that he's just not willing to give up, but I can't imagine when he's gone that I'll keep that shit up.

"Well, she's going to look gorgeous in the gown the sisters made, and assuming I can get a tux to work with this sling, I'll be like I always am. If we're being honest, though, it's not me anyone's coming to see. It's her, don't you think?"

"She'll definitely be the novelty, but don't sell yourself short, Maddox. You're my first born, so people always pay attention to you. You're a Rule, after all."

I imagine at one time that kind of thing meant a lot to people, but I have a hard time thinking that anyone comes to these yearly events to see me. My father makes sure they're a spectacle, and he revels in the fakeness of it all. It's like it gives him some kind of boost of energy to keep going for another year.

I've already decided when he's gone that I won't be holding the ball or anything like it ever again.

ABBI COOK

Gathering people I have no interest in seeing to show off my home isn't my style. It never has been.

He would be horrified to find out my plans for after he's passed on, so I pretend for his sake because I don't want to have yet another discussion of how I don't want to be a carbon copy of him.

The old ways live on in Stephen Rule, but they'll die with him.

"I haven't seen much of Willow around the house lately. Is she under the weather?" he asks as he walks through the ballroom, his focus intent on where tables will be placed and who will sit where.

His not-so-sly way of asking if she's already pregnant makes me smile. "It's only been a few weeks since the wedding, and ten days of that have had been me recuperating from getting shot."

He scowls, unhappy at my non-answer answer. "I was just wondering. Remember, you need an heir to take over once you're gone. You're already twenty-eight. By the time you're my age, you want to know the next generation is ready to take over."

"I'm sure it will happen. That's assuming everything's okay with her."

I don't know why I say that. There's been no indication there's anything wrong with Willow in that department.

But the mention of her possibly not being able to do the one job he expects her to do doesn't seem to bother him. In fact, he appears to believe in her ability to have children even more than I do.

"Oh, I'm not worried about that. Willow will give

144

you as many children as you want. That I'm sure of. You just have to do your part."

This conversation feels strange, especially considering the kindness she's shown me since I've been laid up. I give him a smile like I agree with what he's saying and quickly change the topic.

"I should be able to come back to work right after the ball. The doctor says everything's looking fine."

My father stops his march around the ballroom and nods his approval. "Good. Very good. Everything is all on schedule with Helix, so you take all the time you need."

Just the mention of my brother essentially taking my place sets my teeth on edge. Whether my father sees it or not, I know what Helix is up to.

"I'll be fine. No need to worry about me not being one hundred percent."

My attempt to reassure him about my ability to do my job misses the mark entirely because my father's focused on the ball. "You and Willow will be the toast of the night on Saturday, I have a good feeling you're going to be telling me there's a child on the way any day now, and we're going to be back to business next week. Very good, Maddox."

I'm struck by how pleased he looks at this moment as he stands in the middle of the room smiling at me. I don't think I've ever seen him this happy with me.

"I better get going. I have to make sure the sisters have some way to make this sling work with my tux."

"Be sure to tell them I'm looking forward to seeing something spectacular on Willow this Saturday."

"I will."

I hear a hint of a threat under that statement, but he has no reason to doubt the sisters. While Sonia, Ilona, and Laney have never been invited to any ball the Rule family has held or any other social event, they know what's expected of their designs.

"I think this is going to be the best event in years," he says in a faraway voice as he walks away across the room.

There's a lot riding on this year's ball, even if I don't give a damn about it. For one night, Willow will be the center of all society's attention. To me, what anyone thinks of her doesn't mean a thing, but to my father, it's the culmination of the work of a lifetime.

I still don't truly know why he chose her for my wife, but for one night, everything will be riding on her and her alone.

At least in his mind.

CHAPTER FOURTEEN

*M*addox

LOST IN THOUGHT ABOUT THE BALL, I HEAD OUTSIDE to find Willow where she usually spends her days. I can't help but admit I'm a little jealous. No, I wouldn't appreciate being forced to stay on this estate day in and day out, but the idea of lounging around in the sun all day and then spending hours flipping through magazines doesn't sound like the worst thing in the world.

I find the chair on the patio empty and her glass of iced tea on the table beside it. Looking out across the lawn, I scan the area but she's nowhere to be found.

Maybe she's upstairs. It is hot out, so that would make sense.

As I turn to walk back into the house, I hear her

giggling in the distance. Where is she and why would she sound like that? It's not like there's anyone here on the estate she spends time with other than me.

I step onto the grass and begin walking toward the sound, which continues like someone's tickling her. I can't explain it, but the sound makes me ball my fists in pure anger. Am I confusing giggling with something else? Is she being hurt?

My legs move faster as the possibility that something's happened to Willow races through my mind. Logically, I know no one could be hurting her, but I'm not being controlled by my brain now.

Hurrying around the house, I see her under an oak tree, but she's not alone. Helix is sitting there with her like the two of them are the best of friends and have been for all their lives.

But how is that fucking possible? He's known her literally as long as I have, and he hasn't even slept with her. Shouldn't that mean she should act like this with me?

I stop dead as a single, horrible thought fills every inch of my mind. Has she been with Helix? He hasn't had to spend his days away from the estate doing what our father orders him to do, so he's got more than ample opportunity to be with her. They could spend hours every fucking day in bed.

My bed. The bed I share with Willow.

The two of them sit like best friends talking as if any of this is okay. I know my brother. I've watched him do that brooding guy bullshit to get into a woman's pants in the time it takes for him to finish a goddamned beer. He's slick. He knows how to say just enough to make them want to practically drop their fucking panties they're so wet for him.

He's dark and bad and all they want to do is fix him. Of course, none of them can, but that doesn't stop them from trying. Most susceptible to his act are the sweet ones.

Like Willow.

My head throbs from rage as I look at him sitting there with her while she talks, probably thinking he's some poor misunderstood deep thinker she can reach if she's kind enough to him.

When I see her touch his arm and giggle again, all I want to do is pound the fuck out of him. He has no business hanging out with her, sitting beneath that tree like some asshole douchebag musician hanging out on campus charming coeds into fucking him.

No, he doesn't have a guitar with him, but it doesn't matter. I'm not thinking logically at this moment.

Nearly blind with rage and not sure who I'm angrier at, him or her, I march over to where they sit having the time of their lives. They don't even notice I'm walking directly toward them until I stop and clear my throat. Only then do the two of them finally look up at me.

"Having a good time?" I bite out, barely able to control my temper.

In typical Helix fashion, he shrugs, even though

I'm sure he understands I'm pissed. "Just hanging out telling Willow about when we were kids and all the trouble we got into."

A smile lights up her face, and she asks, "Did you guys really rig all the hoses to point directly at the gardener's shack when he told you to stay off the grass? The way Helix told the story, the poor guy nearly had a heart attack."

That story never fails to make me smile. Except for now. This time, it doesn't even take the edge off how fucking angry I am at this moment, and I glare down at her, even as she continues to smile at me.

"Willow, get inside. Now," I bark, leaving no room for her to misunderstand how much she doesn't want to argue with me today.

Yet, of course, since she's goddamned Willow, she can't stop herself from asking me why. "I was just enjoying the nice day. Why do I have to go back inside?"

"Because I fucking said so. Now, Willow."

Helix watches all of this knowing full well I'm close to losing it, so he says nothing. He's seen me this angry before. Since he clearly likes his new friend and sister-in-law, he understands she's only making things worse.

I watch as tears fill her eyes. She turns to look at my brother as she fights back her urge to cry. "It was nice talking to you, Helix."

He gives her a tiny smile but doesn't respond. Good. I don't need any more reasons to want to beat the hell out of him.

With all the defiance she has inside her, she gets up onto her feet and stands toe-to-toe with me, barely holding back the tears when she tilts her head back to glare up at me. "I guess I'll go inside. Nice seeing you again, dear husband."

My eyes narrow as I fight the urge to cringe at how hurt each of those words sounds when they hit my ears. So much for the truce we made when I was laid up in bed.

I hear her start to cry as she runs across the grass back to the house. Something about that sound and how much sadness fills it makes my chest ache, but I push that feeling away and focus on my brother.

"Don't bother with Willow again. She's not your plaything, Helix. Go find someone else to get friendly with."

He smiles up at me with that cocky grin that says he thinks he knows way more than he actually does. "So you keep her chained to the house here while you do whatever you want, and if she dares to talk to your family, she's punished and sent to her room? Nice thing you have going on there."

"Nevermind what I have going on. Just stay away from Willow. Am I making myself clear?"

Unlike my wife, Helix doesn't wither under my thinly veiled threat. Standing up, he brushes dirt off his pants and sighs like having to deal with me is the biggest hassle he's going to encounter all day.

"Whatever, man. This was nothing. She was sitting here, so I thought I'd make nice with the person my brother's married to."

"I know you, Helix. I've seen you with women. Remember who you're talking to."

My brother chuckles, like any of this is funny. "Whatever you've cooked up in your twisted brain, it's fiction, Maddox. Not that I think she's madly in love with you or anything because let's be honest, why the hell would she be? You give her no freedom, and you yourself have bragged that you haven't kept it a secret that you consider this whole marriage a fucking sham. Maybe you should ask yourself why seeing the two of us simply talking bothered you so much, though."

Damnit, I hate when he tries to pull this psychobabble shit on me.

"I don't need to ask myself anything. What you need to do is stay the fuck away from Willow. Got it?"

He gives me a shrug, like all of this is boring him, and begins to walk away. Grabbing his arm, I stop him to make sure he understood my point.

"I mean it, Helix. Don't push me on this."

"What's your problem, Maddox? Worried I could have her? I could. In a fucking heartbeat. She's miserable and lonely. I wouldn't even break a sweat. I wouldn't do that to you, though. We're brothers, remember?"

All the rage I felt when I first saw him sitting with Willow surges through me, and it takes every ounce of control I possess not to deck him. Cocky fucker. As if being brothers would mean anything if he wants her. We've been down that road before, both ways, and blood has never shown itself to be thicker than anything.

Taking a deep breath in, I try to calm my emotions as my head continues to throb like someone's got a jackhammer inside my brain and they're going to town in there. Now to deal with Willow.

I FIND HER IN THE HALLWAY NEAR THE LIBRARY, AND when she sees me, she immediately spins around and heads in the opposite direction. By the time she reaches the stairs, she's practically running to get away from me.

"Willow, I want to talk to you," I say as calmly as I can force my voice to sound.

She says nothing and never turns around to look at me. In fact, she begins to take the steps by twos.

"Willow, I'm talking to you."

Still she remains silent.

By the time she reaches the second floor, she's running. I'm not sure where she thinks she's going that I won't follow. Wouldn't it be easier to just talk to me instead of breaking into a full sprint and then having to talk to me all the same when I finally catch up to her?

She disappears into our bedroom, and I follow her about twenty seconds later to find her standing next to her side of the bed. The site of our truce is once again our battlefield.

"Willow, when I say I want to talk to you, I expect you to listen."

Her expression changes from angry to hateful, and she squints her eyes at me. "You can say whatever you want, Maddox. You can even trap me in this room and force me to listen. That doesn't mean I have to care about a word you say."

Jesus, this is not what I wanted to do today. Does everything have to be an uphill battle?

"I wanted to explain what happened out there."

Never once in my life have I said those words to a woman. I've never felt the need to explain a damn thing to any woman I've ever known. That I somehow am compelled to do it with this one baffles me, frankly.

My attempt at rekindling our truce fails. Shaking her head, she continues to glare at me. "I don't care, so don't bother."

"I don't want to fight with you, Willow. We got along pretty well for the past few days, haven't we? I'd like that to continue."

"Then why won't you let me have one thing that makes me happy? I was just talking to your brother. I have no one here to do anything with. He's your brother. What was the crime in us just talking?"

The king size bed between us means I could lean over and touch her she's that close, but it feels like an entire world separates us at this moment. I can't explain why I reacted like I did. Well, I can, but I don't want to.

"I have no problem with you being happy. I had the sisters come here to make you anything you wanted."

The anger fades from Willow's face, but she frowns at me now. "You had them come here for you, not me. I was fine with my old clothes. That wasn't to make me happy but to make you happy, Maddox."

"Do you think I don't want you to be happy here? Do you think I enjoy being married to someone who at best barely tolerates me and at worst would wish me dead, Willow?"

That makes her tear up, probably because it's true.

"I don't wish you dead, Maddox," she says in a soft voice on the verge of crying. "That's why what you did out there with your brother hurt so much. It's like no matter how much I try to show you I deserve kindness, all I get in return is cruelty."

She's not wrong. I hate admitting it, but she's right. The problem is as much as I don't want us to continue this vicious cycle, my instincts make it hard to stop it.

"Come here."

Hesitating, she reluctantly walks around the bed to stand in front of me. Always a face-off with her.

I lift my good arm and pull her to me, loving the feel of her body against mine like some guilty pleasure. "I'm sorry."

Willow rests her head on my chest and relaxes in my hold. "For what?"

There's too much for me to answer for with that question, so I whisper against the top of her head, "Everything."

Tipping her head back, she looks up at me with those watery blue eyes I love. "Would you like to call our truce again?"

I let out a sigh of relief and smile as I cradle her beautiful face. "I'd like that. Truce?"

"Truce."

When I press my lips to hers in a kiss I've craved from the moment I saw her sitting under that tree with Helix, I hope more than she can know this truce will last.

CHAPTER FIFTEEN

 illow

NEARLY TWO WEEKS OF MADDOX RECOVERING WITH me by his side has made our relationship blossom. I think we've grown closer, like we're starting to trust one another.

At least I feel that way after that incident with Helix. I don't know what that was all about, but I have a sense it was more about the two of them and less about me.

He says next to nothing about what he thinks about me. He seems to appreciate how I've helped him get back on his feet after getting shot. I believe that because he appears far more relaxed around me now compared to right after we were first married.

But sometimes I catch him looking at me in a way that reminds me of how an animal eyes up its prey. I don't see caring or concern in his eyes but a hunger, like at any moment he wants to devour me.

In truth, I know very little about the man I'm married to. My husband works for his father, although I'm not necessarily sure what that job entails other than being around men with guns. While I've been able to get little out of Emily about the family I've been thrust into, she has intimated that Stephen inherited a great deal of money and the Rules are quite wealthy. As in obscenely wealthy. When I asked what he makes his current income from, she clammed up and refused to discuss another word of any of it.

Maddox and his father do something dangerous I gather, mostly because my husband was shot while working. I haven't mustered the nerve to ask him what exactly his job is yet, even though we've spent the last ten days together nearly every hour of the day. I while away the hours flipping through magazines or watching TV while he sits next to me and says very little. At times I think he forgets I'm there, but then I'll see out of the corner of my eye him staring at me and I have the surest sense he's watching me with that hungry look that both frightens and intrigues me.

He's mentioned this ball tonight a few times, but he acts like it's simply a responsibility for us to appear at, something perfunctory and nothing else. The sisters came to help him with his tux, but while they buzzed around him like bees on a flower, he didn't seem to care much about any of it, although his interest piqued when they brought in my dress.

All of this marches through my head as I stand in front of the mirror and stare at the woman looking back at me. After Sonia and Ilona helped make sure my dress fit perfectly and completed some minor touch-ups, they left, but Laney remained behind to help me with my hair. The way I usually wear it isn't acceptable, it seems, so armed with a curling iron and enough hairspray to double the size of the hole in the ozone, she made me into what she called a belle of the ball.

Her final words to me right before she left echo in my head. "You're going to be the most beautiful person at the ball tonight. Don't you dare think anything else, okay?"

I told her I wouldn't, and now that I look at myself dressed in this long white dress that hugs my body in ways no clothing has ever done for me before, I let myself believe she might be right. I don't know how the sisters did it, but this dress makes me look like I have a great chest. Maybe it's the way the thin straps that go over my shoulders pull everything up. I don't know what it is, but I love it.

A blush covers my made up cheeks at the knowledge that I'm wearing absolutely nothing under this dress. When I begged Laney to let me at least wear a thong, she flat out refused. Something about it ruining all her hard work and that I shouldn't be a prude.

My fingers trail over the back of my neck and near the curls that hang from the bun. Somehow, she made my average brown hair look like a movie star's.

She made me look like someone who belongs in this house.

I wait for Maddox to come up after leaving hours ago, but as it gets closer to six o'clock and time for the party to start, I wonder if I missed a detail he told me about meeting him somewhere instead. For a few minutes, I pace back and forth across our bedroom, unsure what to do, but then a knock on the door rouses me from my thoughts.

Opening it, I see Emily standing in the hallway. "Is something wrong? Where's Maddox?"

"I've been sent to bring you downstairs. The ball is just about to begin."

I notice she doesn't say anything about my dress or my hair. Disappointed, I join her in the hallway and we start on our way down to the ballroom. "What does it look like?" I ask her as we walk down the stairs.

"Oh, it's even better than it was last year. This year's theme is wedded bliss. Mr. Rule had them decorate it in honor of your wedding to Maddox."

Images of those white honeycomb tissue wedding bell decorations all over the room fill my head, but I'm sure the ballroom doesn't look like that. Wedded bliss does seem like an odd theme for a ball, though, but what do I know? I've never known anyone who's attended a ball.

I just have to keep telling myself what Laney said was true. I'm going to be the most beautiful person there. Well, maybe not the most beautiful but one of the most beautiful.

"Are there a lot of people here?" I ask, just now

160

realizing I'm going to be meeting people who all know one another but are strangers to me.

"Yes. This year Mr. Rule made sure to let everyone know that this will be their chance to meet you as Maddox's wife for the first time, so the ballroom has more people in it than I've ever seen."

My stomach drops, and I step off the last stair onto the main floor as my knees shake. Where is Maddox? Why isn't he here to walk into the ball with me?

I frantically scan the area for him, but he's nowhere to be found. Why?

"Am I supposed to wait for Maddox so we can enter together?" I ask as Emily continues to walk toward the ballroom doors.

She doesn't answer me, making this all feel even more terrifying. Why wouldn't he be with me if the entire theme of the ball is wedded bliss?

Emily stops at the doors and lets go of my hand. "They'll be here to take you in."

They? They who?

Before I can ask who she means, she walks away and leaves me standing there alone. Why didn't she just say Maddox will join me?

A noise behind me makes me turn around, and I see Mr. Rule dressed in a tux and smiling at me. I've never seen him so happy in all the time I've lived at this house.

"You look beautiful, Willow. Your mother would be so proud of you tonight. If it's possible, you look even lovelier than she did when she attended the Rule ball."

I don't understand what he's talking about. My mother never came to this. I can't ask him the million questions I have right now about that, though, because even more important ones fill my head.

"Why isn't Maddox here? Where is he? Is he okay? Shouldn't he be here to escort me into the ball?" I ask as Stephen stands there staring at me.

He offers me his arm and takes hold of mine. "You'll see him in a few minutes. As the master of this house, it's my honor to escort you into the ball."

"But he's my husband. I thought he'd do that."

Stephen ignores me and takes a deep breath in, letting it out slowly. "Ready?"

I'm anything but ready. He doesn't wait for me to respond and gives the signal for the doors to open. I hear the sound of instruments and the low murmur of people talking, and then everything goes quiet as we step into the ballroom. I scan the room looking for Maddox, but still he's nowhere to be found.

The silence around us is deafening and makes it impossible for me to ask where my husband is. For weeks, I've grown to trust him, and now when I need him most, he's abandoned me.

White fabric drapes from the ceiling for the full length of the room, like billowing clouds obscuring the plain area above it, and an enormous crystal chandelier hangs in the center of the room. Round tables covered in white tablecloths fill the half of the space we have to walk through to reach a dais at the other side of the room where there's an area for dancing.

If I didn't know better, I'd say it looks like the wedding reception Maddox and I never had. Men in tuxes and women in ball gowns of all colors and styles watch Stephen and me as we make our way through the crowd that watches in silence. It's eerie how they don't speak or clap or make a single noise. The only sound I hear is the tapping of my shoes on the floor with every step I take.

No one around us moves, except out of the corner of my eye I see someone near the wall to my left take a step forward and then stop. My head snaps in that direction and finally I see Maddox. Dressed in his tux just like every other man here, he looks stunning. I want to run to him so he can protect me, but he stares off angrily across the room instead of looking at me.

I follow his gaze and see another man dressed just like him who resembles Stephen standing against the right wall. I've never seen this man before. Is he Maddox's uncle? But he looks too young to be that.

He can't be another brother. Can he?

Quickly, I look for Trace, Helix, and Julian and find them toward the back of the room. Dressed like all the other men here, they seem like they always do, but I notice their attention is on that man off to the right too.

My mind frantically runs through what I've been told about the fifth Rule son. Nick is away in Europe at school and has been for months. He could have returned for this, though. It seems the ball is very important to his father, so that would make sense. But

Nick is the youngest of Maddox's brothers, so this man can't be him. He looks too old.

Who is this man, and why does my husband look so unhappy to see him?

When we reach the dais, Stephen guides me up a ramp and directs me to stand in the center of the platform. I feel everyone's eyes on me, watching my every move as if there's something important about me.

When Stephen finally speaks, he sounds like a game show host showing off the prizes contestants can win. "Ladies and gentlemen, welcome to the Rule ball! I hope you've been enjoying yourselves. Tonight's a special night indeed for me and the entire Rule family because we have a new member in our midst. Let me introduce you to Willow Rule, my daughter-in-law and hopefully not too far off in the future, the mother-to-be to the next generation of our family."

My eyes glaze over at the number of men and women standing in front of us, their gazes turned our way in rapt attention as they clap enthusiastically at Stephen's announcement. Who are all these people? In the entire month I've lived here, I've never seen a single person visit, except for business associates of Stephen's, but now this enormous ballroom is filled with people eager to hear about me?

And why isn't Maddox standing up here with me? I look over to where he was standing just a minute ago but don't see him now. When I turn my head to look for the other man, he's missing too.

"Now enjoy your time and be sure to eat and drink

to your heart's content," Stephen says to the crowd as they continue to clap.

A second later, he whisks me off the dais to behind a curtain at the back of the room where Maddox waits. I instantly see in his eyes something's wrong.

"Where were you? Why didn't you bring me in? What's going on?" I ask, peppering him with questions even as I'm afraid of the answers.

He takes my hand and smiles in that sexy way of his. "You look incredible, Willow."

"Thanks, but what the hell was all that? And who's that guy who looks like your father but was standing on the other side of the room opposite you? Is he a relative or something? This is all so strange. Can we just go back to our room now? I don't like this at all, Maddox."

He shakes his head and frowns. "This is the biggest night of the year for the Rule family, so no going back to the room yet. We just have to get through tonight and we'll be fine."

"Get through tonight? What does that even mean? I don't understand why that was so weird. Why did your father have to bring me into the ball instead of you? Everyone was so quiet, like it was some somber ceremony. It was so strange."

Maddox trails his finger along my collarbone and over my shoulder and sighs. "It's just the way things are. It's just tonight, and then after that, everything will go back to the way it was before."

Something in the way he says that unnerves me.

"So what happens now? Do we have to dance or

something? The food smells terrific, so if you tell me we get to eat, I'd be thrilled to hear that."

I see in his eyes something else is about to happen that won't make me anywhere as happy as if I got to eat. Slipping his arm around me, he pulls me close to him and stares down into my eyes. In his, I see a darkness I've never witnessed before in them, not even on that first day here.

"You need to do something for me, Willow. Can you promise me you'll do as I tell you to?" he asks with so much seriousness in his voice I can't help but be frightened.

"Okay. What's going on? What do you need me to do?"

"Promise me you'll remember all those hours you and I spent upstairs after I got shot. Can you do that for me? Can you promise whatever happens tonight won't make you forget all that time we spent together?"

"You're scaring me. What's going to happen tonight? Please don't let anyone hurt me. I know I don't fit in with you and all these people, but don't let them do anything to me."

He moves his hand up to stroke my cheek and shakes his head. "You are the most beautiful woman here. You fit in with me perfectly, so don't ever think you don't. As for all those people out there, they mean nothing. Never forget that. Nothing. Don't let a single one of them ruin this night for us."

Absent in all this lovely talk of his is a promise to not let anyone hurt me. He looks like he cares about me as he stares down into my eyes and says all those nice things, but why won't he say he won't let anyone hurt me?

"Maddox, please! Promise me you won't let anyone here hurt me. Why can't you say that? You asked me to promise you something, now I'm asking the same. Don't let them hurt me, please!"

I wait to hear those words—"Willow, I won't let anyone hurt you tonight"—but they never come from his mouth. Instead, he leans down and kisses me sweetly, and I don't know if I imagine it or if it's just what I want to be real, but I sense he cares for me in that kiss.

Caressing my face, he whispers, "I'll be right here with you the whole time. We'll dance and then we'll get something for you to eat, okay?"

"So that's all we have to do? Why is your father acting so oddly?" I ask as my heart races in panic. "Is something wrong that I need to know? Please tell me."

"I can't, but don't worry. I'm right here with you."

I feel like I'm going to be sick listening to all these cryptic warnings. What is going on and why is Maddox acting this way?

Terrified, I grab hold of Maddox's hand and grip it as tightly as I can. "Why won't you tell me what's going to happen? Please, just tell me! I hate surprises. Just tell me, or even better, let's just go and leave. I can see you don't want to be here. Why can't we do that?"

He lifts my hand to his mouth and presses a kiss onto my knuckles. "Because this night is about us, so we can't just leave. Like I've said before, being a Rule is all about responsibility to this family."

What the hell does that mean? If this ball is all about wedded bliss, why are the two people who are the stars of this show not allowed to be happy?

"What's going to happen, Maddox? You've been to one of these balls before. Tell me so I can know!"

"Not like this one I haven't. I just need you to always keep in mind that I'm right here. I'm not going anywhere, Willow."

A million horrible ideas flash through my mind, each one more terrible than the one before it. "What does that mean not one like this? What's going to happen? It's just a party, right?"

The problem is it doesn't feel like just a party. I sensed something felt wrong with Stephen, and now Maddox seems off too.

"It's going to be fine. We'll have a good time. It's just that we all have our roles to play in this world, Willow. I keep telling you that."

Disgusted by the man I thought I'd grown to care about in these past few weeks, I push him away, making sure to thrust my hand into the shoulder where he was shot. He winces in pain, and I watch wishing I hurt him more.

"I'll never forgive you, Maddox. I don't care if we're married until the end of time. I'll never forgive you if something happens to me tonight. Never!"

Behind me, I hear someone clear their throat and turn around to see Stephen glaring at me. I must be ruining his little party with all my protests against not wanting to take part in this monstrous charade.

"It's time for you two to take center stage. Tonight, you become an official member of the Rule family, Willow."

When he reaches out to take hold of my hand, I yank it away from him. "What does that mean? Why are you all acting so strangely? I'm married to Maddox and this whole thing is supposed to be about wedding bliss, so just let us be. We'll dance and eat and then let us be."

"Your wife is an excitable one, Maddox. I would have thought you'd had enough time to do something about that."

I don't recognize the voice saying those words and look around to find out who's talking. Behind me standing next to Maddox is the man from the other side of the ballroom. Now that they're just inches away from one another, I see the man not only looks like Stephen but Maddox too.

"Who are you? Why are you talking to my husband like that?" I ask, but the man only smiles.

"Ignore him, Willow," Stephen says flatly. "Tonight is for this family to have a good time."

Spinning around to face him, I don't know what he means by a good time. So far, I don't understand how any of this has been fun for anyone. And who is this man who continues to stand here after Stephen has told me to disregard what he's saying?

"My name is Asher," the man says in a deep voice

that instantly frightens me, even though I've never met him before in my life. "Asher Rule."

Asher Rule? Who is this person?

I look back at him and study his face. He's too old to be a sibling to Maddox. The slight hint of lines around his eyes and the few stray gray hairs tell me that. So he must be his uncle.

Before I can ask any questions, Maddox takes my hand in his and smiles. "It's time for us to get out there. No more talk about any of this."

Stephen throws Asher a nasty look and gets a chuckle in return, the kind of laugh that sounds ominous and threatening even in its seemingly happy way.

"Yes, let's forget this and get out there to greet our guests."

Neither man speaks another word, practically ignoring Asher, and as we leave the relative quiet found behind that curtain, I look back and see him watching me. His dark eyes fix on mine, locking our gazes uncomfortably as Maddox pulls me up onto the dais.

I don't know what's happened between these three men, but I sense nothing good will come from Asher's arrival in this house.

CHAPTER SIXTEEN

illow

CLUTCHING MADDOX'S HAND SO TIGHTLY MY fingers ache, I walk out onto the dais with him and watch the crowd of guests erupt into clapping and cheers. It's surreal to see all these people I don't know excited about us merely walking out in front of them, and I look over at Maddox in the hopes that he's more comfortable with it than I am.

He's not. I know by the smile he's plastered onto his face that he hates this. I don't understand why this is such a big deal or why any of these people care at all about our marriage. Don't they know we just met a few weeks ago and our wedding was nothing but a sham?

"Ladies and gentleman, I'm so happy to introduce

you to Mr. and Mrs. Maddox Rule," Stephen says loudly as he strides over to stand next to me.

I can't place why, but I have the surest sense he's chosen to position himself just inches away from me instead of on the other side next to Maddox because he's protecting me. Stiff and uncomfortable, he's practically announcing to anyone who's paying attention to him that he's worried about something.

Glancing over toward the area behind the curtain where we just came from, I see Asher still watching, his gaze set on only me. Why would he be looking at me like that? He's never seen me before tonight, and that's been for a total of mere minutes.

I reach over and grasp Maddox's wrist with my other hand, desperate for something that will make me feel like I'm safe. Stephen continues to talk to the guests about how happy the Rule family is to be growing and how much he hopes to be able to say it will be growing by even more still in a few short months. Maddox's reaction never changes, and he continues to smile that almost painful grin even when he looks over at me.

All I want to do is run away from this ballroom. Even being trapped in our bedroom would be preferable to being stuck here on display for all these strangers and forced to pretend this night and what Maddox and I are to one another are anything close to normal.

"So now it's time for the happy couple to have their first dance together. Maddox and Willow, if you will, take your place on the dance floor."

Maddox begins moving toward the stairs even before the last of Stephen's words filter through my brain, and I have to practically run to catch up with him before he starts dragging me across the dais. The guests clap again, and I see Stephen next to me oddly following us with a smile on his face. It's not forced like his son's, but it doesn't go all the way up to his eyes, which tells me he's not as happy as he wants everyone to believe either.

At the stairs, he and Maddox help me down the three tiny steps. They hover over me like I'm some prized thing they adore, a marked change from how they've treated me since the day I got here four weeks ago.

I feel Stephen release his hold on my arm and then it's just Maddox and me in the center of attention, all those eyes on us expecting to see a husband and wife have their first dance as a married couple together.

Or do they? I don't know. Maybe they're all like Stephen and force their children to marry people they don't love. Or maybe they themselves have been forced to marry someone against their will. Perhaps they understand exactly what they're seeing and tacitly approve because it's all they've had in their lives.

Maddox presses his hand to the small of my back and gently pulls me closer to him as he takes my right hand in his left hand to begin our dance. I don't recognize what the musicians play, although it wouldn't have been what I would have chosen. Then again, I wouldn't have chosen to marry this man at all, so worrying about everything after that is pretty much useless.

"Remember what I said, Willow. Just stay close to me and you'll be fine," he says in a low voice in my ear.

Like everything else he's told me tonight, that doesn't make me feel any less anxious. I wish I could be fine. He presses against me as we gently move to the music, and my body reacts to the closeness against my will. I don't want to enjoy the feel of him. He's cruel and cold, and I suspect he's still sleeping with other women.

Yet even believing that, I close my eyes and revel in how exquisite he is when his thigh brushes up against mine. The man I was forced to marry is nothing short of gorgeous. It's a beauty like one can find in an ice carving, though. Cold and sharp, he's dangerous to the touch.

But will he ever melt for me?

I wonder that as I feel his warm breath drift over the shell of my ear and travel down over my neck. He feels like the kind of man I'm used to, but all it takes is one word from him and I'm chilled to the bone with fear. That he keeps saying I'll be safe and fine if I stay close to him belies almost everything he's said and done to me since the moment I walked through the front doors of this house.

The last notes of whatever music the band has been playing drift off into silence before the guests join us on the dance floor, but I feel no sense of security surrounded by them. They don't know me and I don't know them, so who's to say people who consider the

Rules as friends won't simply allow something horrible to happen to me right here in front of their eyes.

"Another dance?" Maddox asks in a way that says he isn't asking my permission but merely informing me of what's about to happen.

I give him a tiny smile, unsure if I'm happy to submit to his wish or simply too afraid to be released from his hold amongst these people. "It's our night, so I guess it's only right. But what about your arm? Does it hurt because you aren't wearing your sling?"

His icy façade softens for a moment, and I regret what I said to him before. That happens from time to time, even more in the past couple weeks as he's been recuperating. All it takes is a flash of kindness to make me wish things were different between us. Yes, he forced me to marry him, or more correctly, his father did, but with each passing day as I tell myself I hate him and sometimes let that emotion slip out in front of him, I wish we could be like normal couples and have some kind of happiness.

I feel someone's hand against my back and turn to see Asher standing to my right. He gives me a smile before glancing over at Maddox. "May I cut in?"

My gaze locks on his as I wait for him to tell his uncle no, but he looks over my head and winces before sliding his hand away from me. Nearly emotionless, he answers, "Of course."

Stunned, I watch him step back while Asher brusquely presses his hand against my back and roughly pulls me too close to him, his body pushing against mine and making me uncomfortable. When I try to step back away, he holds me like his hand is made of iron and shakes his head, his smile never fading the entire time.

"It's remarkable how much you look like your mother, Willow," he says, surprising me.

In that instant, everyone in that room fades away and I focus my entire attention on him. "You knew my mother too?"

"I knew her like no one else in the world did," he says in a faraway voice.

I wait for him to continue talking, desperate to know what that means, but he says nothing more and I'm left wishing we weren't dancing to this stupid music at this damn ball I never wanted to attend in the first place. I want to hear about my mother. I know he couldn't have known her during my lifetime because I would remember something of the name Rule being part of our lives.

No, this man knew her when she was young, a time in her life that's like a vacant spot in my knowledge of her. Whenever I asked my father about her life before she met him, he'd give me some pleasant but vague statement about how she was a different person then and the past doesn't really matter.

But it matters to me. I always felt like there was a piece of my mother I never knew, and now this man and his brother have both said they knew her. I want to know how and anything else they can tell me.

"When did you know her?" I ask, barely able to contain my curiosity.

His eyes sparkle as he turns me around the dance

floor. "When we were young and life was all the two of us could ever imagine it could be."

The way he says that sounds so magical, and I can't help but think he knew her not merely as a friend but as someone he truly cared about. For a split second, I feel bad for myself that Maddox and I likely won't ever be like that toward one another, but I have to push that away for the moment. That regret can wait for another time. Right now, I want to hear all Asher can tell me about my mother when she was young.

"I've always wanted to hear about my mother back then. Were you teenagers when you knew her?" I ask, desperate to know what he meant by the two of them imagining a life between them.

Asher nods and lets out a sigh. "Even younger. She came to live here when she was only seven. I was eleven at the time, but I knew from the moment she walked into my life that she was special."

"How? What made her special?" I ask, leaving aside my surprise that it was here that my mother lived after her parents were killed in that car crash. My mother always said she lived with a foster family, so I assumed something far different than the Rules.

He levels his gaze on my face and sighs again. "You have the same look in your eyes when you're curious that she used to get when she wanted to know about something. She used to love to ask questions. Stephen never liked having to listen to her ask them, but I never tired of answering every one she had."

I smile at that while the memory of my father

always saying I was just like my mother with all my questions fills my head. So often when he said that, he sounded frustrated, but now I have to wonder if he saw my curiosity the same way Asher saw my mother's.

Stephen not wanting to answer a little girl's questions doesn't surprise me. He hasn't answered a single one of mine since I got here, and his son is just like him. They speak in cryptic riddles more than anything else, and yet they're surprised when I ask how or why because I don't understand what they mean.

"How much younger are you than your brother?" I ask and watch Asher look over my shoulder in the direction of where Stephen stands on the edge of the dance floor.

"Four years. Maybe that's why he always found your mother so annoying. Eight years is a long time, especially when you're a man of eighteen and she's a girl of ten."

What Stephen said to me when he mentioned my mother right after I came here flashes through my memory. "He seemed to remember her fondly when he talked about her to me. He said she was the sweetest person he'd ever met."

Asher responds with a sneer and a nasty look over my shoulder I imagine is meant for his brother. "The years have made him look back on that time far differently than it actually was. I guess I don't blame him, though. No one wants to think they treated a young girl like a pest when she so obviously just wanted someone to care about her."

The music ends, and as much as I'd dreaded dancing with Asher, I'm sad when he lets me go and steps back away from me. "It's been a pleasure, Willow. I hope we get to talk more while I'm here."

And then he's gone, swallowed up by a group of guests and behind Maddox as he steps forward to take me in his arms again for the next dance. Asher's smiling face is replaced by my husband's angry expression, and it doesn't take long after the music starts again for me to understand just how furious he is.

"You seemed to have a nice time dancing with him. I would have expected you to be unhappy, but you were all smiles the whole time. Don't think that others didn't notice too. I'm sure that more than one person here is wondering why you're smiling for him but not with me."

Maddox tightens his hold on me as a much slower song begins to play, and I feel his hard body crush against mine. I can't pull away or find any freedom, no matter how much I try and still be subtle so the people dancing around us can't tell how I truly feel about him, so I give in and let him hold me tightly.

"He says he knew my mother when she was a little girl. I like hearing stories about her back then. That's what I was smiling about. I don't even know him," I say as I look up into my husband's dark eyes and wish I could see some faint hint of kindness in them.

But his expression only hardens at hearing my

explanation. "I don't want you talking to him anymore, Willow. Whatever he has to say doesn't affect us."

"So it doesn't matter that finding out what my mother's life was like as a child here makes me happy? Did you know she lived with your family after her parents were killed?"

A flash of surprise lights up his face for a moment, but then it disappears. "No, I didn't. Perhaps if you want to know about that you should talk to my father then. But no more talking to Asher."

Frustration builds inside me and makes tears well in my eyes. "Your father wasn't as close to her as your uncle was. He was so much older than her that he thought she was a nuisance. How is he going to tell me anything nice about her then?"

Maddox presses his mouth into a thin line across his face, a sign he's frustrated with me now too. "I don't know, Willow. I just don't want you to talk to my uncle again. Don't make this a problem tonight."

I turn my head, hating that this man so easily can make my emotions spill out all over the place. It's like he senses something brings me a tiny flicker of happiness and has to snuff it out before I get to enjoy it.

"And if I do?" I ask, unable to stop myself, even though I know I should fear his response.

His hand slides up over my shoulder blade and closes around the back of my neck. In my ear, he whispers in a ragged voice edged with rage, "Don't test me on this, Willow. You won't like how it turns out."

As we dance until the end of the song, I know that's not an empty threat. Maddox doesn't make those.

But I can't miss a chance to learn about my mother from his uncle. No matter how dangerous it is.

CHAPTER SEVENTEEN

*M*addox

MY FATHER SITS BEHIND HIS DESK STILL RAVING about this year's ball three days later. I don't understand how he can think it went anywhere close to well after that goddamned brother of his showed up just hours before.

"I know I've said this to you more than once, but Willow just impressed me beyond what I ever imagined she could do. Do you know I'm still fielding calls from people who want to say how lovely they thought she was? And the sisters tell me they've gotten enough requests for designs and orders to last them through the end of the year after the ball and Willow's gown."

"Great. I'm happy it turned out so well for you," I

mumble while I count the seconds before I get to leave his office.

I barely feel the heat in here today. It's obscured by the near constant rage I walk around with ever since Asher's arrival on Saturday. I even think my father could push every button I have and still not make me any angrier than I've been for days.

"You must be so proud of her. I don't think I've ever seen her happier than that night," my father coos, still stuck on the same fucking topic I wish he'd just get over.

"Yeah. She was the prettiest dog in the show."

My poor attempt at sarcasm comes off wrong even to my ears, but I'm not in the mood to apologize. The disapproval written all over my father's face says it fell flat for him too.

"How have things been with you two?" he asks, thankfully changing the topic but unfortunately to the same one he usually fixates on.

Our upcoming child.

I don't feel like lying today, so I shrug and admit the truth I know will upset him. "Well, since I don't get home until she's asleep every night, I guess you could describe how things have been between us as chilly. Or maybe the word nonexistent works better. Let's just say I'm happy I don't have to rely on my lovely wife to get off or I'd be walking around with blue balls."

His expression immediately turns dark, his jet black eyebrows drawing in like angry slashes. "Is it so much to ask that you sleep with your beautiful wife? Why can't you do that one thing?"

I open my mouth to tell him I'd be happy to but since I didn't want to get married in the first fucking place, giving up my own life to just get sex from her doesn't seem like a very good trade off. Before I can get a word out, though, Asher appears in the door and decides to join in the conversation.

As if anyone fucking asked him.

"You have a lovely young wife and you ignore her? No wonder she comes to find me every day. She's desperate to have some decent conversation. It's obvious you're not offering her that."

Rage tears through me at hearing Willow disobeyed me by seeking him out, and I leap out of that leather office chair, ready to put a bullet into him. Pulling my gun, I aim at his head and let my temper go like I've wanted to for days.

"Who the fuck do you think you are? Don't talk to my wife ever again, or I swear to God I'm going to get rid of you and all the fucking hassles you bring with you."

For a long moment, I stand there with my gun pointed at him, prepared to do what I've wanted to do from the moment he showed up that day. He looks at me like he can't believe I'd actually go through with it, and out of the corner of my eye, I see my father shake his head.

I don't waste time waiting for Asher to say something back to me. I don't give a fuck to hear anything he has to say anyway. Pushing past him, I stuff my gun into the back of my pants and march upstairs to find the person I'm even angrier with than goddamned Asher.

With each step, I grow more and more enraged. By the time I reach the bedroom, I want to kill her for how she makes me feel.

She sits on the bed reading some book and doesn't even look up when I storm in. Has she gotten so strong in just a single month that I don't frighten her anymore?

That's a mistake she shouldn't make.

"Have you been talking to Asher even after I explicitly told you not to?" I snap.

Willow closes the book and looks up at me as I make my way toward her around the bed. "He tells me about my mother when she was young and lived here, Maddox. It's nothing bad. I swear."

"Nothing bad? I told you not to do it, and still you do it anyway. Sounds pretty fucking bad to me."

Where the hell did the terrified girl of four weeks go? The one sitting in front of me now tilting her head up defiantly to meet my gaze isn't the one I married.

"Why can't you just let me have this? I ask for nothing from you, and you graciously give me just that. Nothing. You go out every night and live your life while I stay here, forced to live my life only on this estate. Getting to hear him tell stories about her is a tiny thing that brings me incredible happiness, so of course, you'll move heaven and earth and fight hell and high water to make sure I don't get to have it. You're a real son of a bitch, Maddox."

Unlike every other time we've fought, she has no tears to make those blue eyes all watery tonight. Instead, she's all courage and insolence in a tiny package I could crush with my bare hands if I want to.

I take a step toward her, but she doesn't flinch. Her gaze never wavers, this brand new brave wife of mine.

"You want son of a bitch? Good. That's all I have for you tonight, so get ready. I already threatened your new best friend, so now I'm going to tell you the same thing. Don't talk to him anymore. If you do, I swear to God, Willow, I won't be responsible for what happens to you."

She surprises me when she jumps up off the bed and stands toe to toe with me. "Just say it, Maddox. Don't be a coward. Say the words you want to say. If I don't do what you want me to do, you're going to kill me, right? That's going to make having that baby your father wants pretty damn hard, but I guess you can get one of those whores you spend every night with to give you a child. In fact, why don't you just let me go live my own life and you can get one of them to do that right now?"

"Enough! I'm done playing games with you. No more talking to Asher! Do you understand me?"

I instantly recognize the hurt that flashes in her eyes when I ask that question. I know I've had that same look in my own eyes hundreds of times after hearing my father utter those exact words, as if I'm too stupid to understand a basic command.

Her reaction tells me she hates that question just

like I do. Willow pushes her hands into my chest, her anger spilling out when she asks through gritted teeth, "Do I understand? I'm not a moron, Maddox. I understand a lot. I understand that no matter how kind I am to you, you're cruel and heartless to me. I understand you've never even tried to be good to me, even though I'm your wife. I understand you lecture me on duty to this family, but you have no idea what your duty is to me. You talk about duty, but you don't act like you have any duty to me or this marriage."

She stuns me with how brave she is now, and for a few moments, I don't know what I want to say to her. It seems she wants to poke the bear, but I doubt she's ready for when the bear returns the favor.

Grabbing hold of her wrists, I stop her pushing, which was getting her nowhere since I'm so much bigger than her, and squeeze them tightly. I want to see her eyes fill with tears. I want to see her feel bad for talking to my asshole uncle.

If she won't give me that any other way, I'll take this way.

And right on cue, it doesn't take more than a few seconds of pain for her to react just as I want. "Maddox, let go of me. You're hurting me. Let go!"

But I don't let go. Instead, I keep my fingers around those tiny wrists of hers and smile as her eyes turn that watery blue I love so much.

"Why? You have no problem causing me pain, so why shouldn't I give you the same in return?"

"Please, Maddox. How can you say I've caused you pain? I'm barely half the size of you," she says like she truly doesn't understand the game we're playing here.

Still I don't let her go.

"How do you think it feels when Asher tells me you come looking for him every day and he's sure it's because I'm not giving you what you need? How do you think that feels, Willow?"

She doesn't answer at first, like she's trying to understand just how fucking bad that hurts me, and then she frowns like she does know how that feels. But she doesn't. That's clear when she finally speaks.

"Why would you care if anyone thought you didn't give me what I need? You're more than proud of that, aren't you? If you weren't, you'd stay home at night and be here with me instead of out with God only knows who."

"Because I'm your fucking husband, and I don't need my uncle acting like he knows what my wife needs better than I do," I bark at her.

Willow tugs her hands away from my hold and meets my anger with her own. "Then treat her like she's worth your time and not a hassle you never wanted in the first place!"

Something changes inside me at that moment. She wants me to show her what she's worth to me? Fine. I'm done holding back with her.

I reach out for her and wrap my hand behind her head to pull her to me. I crave her mouth on mine to take away this feeling I've had since that fucking Asher accused me of not giving her what she needs. My body aches for her to see he's wrong.

The first taste of her lips makes my cock hard as steel. She's sweet like peaches on my tongue, and I'm like a starving man who wants to devour her. Willow doesn't fight my desire, ratcheting it up notch by notch with every time she returns my kiss with as much need as I have inside me.

No, this isn't the girl from a month ago, and I'm not the man I was that day either. Then I didn't give a damn about her or what she needed. Now the idea of her thinking someone else can be what she wants or needs nearly makes me go blind with rage.

Her fingers fumble with the buttons on my shirt, like needy little things teasing me with what's to come. I push her hands away and rip the fucking thing off myself, desperate to feel her touch on my skin. The white buttons fly everywhere, hitting the wood floor with tiny tapping sounds as they scatter across the room.

"Not one more fucking time, Willow. Never again. I don't want you talking to him," I groan as I stuff my hand into her hair and tug hard so she has to look into my eyes and see she's not the only one who fucking feels something here.

She doesn't answer, but she will obey me this time. I'll see to that.

Right now, though, I don't want to think about that goddamned uncle of mine, what he has to tell her about her mother, or another soul living or dead in this world. For tonight, all I want to think about is how she feels against me and how it feels to fuck her without holding back for the first time.

"Maddox, I want to feel like you don't hate me," she says on a tiny sob.

Her hands run over my torso, leaving trails of need that feel like fire on my skin. Her eyes wide, it's like she's seeing my body for the first time and she wants to explore every inch of it.

"I don't hate you, Willow," I moan before stuffing my hands beneath her shirt.

Her skin is warm and soft, and I dip my head to taste the spot just below her collarbone. I sink my teeth in just enough to make her feel a twinge of pain, and she cries out above me. When I lift my head, I see her eyes filled with tears again.

"Why do you want to hurt me?" she asks in a soft voice, dropping her hands from my body.

I instantly miss her touch and seek them out, bringing her fingers to my mouth. Pressing a kiss onto them, I answer her honestly. "It's all I am."

She slides her hands along my jaw and cradles my face while she shakes her head. "I don't believe that, Maddox. I've seen something else in you. Something good."

No, she hasn't. She wants to think she has, but I've given her nothing but pain all this time. She wants to believe I'm like her, but I'm not.

My hands rip off her shirt from her body and make quick work of her bra. Cupping her breasts in my hands, I squeeze the tender flesh and leave red marks that will be black and blue by tomorrow.

"What good have you seen? Don't lie to yourself. I know what I am. You do too."

Her eyes slowly close at the feel of my mouth on her sucking a pebbled pink nipple between my lips. I nip her with my teeth to hear a soft moan escape from her throat and know when she slides her hand around the back of my head to keep me there that she likes a little pain with her pleasure.

"Please, don't make me think there isn't any good in you, Maddox. It's the only thing that's made me think I can survive here."

She doesn't finish her thought, but I know the truth. The only real happiness she's found here is talking to Asher about her mother, and I've taken that away from her because I am that cruel person she's come to know. I can't change that or who I am, but I can give her something no one else has ever gotten from me.

"You'll survive because I'm your husband and I'll protect you. I swear to you."

If she was as untrusting as I am, she'd ask who would protect her from me, but I see in her eyes my promise is enough to make the unhappiness completely disappear from them, and as heartless as I am, that makes me happy. I don't want her to have nothing good in her life. I just want to be the one who gives that good to her.

"Then show me I'm worth protecting," she says, her tender plea coming out as a sob when I tug her shorts down to allow me room to get my hands under them.

Willow undoes my zipper and reaches into my pants to palm my cock. The mere touch of her hand on me makes me want to be inside her so fucking bad. When she tightens her grip and strokes it from base to tip, I can't wait any longer.

I rip her innocent white panties off and push her hand away to get my own pants off, needing to be inside her. We're all hands searching for flesh and release, two bodies craving the one thing they desperately want to share.

We're raw and vulnerable, something I've never let myself be before with anyone, and I don't try to hide it. It's almost as if I need to show her I'm something more than just cruelty, for once.

CHAPTER EIGHTEEN

illow

MADDOX TEARS AT ME, MAKING WHATEVER WE ARE to one another come to the surface. I've spent weeks trying to hide the effect he has on me, but tonight, I can't do that anymore.

And even more, I don't want to.

I don't understand why my talking to Asher about my mother when they were young bothers him like it does, but as much as I want to hear more about her back then, I'll give that up if Maddox can give me what I crave.

That sense of someone here caring if I live or die or even that they miss me when I'm not around.

I know I can't change him, but I also know there's some tiny sliver of good somewhere deep inside him. If he's willing to share that with me, then I'm willing to do as he demands.

He stares down at me with more need than I've ever seen in another soul, but even as much of what Maddox is frightens me, what I see in him eyes now doesn't scare me at all. I understand need.

The need to feel like you aren't alone.

The need to believe someone wants you just as you are, without alteration and without concession.

The need to have another person desire what you are for just that and nothing more.

"I don't think I've ever been with a woman who asks so many questions when we're not fucking and then says so little when we are," he says as his gaze travels over my body, followed by his hands that roam over my skin, leaving marks along the way.

My hands continue their exploration of his body, and with every inch I touch, I want him more. The hardness of him, the utter opposite of who I am, makes my desire soar.

Maddox grabs my face and forces me to look up at him. Gently holding my jaw, he smiles in that sexy way I know so many women have seen and loved.

"I like that you're quiet, though. Don't think I don't."

"I'm sorry I'm not like your other women," I say, suddenly self-conscious about him silently comparing me in his mind to the ones he still sees to this day when he's not in this house.

"I don't have other women. None of them are mine. Women have always been a way for me to forget everything my life is. Nothing else. But they aren't mine. I never wanted them that way."

"What way?"

"The way I want you," he answers before crushing my mouth with his in a kiss that takes my breath away.

The way I want you.

I want to ask what that means. He thinks I'm quiet because I don't have anything to say, but that's not true. I have a lot to say, but I'm afraid to give voice to those questions, like what do you feel and how do you want me because I'm not sure I can handle the answers he'll give.

For as much as I adore the hardness in his body, that same hardness in his nature isn't something I've grown strong enough to handle yet. It's only been a month in this place, and no matter how hard I try, I'm still the soft soul I've always been.

We tumble down to the bed, our hands searching out parts of the other person while our kiss remains unbroken. I feel his hard cock between my legs, brushing up against my tender skin and making it nearly impossible to not beg him to do what I've wanted him to do for weeks.

You see, as much as Maddox is someone I want to hate, I don't know if it's time or the loneliness of this place, but every day I grow to want him closer to me, even if he's never known that. To have him turn to me and say he wanted what I so desperately craved is all I've wished for with every passing hour. He has no idea how much it hurt to know every night he willingly chose to leave me here alone while he went out to spend time with other people.

I tilt my hips to feel him push against my needy clit, and he takes the hint instantly, rolling his hips so his cock grazes that tiny bundle of nerves that yearns for attention. I slide my hands over his back, raking my fingernails across his smooth skin on my way down to cup his ass. He lets a low moan escape from him next to my ear and then closes his fist in my hair, tightening just enough to send a wave of sharp pain along my scalp.

He pushes my legs open with his hand, forcing my thighs apart until my hips ache. Looking down at me for a moment, he seems strangely calm while a storm rages inside me that can only be abated when he finally fills me.

And then with one thrust of his hips, he pushes his cock into me and all that calmness I saw in him a second ago disappears, replaced by a fury I'm not sure I can handle. His hand in my hair tugs hard, forcing my head into his muscular shoulder as he begins to pound into my body like a man possessed.

In my ear, I hear him moan my name like some mantra or promise I don't understand. "Willow…Willow."

Over and over, he repeats that single word between grunts and groans and something I can't distinguish that sounds like words meant to tell me he cares. They flow into my ears and fill my brain with the music of our fucking, inching up my desire for more and more of him with every syllable.

It's animalistic and raw, but it's so quintessentially Maddox.

I clutch his shoulders, my fingernails digging into his back, and ride each thrust of his cock. The rhythm and how exquisite he feels when he touches that spot deep inside me make how much my hips hurt fade away until all I have is my need and his cock satisfying it.

My orgasm comes over me like a freight train, taking me by surprise at first and then leveling me until I have nothing left to give. I struggle to keep my legs around Maddox's waist, but I lock my ankles against the small of his back and press hard to hold on to him as the last thrusts of his fucking me happen and then he stills on top of me. His cock twitches inside me before he fills my body with all he has while we lay there silently, the only sound in my ears the racing beat of my heart slowly easing down to normal.

Maddox lets out a heavy sigh into the pillow next to me that makes the side of my head and my neck warm. For a long moment, it's as if the world stops and the only two people in it are us. In the haze my mind's in after sex, I think about how different things might be if that was true.

What if he didn't have to work for his father doing whatever they do that involves people shooting at him? What if he and I met not to have to get married quickly but because fate put us together in some time and place that gave us the chance to get to know one another? Would we have ended up in this bed in this house as we are today?

As if he reads my mind, he rolls off me and props his head up with his hand like he wants to answer those questions. Did I say them out loud, I wonder as he stares into my eyes? I don't think I did, but he's looking at me like we're in the middle of a conversation.

"I don't know if I've ever told you this, but I hate that the whole idea of sex with us is only so my father can get that grandchild he so desperately thinks this family needs. I never didn't want to be with you, Willow. I just didn't want to give him that, and you got caught in the middle."

The words hit me hard, even though he says them in the nicest voice he's ever used with me. I force a smile and nod. "I guess I can understand. Can you understand how much it hurt that I never knew that and thought you just didn't like me at all? I thought that's why you went out every night and went with…"

I can't finish my sentence now after what we've just done. I'm too vulnerable and admitting that truth hurts too much.

When I turn my head to look away because I don't think I can handle seeing him at that moment, he takes hold of my chin between his fingers and gently pulls me back to face him. My instinct is to close my eyes so I don't have to see the pity or cruelty in his expression. That won't help me when he says something to answer my question, but it's a tiny bit of armor I can wield against the hurt I fear is about to come from him.

"Why won't you look at me, Willow? I want you to see me when I say this."

I shake my head, hating that all the wonderful feelings of the time we spent together are about to be ruined. But Maddox won't relent.

"Open your eyes and look at me. You asked me a question, so I deserve the chance to give you an answer."

I do as he orders and brace for the pain his words will bring. I'm not even sure he understands that his answer will hurt.

"When I went out, it wasn't to be with other women because I didn't want you. I didn't know how much it hurt you, and for that, I'm sorry. I don't think I understood how anything I was doing could hurt you until today."

Surprised at how he isn't trying to be cruel at this moment, I let myself open up a tiny bit and ask, "What happened today?"

His expression hardens right in front of my eyes, and I brace for that harshness that's so much a part of him to come roaring out of his mouth. But it doesn't. Instead, he shakes his head and takes a deep breath.

"My uncle said that I wasn't giving you what you needed. There's nothing worse for a man to hear than he's not able to do what's expected of him," he says quietly.

I consider trying to explain that I think Asher meant talking about things I'm interested in, particularly his memories of my mother, but I decide against that. Pitting Maddox against his uncle isn't what I want while we're lying here still naked in bed bearing our souls to one another.

"Maybe we weren't doing that for each other. We've only been married a month, and we barely know each other still."

That I'm actually trying to shield his feelings is something I couldn't have imagined even a few days ago. I don't want to lash out now, though. This is the first time I've ever seen Maddox open up, and to attack him now could mean he might never let me in again. I don't want to risk messing up like that.

He takes another deep breath and lets it out in a rush. "I don't know. Six months ago, I celebrated my birthday and acted like I had since I was sixteen. Drinking and taking whatever drugs I could get into me was what I looked forward to after a long day at work. I'm not really husband material, as you can see, but that didn't matter to anyone. So when we got married, I figured I'd be able to keep living my life as I always had. The problem is when I came back each night, you were here reminding me of what I wasn't doing right."

I never would have guessed. I thought he didn't care about any of this.

"And my asshole uncle blows into town like a bad wind and the first thing I see is he can make you smile after literally two minutes while you've lived here for an entire month and I've never done anything to make you smile. That kind of thing sticks with a guy, even if he doesn't show it."

As crazy as it seems, I can't let that confession go without trying to explain myself to him. "It's just that he knew my mother, which to be honest, is still the most incredible thing. I guess you wouldn't think that, but to be here in a place where my mother lived for years is just amazing to me. Because she died when I was five, she never told me a thing about her childhood, and to be honest, it's like there's a hole inside me where all those memories should be. Your grandparents took her in, she had this entire estate to enjoy, and it's obvious at least one of their kids was friends with her. That's the only reason I was smiling, Maddox. That whole ball terrified me because I felt like I didn't belong, but just getting to hear someone tell me even the tiniest thing about my mother made me forget I stuck out like a sore thumb among all those people."

Maddox runs his finger along the outline of my mouth and shakes his head. "You aren't any less than anyone who was here that night. You're a Rule now, Willow. That means something in this world."

"What does that mean for someone like me?" I ask as I turn to look at him, wishing he'd give me the answer. "I'm just some girl your father took to marry you. I might have that last name, but I'm not really like your family. You've had money and power all your life. I've had neither and still don't here. All I have is a name that's worth something more than the name I used to have. It's not the same."

He doesn't answer at first, studying me like he isn't sure what to say because I'm telling the truth. He has to know it like I do.

Twisting his expression into a grimace, he says, "All of that may be true, but you are in this family now. I realize I haven't done much to show that, although I have to say in my father's mind that ball was literally all about you, but the fact is you're a Rule."

"I don't get to leave this estate, Maddox. What good is having some name if the only people impressed are the maid, who tolerates me constantly trying to talk to her, and the gardeners, who don't even bother to tolerate my attempts at conversation and simply ignore me? It's not the same, and you know it."

As much as I know it's a risk to push him, I can't resist and ask, "Why is it that I can't leave this place? It's not like you wouldn't just come to my father's and bring me back here if I left."

"It's the only way you can be kept safe right now," he answers, surprising me with how honest he sounds.

"Safe from who?"

I see by how his expression grows dark that I probably don't want to know the answer, so I quickly change the topic. "What do you like to do, other than going out?"

My question makes him look at me oddly, like it's the last thing he thought I'd ever ask him. "I don't know anymore. It's all I've done for so long that I don't think there's anything else I like to do. For as long as I remember, I worked for my father and went out with my friends at night."

He sounds sincere, but I can't believe he doesn't have anything else in the world that makes him happy. "What about before you started doing that every day? What did you like to do as a kid?"

Without missing a beat, he says, "I liked watching old horror movies. The black and white Frankenstein movies with Boris Karloff and Bela Lugosi as Dracula. I'd hide up here in my room and watch them for hours on a Saturday afternoon."

Something in the way his eyes light up when he talks about watching those movies as a little boy makes me smile. For as hard and unyielding as Maddox is, there's something that made him happy once. I like knowing that.

"Do you ever watch them now?"

The happiness fades from his expression as she shakes his head. "I haven't in years. I grew out of that."

"Would you like to watch one of those movies with me sometime? I'm sure we can find one somewhere," I tentatively offer, hoping to not ruin whatever progress we've made tonight by pushing too hard.

"You like horror movies?" he asks in complete surprise.

I hate that I have to admit the truth of how terrified they make me, but I don't want to lie to him at this moment. "Actually, they scare me to death. I always have nightmares after watching something scary."

He laughs at my confession, his turn to surprise me. "They aren't the kind of things that give you nightmares. They're not even really scary. I mean, ax murderers are scary. That shit really happens. Psychos breaking into your house and terrorizing your whole family. That's scary. But Frankenstein and Dracula? They're Halloween characters."

"Well, they give me nightmares. Anything spooky like that does. I can't help it. They just do."

Maddox rolls onto his back and chuckles. "Scared of Frankenstein. Next thing you'll tell me you're afraid of Boo Berry and can't eat the cereal," he says, teasing me as he wraps his arm around my shoulder to pull me to him.

While I get comfortable, nuzzling the warm space between his jaw and shoulder, I defend myself. "I'm more of a Count Chocula kind of girl, to be honest."

Pressing his lips to the top of my head, he says with a laugh, "Well, then there's hope for you yet, Willow. Not to worry. We'll get you straightened out."

And with that, I'm not sure if he means my choice in cereal, my dislike of his favorite kind of movies, or my role as his wife. For the moment, I don't want to think about the answer to that question, though. I just want to relax against his warm skin and breathe a sigh of relief, one of the first I've enjoyed since I came to this place.

For a long time, we lie there silently while his fingertips drift over my skin, but I want to know more about the man I'm married to, so finally I quietly ask, "Why didn't your father remarry after your mother, Maddox? He had all these children to take care of himself."

My question makes him laugh. "Trust me. My father never really took care of any of us. But there have been other women. Helix's mother was first. Then Julian and Nick's mother."

I look up at him, shocked at what he's just said. "So you aren't all brothers from the same mother?"

Maddox shakes his head, pursing his lips. "Nope. Trace and I have the same mother. Then my father got together with Jessica, Helix's mother. She was here for about as long as it took to meet us before she left. I guess a two year old and one year old weren't in her plans. She gave birth to him somewhere else, and then my father brought him here. After her was Celeste. She was around for about three years, but she died giving birth to Nick."

"Oh my God! That's terrible. And what about Helix's mother? She must have been devastated when your father brought him here to live without her."

A look of almost pain crosses Maddox's face before he answers, "She killed herself right after. I think that's why my father is always so easy on him. He feels guilty for what he did. As if the rest of us didn't lose our mothers too."

The edge in his voice grows harsher with every word, so I hug him to me and kiss his cheek. "I'm sorry. I didn't know when I asked that any of that had happened."

Nodding, he wraps his arms around me and holds me tightly to him. "You don't have to be sorry, Willow. Of all the people here, you're the only one who doesn't have to be sorry for anything when it comes to me."

CHAPTER NINETEEN

*W*illow

THE NEXT AFTERNOON, THE ENTIRE HOUSE SEEMS TO have an odd feeling to it. People I know don't work here buzz around in and out of the ballroom like they're preparing it for another event, but I haven't heard a thing about it. Emily informs me that I can't eat in the dining room for dinner, so I have to eat upstairs in my room. And when I ask her why, she mumbles something about it being the way it has to be and rushes off before I can find out what the hell that means.

Maddox and the rest of his family seem to be nowhere to be found too. What is going on?

I finish my dinner of salmon and roasted potatoes in my room and carry my plate downstairs, hoping to find out what everyone is so busy preparing for. I see groups of men outside walking along the driveway, but they don't come in through the front door.

Who are they and where are they going?

I catch Emily on her way out of the kitchen just as it's getting dark out, grabbing her as she tries to shuffle past me with a stack of linens and towels in her arms. She stops, but I sense her reluctance to talk to me almost immediately.

"What's going on? Is Stephen having a party here tonight?" I ask, wondering why Maddox wouldn't have mentioned it to me. "Two events in less than a week seems like a lot for him."

Emily shakes her head and frowns. "Don't worry. You won't have to attend. Trust me."

Trust her? I'm just starting to trust the man I'm married to.

"What do you mean?" I ask, curious but not at all unhappy about not being invited to attend yet another get-together with all those people who are strangers to me.

She leans toward me, almost knocking over the pile of linens she's holding, and whispers, "It's men only tonight. Mr. Rule has parties for his club and tonight's one of them. So no women allowed."

Relief mixes with confusion. No women allowed? What kind of club is this? And what year are we living in that women aren't permitted in a club?

"What kind of club? Will Maddox be going?" I ask, not expecting Emily to know the answer to whether or not my husband will be at this men's only party.

"It's his exclusive club for men like Mr. Rule. Just stay upstairs and you'll be fine," she whispers before hurrying away toward the ballroom.

I consider following her to see what's going on, but instead I rush up to the bedroom to see if Maddox has finally appeared after being missing all day. I catch him just as he's getting out of the shower.

He smiles at me as he knots the towel around his hips and pushes his wet hair off his face. "What's up? You look all frazzled."

And then in a flash, his smile disappears and his face darkens. "Did something happen with Asher? Tell me if it did, Willow."

"No. Nothing happened. I haven't seen him all day. In fact, I haven't seen anyone in this house all day, other than all those people who seem to be getting the ballroom ready for something. Your father isn't having another ball, is he? Is that why I needed more than that one dress?"

Maddox's smile returns, making him look entirely too sexy as he stands there with just a white bath towel slung low across his hips. "No, there isn't another ball tonight."

"So it's something with your father's males only club?"

He narrows his eyes for a moment like he isn't sure he wants to admit that fact, even though I already know it. "Who told you that?"

"Never mind who told me that. Is that right? Is it something to do with that club of his?"

Waving away my questions, he walks over to me

and kisses me softly on the lips. "Don't worry about that kind of thing. My father loves getting together with his friends and talking business."

Tiny droplets of water drip from Maddox's hair onto his shoulders, and I reach up to dry them with my fingers. "Are you going?"

"I usually do, but I think I get a reprieve this time," he says as he brings my hand to his lips and presses a soft kiss onto my fingertips. "I might just stop in to say hi and then leave."

"So it's just a bunch of old guys sitting around talking business?" I ask, searching his dark eyes for the truth I have a feeling he's hiding from me.

"Pretty much. They smoke cigars too. Well, the old guys do. It's nothing to be bothered with. You don't have to do anything but stay up here and relax."

Now I know there's something he's not telling me.

"Are your brothers going?"

He nods and chuckles. "Yeah. They never miss these meetings. All except for Nick, of course, since he's still in Europe."

The way he says his brothers never miss these meetings make them sound like something fun. But if it's just a bunch of men sitting around smoking cigars and talking business, why would they want to go at all? I don't know them well, but I haven't gotten the sense that any of Maddox's brothers would enjoy a night like that.

I slide my palms over his chest and abs until they come to rest just above the towel. "Is there something you aren't telling me? This all sounds very weird. Like why did I have to eat up here instead of us having dinner downstairs in the dining room? And why do I have to stay in this room while this meeting is going on? Why is your father making me do that?"

Maddox pulls me to him so I feel the hardness of his body press against mine. Wrapping his arms around me, he kisses the top of my head. "It wasn't my father. It was me. Now don't fight me on this and I'll be back up in a little while."

He steps back and I see the outline of his hard cock under the towel. Why doesn't he want to stay here if he's already aroused?

"Okay, but do you have to go already?" I ask, reaching out to loosen the towel from around his hips. "It looks like at least one part of you doesn't want to go yet."

Even though he's clearly excited, he gently pushes me away. "I promise I won't be long. Just wait for me and I'll be right back."

And with that, he turns his back to me and walks back into the bathroom to get dressed. Five minutes later, he emerges dressed in black pants and a grey dress shirt.

Leaning down, he kisses me while I sit on the edge of the bed still utterly baffled about what's going on downstairs. "Get comfortable, and I promise I'll be right back, okay?"

I don't know why, but I hold onto his hand as worry rushes through me. "Please promise me everything's okay, Maddox."

A sexy smile lights up his dark eyes. "Everything's fine, Willow. Now stay here and wait for me."

The door barely closes before I'm up on my feet to follow him. I don't know why, but my gut says something is very wrong. I don't know if he's in danger or I am, or maybe it's the both of us, but there's no way I can stay in that room and wait for him to return.

By the time I reach the stairs, he's already disappeared. Is he running to get to this boring old guy meeting? What's his hurry?

I take the steps by two, nearly tumbling down the last five or so when my right foot slides off a stair. Adrenaline courses through me, making my heart race. All I want to do is know what's going in the place I live. Why does everyone in this damn family have to be so secretive?

All the staff and workers who had been milling around all afternoon are gone now, so I head toward the ballroom without meeting a soul. The hallway there is dark, just like it was that day Maddox took me there to meet with the sisters, but I hear voices coming from the room.

The sound of footsteps behind me stops me dead, and I turn to see Maddox shaking his head at me. How did he get there?

I freeze in place as he marches toward me and grabs my wrist. "You never listen, Willow. Why can't you just do what I tell you to?" he asks in a low voice tinged with anger.

"Why are you mad at me? Why can't I just know

what's going on if it's just a meeting of some old guys and your brothers?"

He doesn't answer before he pulls me across the hall to a door. "Come on. You know what they say about curiosity killing the cat."

I don't bother telling him the rest of that saying that satisfaction brought him back. I doubt he'd appreciate that at this moment.

We walk down a dark passageway to another door while I listen for any sounds like I heard outside the ballroom doors. I don't know where he's taking me, but whatever this is, I can't hear anything but the sound of our footsteps.

"Maddox, what are you doing? Is this some secret way back up to our room?"

He stops in front of a door and whispers, "No. I'm going to show you what's going on."

Pushing it open, he flicks on the light switch to reveal a room the size of a large closet with a table and curtains hanging halfway down the wall. It reminds me of the dressing room we used when I was in plays in high school.

"What is this? Why did you bring me here?" I ask as he releases his hold on my arm and moves over toward the curtains.

"You're always too curious, Willow. So many questions. But this time I've decided to answer the one about the meeting tonight. Behind this curtain is a window only we can see through. On the other side is a mirror. So we'll be able to see them, but they won't be able to see us."

I don't say anything, and he pulls open the curtains to reveal the ballroom, but it doesn't look anything like what I've seen the ballroom look like before. Gone are the round tables and chairs from the ball the other night, and in their place are couches and large pillows on the left side of the room while on the right side are leather chairs and tables near a bar.

The two sides of the room couldn't be any more different. Seated on the right side are a group of maybe twenty older men smoking cigars and drinking liquor while they discuss amongst themselves, but on the other side of the room is nothing less than what looks like an orgy. Younger men sit or lie naked on couches with women on top of them, while others have sex on the colorful pillows.

My eyes open wide to take in this incredible scene in front of me, but I don't know exactly what I'm looking at. Turning to face Maddox, I see him smiling at me.

"What's going on? I thought you said this was just a meeting. This doesn't look like any meeting I've ever been to."

He points toward where his father and other older men sit on the right side of the ballroom. "That is just a meeting. That's what they always do at the Order's parties."

"The Order?"

Maddox nods. "The Order of Impuratus. Or the Villains Club, which is what my brothers and I call it."

"Are they in there?" I ask, curious enough to

wonder but unsure if I want to look back out that window to see where in the room they are.

"Yeah. They aren't members yet, but since my father controls much of what goes on with the Villains Club, he makes sure they get to enjoy the perks of the Order."

Taking my chin in his fingers, he turns my head and points toward the left corner of the room. "See that girl getting it from behind and blowing another guy? That's Trace fucking her and Julian on the receiving end of a blowjob."

I feel my mouth drop open as I watch two of his brothers with a blond, the three of them looking like they're having the time of their lives. Nearby, another man lays on pillows on the floor while a dark haired woman rides him like he's a bucking bronco.

"Oh, my God!" I say with a nervous giggle as Maddox slowly slides his hands over my shoulders.

My eyes scan the room and I see a man I know I've seen on TV just in the past week. Pointing to direct Maddox's attention, I ask, "Is that our new senator? I just saw him on the news. His wife is young and gorgeous. That's not her, is it?"

He lowers his head so his chin is resting on my shoulder. "No, I don't think so. That's just one of the girls for tonight."

"Your father and uncle?" I ask, afraid to know the answer to that question.

"My father's on the other side talking business. I have no idea where Asher is," Maddox answers flatly.

Looking more closely, I see out of the corner of my

eye a man with three women toward the center of the room. Pressing my nose to the glass, I try to make out what they're doing. Two women sit draped over the man's legs taking turns with his cock while a third lays next to him as he kisses her.

Then it dawns on me. That's Helix.

"Is that…"

In my ear, Maddox groans as he slides his hand around the front of my throat. "Helix. Greedy fuck. Yeah, that's him."

I spin around and shake my head. "I shouldn't be watching this. I have to live in this house with them. How am I going to look them in the eye when I see them next time?"

My husband smiles in that way that tells me he thinks I'm being silly. "It's just people having sex. Tonight's a pretty tame meeting, to be honest. I've seen nights where things got pretty wild."

"Were you going to be doing that like your brothers are? Is that why you showered and got dressed to come down here?" I ask, not even trying to mask the hurt in my voice that he'd do that to me.

To us.

He shakes his head. "No. I told you I get a reprieve tonight. My father and the Order demand an heir, so they think I should spend my time devoted to that."

I turn around and look out the window again at the sight in front of me. "So if we already had that all-so-important child, you'd be here like your brothers?"

Maddox wraps his arms around me and plants a

tiny kiss on my neck just below my ear. "No," he whispers. "I won't be doing this anymore."

Looking back at him, I wish I believed those words. "Promise?"

"Promise."

Still, that's not enough.

I spin around in his hold and stare up into his eyes. "Swear you won't, Maddox. Swear. I can't be in a marriage that includes you going to meetings and sleeping with women who are...are they prostitutes? What are they?"

He shrugs like it's all so ordinary to him. "I don't know. I just know they show up and they're ready to party."

"Swear to me you won't do that ever again. I don't want to be like that senator's wife. God, she's stunning and still he's here fucking some random woman. I can't be that for you, Maddox."

For one of the rare times since that day we met in this very house, I see kindness in his eyes. He cradles my face in his strong hands and smiles at me.

"I swear. I don't want that anymore, Willow."

"You don't?"

He glances over my shoulder and then brings his focus back to me. "No, I don't. I want you."

"I want to believe you."

His gaze travels down from my face and he smiles. "I want you and your little sundresses that make me think of bending you over the side of the bed whenever you wear them. I want you and your half a million questions I can't answer."

Then he lifts his eyes and looks into mine. "I want you, Willow. I've had that out there for way too long."

I can't think about him with other women and at meetings like the one behind me. It makes me too jealous to imagine him doing what his brothers are doing right now.

Standing on my tiptoes, I kiss him with all the fear and need that swirl around inside me, desperately hoping he doesn't want that out there. I feel his fingers slide under the straps of my sundress, and then a second later, he pushes it down my body so I'm standing in only my panties.

"Reason number one I love these dresses you wear: no bra," he groans as he cups my breasts in his hands.

Insecurity roars through me, and I open my eyes to look down at how lost they look in his palms. If only I had bigger boobs like those women out in the ballroom.

I watch as he dips his head to take my right nipple in his mouth, sucking gently at first but then harder before he sinks his teeth into my flesh. The mixture of pain and pleasure is exquisite, and I can't stop a moan that says how incredible it feels from escaping from my throat.

He releases his hold on my nipple, and his breath hisses out between his teeth, covering my tender skin. "I love what that does to you. I bet when I slide my fingers under those pink panties of yours that you're going to be fucking drenched."

There's no time to answer before his forefinger glides through my pussy and dips inside me. He's right. I'm already wet and dying to feel his cock inside me.

"See? I told you. My Willow wants it, doesn't she?" he asks while he pushes my panties down my legs.

I kick them aside and practically climb up his body to feel him next to me, my fingers fumbling with his pants and zipper to get them open. Reaching in, I palm his hard cock.

It's thick and heavy in my hand when I stroke him from base to tip. Maddox stuffs his hands into my hair and tugs hard, kissing me like he's never kissed me before. His lips and mouth devour mine, and he makes a low, sexy sound that I swear hits me somewhere deep inside.

He slides his hands down to cup my ass and lifts me off the ground. I quickly wrap my arms around his neck to hold on as he turns around and walks us toward the wall.

"Are you sure they can't see in here?" I ask, suddenly worried about putting on a show for the people on the other side of the wall.

As he lowers me down onto his cock, filling me so perfectly I instantly don't care who can see what, he says, "Nobody can see a thing, and even if they could, they wouldn't care. Trust me."

Maddox wastes no time on the issue of who's watching or not and begins to fuck me, forcing me to take every inch of him. Each thrust squeezes all the air out of my lungs, and with every time he retreats from my body, I inhale and hold on to his neck.

"This is what I want," he moans and then pushes his hips forward to fill me again. "My wife's pretty little cunt."

When he talks like that, he makes me run wet with need. I rake my fingernails across his shoulders and beg, "Don't stop. Oh, God...that feels so good."

With every thrust, my back and head slam against the wall, but I don't care. The pain is drowned out by the feeling of utter pleasure every time his cock touches that spot inside me that drives me wild.

"Time to change things up," Maddox says, and then a second later, he spins to the left and I'm lowered onto the table.

The different location means he has to pull out of me for a moment, and I grasp at his open shirt to draw him back to me. I can't reach him, though, because I'm too far back on the table, so he yanks my legs toward him, tugging me to the edge.

I watch with rapt attention at every move he makes. How he licks his lower lip while he stares down at me. How he takes his cock in his hand and strokes it once and then twice, his eyes narrowing before he directs it back to where I so desperately want him to be.

How he smiles as he leans forward and puts his hand around my neck just as he thrusts his hips forward, filling me with his cock. "My beautiful Willow."

Reaching out, I run my fingernails over his chiseled abs and down toward his hips, loving how his skin quivers beneath my touch. He closes his eyes for a moment before pushing forward, moving the table and me. The rough sound of the wooden table legs scraping across the floor contrasts with the sensation of him pistoning into me, in and out, his smooth skin dragging across my wet, tender skin.

I wrap my legs around his waist to hold him close, hoping to stop the noise the table continues to make. He's stronger than I am, so I lock my ankles and press hard against the base of his spine. He tightens his hold around my neck and pumps hard into me, but at least that sound stops.

My release begins deep inside me in that spot he grazes with every thrust into my body. It unwinds with every movement he makes. His touch sets me on fire anew over and over, and when he leans down to kiss me, I love the feel of his lips against mine.

A craving like I've never felt before twists around my heart, making my release race through me. I arch my back and push my heels as hard as I can into his lower back. With one final push into me, he stills and I feel him flood my body with all he has.

The two of us pant as we ride the waves of our shared release. I cling to his neck, and he keeps his hand around my throat, just tight enough for me to feel grounded and safe as the reality that people exist just outside that window a few feet away.

Maddox lifts his mouth from mine and slides his lips over my cheek to my ear. "I had no idea you had it in you to be so fucking good. That's what I get for judging a book by its cover."

"What does that mean?"

He leans back away from me and smiles. "You look like a virgin, a girl too afraid to enjoy herself. I guess looks can be deceiving. I'm not complaining. Don't think that. I just had no idea my little Willow was so good in bed."

I chuckle at his compliment and rap my knuckles off the wood table beneath me. "Good on tables too."

Pulling me up so I'm sitting, he kisses me sweetly and smiles at my joke. "Good everywhere."

As much as I know he's been the last man I ever wanted to marry, three little words form in my head. I don't speak them, but for the first time, I think them about Maddox Rule.

I love you.

CHAPTER TWENTY

$\mathcal{M}$addox

ASHER SITS IN A CHAIR IN THE LIBRARY LOOKING like some wannabe professor type there thumbing through a book but obviously not reading a single word on any page. Typical of him. Everything is a show. His return to this house. His efforts to spend time with Willow. His proclamations of love for my father and this family.

All bullshit. Lies meant to make him look good but are nothing but hollow nonsense.

"Reading anything interesting?" I ask as I stroll past him toward the desk in the corner of the room near the windows that reach to the ceiling. Unlike my father's office, this room is comfortable and bright. I assume that's why he never spends any time in here. I haven't either since high school, but I have a sneaking suspicion Willow likes to come here to read.

"Just browsing through some of Byron's poetry. It really has aged well," Asher says, doing his best pseudo-professor voice for me.

I look at him and wonder if I should waste the time to say that Byron was a pompous jackass, much like all those British Romantic poets. Unlike my uncle, I actually paid attention to my private school education. I didn't enjoy it, but knowing things has always been a hobby of mine. To Asher, bringing up the topic of Byron sounds important because someone told him it was one time. He got nothing out of his years in school.

Unless you count his talent at manipulating people, but I have a feeling that's something he was born with. All the Rules are born with it. He just got a bigger helping of that than the rest of us.

"I was never really a Byron fan. Not really a poetry fan. But I didn't come down here to chat about British Romanticism, Asher."

He smiles like he's considering challenging me to some ridiculous discussion of that fucking topic, but I hold my hand up to stop him before he starts down that path. "Let me cut to the chase. Don't go looking for Willow anymore. Don't try to talk to her. Not about anything. I know you like to travel down memory lane with her about her mother, but it won't be happening anymore. Understand?"

Unlike with my wife, I don't regret pulling that understand shit with him. The insult registers on his face with his eyebrows shooting up into his forehead like he can't believe I dared to speak to him like that.

"Don't you think your wife is old enough to make decisions like this on her own?"

Smug fuck. He doesn't use her name because he wants to rub it in my goddamned face that the woman I'm married to likes to spend time with him.

"Willow doesn't know her way around the Rule family like I do, so in this case, she can't make that decision on her own," I answer sharply, my anger with him rising with each second that ticks by and this asshole doesn't get that he's out of line.

"Have you told her how you feel? What did she have to say?" he asks, as if any of this is up for discussion.

I stand from the edge of the desk and glare down at him, barely controlling my rage now. "Did you not hear what I just said? You chatting Willow up isn't going to happen anymore. Period. I'm not interested in your opinion about this."

Asher sighs and shrugs before rolling his eyes. "Or hers, it seems."

I lunge forward and grab him by the collar, yanking him up out of the chair. The book on Byron he was pretending to read goes flying onto a side table, knocking it over so it makes a crashing sound when it hits the wood floor.

"I'm not fucking playing games with you. I don't care if you're my long lost uncle or not. My father may give a damn about that bullshit, but I don't. We don't share anything except a family name, but that won't keep you safe if you pull any more of your shit. Stay away from Willow, Asher. I won't tell you again. Next time, I'll put a gun to your fucking head and let that do the talking. So do you understand or do I have to make myself even clearer?"

"I understand completely," Asher answers in a shaky voice, his eyes wide with terror.

Releasing my hold on his shirt, I step back and watch him fall into the chair like the pathetic weasel he is. Now to get to work and begin my day.

I walk past him toward the door and hear him say in a cocky voice behind me, "I suggest you keep a better eye on your wife, though. I might understand, but I doubt she does."

By the time I spin around, he's up out of the chair and standing beside the desk with his hand on a metal letter opener. I don't doubt this fuck will pull that on me if he feels cornered, but I'm way past the point that I give a damn what he thinks should happen when it comes to me.

I reach behind me and draw my gun, aiming it squarely at the center of his head. "Unless you've got fucking ninja skills I don't know about, the bullet that comes from this gun is going to blow through your head before you even get a chance to pick that thing up. Make your choice wisely."

We stand there silently eyeing one another up, and I'm more than eager to see just a single finger twitch on the hand he's got on that letter opener. Just one tiny movement and I'll blow his head off.

"Maddox! What's going on here?" my father says

behind me, but I don't turn around to acknowledge him when he walks into the room.

"Your son seems to have a problem, Stephen," Asher says in a tone that's just a hair away from being whiny.

My father stops right beside me. "Answer me, Maddox. What's going on here?"

"Your brother doesn't understand what stay the fuck away from Willow means. I was just explaining it to him," I say, still aiming the gun at my uncle's head.

"Put it away. I'm not going to have family shooting one another here. Put the gun away and let's have a conversation."

I glance over at him and see he's dead serious. What the hell are we going to be discussing?

"Maddox, put your gun away, for Christ's sake! We're all family here. Now let's talk," my father says as I relent and lower my weapon.

Asher steps back away from the desk, as if he ever posed any danger with that silver letter opener, and folds his arms across his chest. Right before my eyes, he changes from a scared piece of shit he was with me to a defiant son of a bitch to my father.

"I've been waiting a long time for this discussion, brother. What should we start with first? How you ruined my life, or how you cheated me out of everything I deserve?"

I look over at my father as my uncle's ridiculous claims threaten to make me laugh. Ruined his life? Cheated him? I've heard the story about how he abandoned this family the day he walked out and never once looked back.

Until recently, that is.

But my father looks like every word Asher is saying hurts him. His expression twists into something that makes it seem like he's in pain, and he sighs like he's been dreading this for years.

"I didn't ruin your life. You know that's not true. I simply didn't let you get away with what you wanted to do. As for cheating you out of anything, you know that's not true either. You received your part of the inheritance like you were supposed to."

Asher's face turns bright red as he frantically shakes his head. "You did! And you've owed me ever since!" he yells, startling me for a moment with how emotional he's become in the span of a few seconds.

Still, my father remains his usual calm self, keeping his voice level while he says, "She couldn't be yours. She couldn't be either of ours. The only difference between us was I understood that and you didn't."

"No, she couldn't be yours because you were too old, but there was only four years between her and me. She loved me, and it ate you alive to see that. So you took her away!"

Who the fuck is he talking about?

Before I can ask my father, he turns to me and nods, letting out a sigh of exasperation as Asher continues to ramble on with his accusations. "This is why your uncle and I haven't spoken in decades. Willow's mother, Cate. He was obsessed with her, and

I knew he'd hurt her, so I told her to get away from this house."

"She loved me! You sent her away because you couldn't have her. You treated her like the help and then took her from me to spite me."

"Willow's mother?" I ask, still reeling from all of this.

"Yes. I told you she lived here as a child. What I didn't tell you is your uncle became completely obsessed with her. Then he took her to the ball and that's when she realized everything I warned her about was true."

He turns toward his brother and continues. "You weren't well, Asher. Everyone knew that. Even she knew that, I think. She just didn't know how to make you stop because she was afraid she'd look ungrateful to our parents. But they knew you weren't well either. The only thing I regret is not pushing our father to get you the help you needed back then. But you left, so I figured that wasn't my problem anymore."

I look over at my uncle and watch as all the blood drains from his face, leaving him white as a ghost. Still shaking his head like he can't believe what he's hearing, he looks like he's barely holding back a flood of emotions.

"Loving someone doesn't mean you're sick. That's why your son is how he is, Stephen. He doesn't know how to care for someone any more than you do. I wasn't the one who needed help. You were. You never showed a hint of kindness or love to anyone, and now you have a carbon copy of yourself in this kid of yours."

I step forward to tell him he can fuck himself, but my father puts his arm in front of me to hold me back. "We're not doing this, Asher. Cate is dead, so this fight between us must end. Don't attack Maddox with what you mean only about me."

The mention of Willow's mother being gone takes all the anger out of him. His shoulders sag, and he hangs his head in defeat. "You took her away, and you never had to pay for that, Stephen. You got off scot free, just like you always have."

My father's body sort of falls slack, like what his brother is saying hurts him. "I didn't take her away. I gave her a chance at a life. She wasn't ours to have."

And with that, Asher falls silent and then walks out past us, broken by all my father had to tell him. I'm a little shocked at what I heard, but now doesn't seem to be the time to ask about the details of what happened between Asher, Willow's mother, and my father.

"You best get to work, Maddox. I have an appointment I have to get to in an hour."

"I'm not happy with him being here with Willow while neither one of us is around to watch him. I'm going to warn the guards at the front gate to keep an eye out for anything odd going on with him."

My father nods, but his eyes are filled with sadness like I haven't seen in years. "I understand. He's harmless now. There's no Cate for him to obsess over."

"All the same, I'm going to let them know. I've

already told Willow to avoid him, and if he has any sense in his head, he got my meaning loud and clear before you came in."

"Okay. I need to get ready for my meeting. Let me know if you run into any trouble with Captain today. I know you two don't always see eye to eye."

Patting my father on the shoulder, I chuckle at that little dose of truth. "He's just so fucking gung-ho. The guy's going to get himself or someone else killed with the way he charges into every situation. Maybe if he'd dial it back a bit I wouldn't hate going anywhere with him."

As we walk out of the library, he nods his agreement about Captain being a pain in the ass. "Have patience with us old guys, Maddox. You're going to be one of us one day, God willing."

CHAPTER TWENTY-ONE

illow

I LOOK AROUND AS I WALK ACROSS THE GROUNDS toward the stables, relatively sure no one even notices when I go anywhere here but still anxious about it today. Maddox left early this morning on an errand for his father, and I saw Stephen drive away a few minutes ago. I don't know how long either of them will be gone, so I have to hurry.

A tiny lick of guilt nips at me after what Maddox and I shared last night. Not the sex, which was incredible, but the hours we spent talking afterward. If he finds out I directly disobeyed him on this one issue that seems to stick in his craw, I worry all the progress we've made will be ruined.

Even more, though, I just want to find out any more I can about my mother before Asher leaves. I have a sense it won't be long before he's gone by the way no one appears to be very happy to have him here, so I want to take advantage of any chance I can to listen to him talk about growing up with my mother and what she was like back then.

I take one last look around before I duck behind the stables out of view of nearly every place on the estate. I've noticed the cameras fixed in trees and on the fences bordering the property, but I've found this is the single spot anywhere here that doesn't seem to be in the line of anyone's view. Once I realized that, I ended up spending as much time just sitting on the ground and enjoying not being watched for at least a few hours each day.

Only a minute later, Asher appears wearing his usual smile for me. "I'm so happy you were able to come, Willow. While I was walking across the lawn behind the house, I was thinking about the one time your mother and I snuck out of the house on a cold winter night with no shoes on with our sleds to slide down the hill at the back of the property. Have you ever been back there?"

"No. I wish we could take a walk there. Did you two have fun? Your feet must have been freezing in the snow!" I say, thrilled to hear my mother was so carefree back then.

"They were," he says and throws his head back to laugh. "I think she handled it better than I did, though. They thought I had frostbite and I'd lose my pinky toe after that. Thankfully, I didn't. You know, we could walk back to that little hill. I don't think anyone would see us. Stephen and Maddox are gone for the day."

I consider his suggestion knowing that if we are found out, Maddox might never forgive me. I can't risk that.

"There are cameras everywhere, though, Asher. This is really the only spot on the estate that isn't near one so it's a little private, at least."

His mood changes with my decline of his offer. Sullen, he nods as a frown settles into his thin face. "Oh, okay. It's just that I haven't been back there in so many years. I promised myself I'd take a walk up that hill because I love that memory of your mother and me and that snowy adventure."

I hate the look of disappointment in his eyes. He has so little joy, as far as I can tell, and getting to tell me this story would obviously make him so happy. Even more, I want to see the hill where they went sledding that night and nearly got frostbite. It sounds foolish, but being there while he tells me the story would make it feel like I'm closer to her somehow.

If Maddox finds out about this, he's going to hate me. I don't want that. After the last few days, I think we can make this marriage work. Or if that's too much to ask, at least we can be friendly. But if he thinks I've betrayed him, he's going to never forget, much less forgive me, especially since he so intensely dislikes his uncle.

This emotional tug of war plays out inside me until I finally have to give in to what I want more than anything else. I can hope my husband will forgive me, but his past behavior toward me doesn't say that's a given. My mother's memory brightening my day and making me happy is a sure thing, and Asher can give that to me.

"How will we get past the cameras? They're everywhere, except right here."

Asher's smile returns, and he squeezes my hand, clearly thrilled I've agreed to go with him so he can tell his story. "Go back inside the house and out the door in the kitchen area that leads to the back of the property. I'll go the other way and meet you there. Nobody will have a problem with you simply taking a walk, will they?"

The sharp tone beneath his last sentence makes me want to defend Maddox, so I quickly explain, "It's not like that at all. Really. He just worries about me getting hurt. That's all."

That's not entirely the truth, but I don't like Asher thinking Maddox is some kind of terrible monster to me. He has been a few times, but recently he's been different and I want to believe he's got more kindness in him than he shows the world most of the time.

"Well, I'm happy to hear that. You're too sweet to be treated like some criminal who should be under house arrest."

"Oh, no. It's not like that at all."

He squeezes my hand again and flashes me a big smile, his eyes wild with excitement. "Go, now! I'll meet you there in a few minutes. Just walk straight back once you get out of the kitchen, but be sure to hurry, okay?"

"Okay. Is that the way you and my mother went out that night without shoes?" I ask, eager to hear about their snowy night escapade.

"Yes, it was. We ran up the hill hand in hand laughing the whole way. Now go and I'll see you in a few minutes."

Asher hurries off, leaving me wishing he'd told me more of the story, but I only have to wait a little while longer. I rush off toward the kitchen, my eye on the cameras everywhere while I try to look as casual and nonchalant as possible. It's not like there's anything odd or out of the ordinary about a person wanting to go for a walk on a beautiful summer day.

I just hope I don't look as guilty as I feel.

Emily sits at the large wood table in the center of the kitchen with the cook talking about something in low tones. Since the cook has never once made an effort to utter a single word to me, despite the fact that I see him literally every day at least once, I give them both a tepid smile as I march through their area toward the door to the back of the house.

"Willow, wait! I want to talk to you," Emily calls after me as I pull the door open to step outside.

"I'm really in a hurry right now. Can this wait until I get back? I won't be long. We can talk at lunch."

She puts her hand on my arm as I turn away, surprising me, and I look back to see her eyes filled with concern. It stops me in my tracks and makes me wonder if something's happened.

"What's wrong? Is Maddox okay?"

"He's fine. I haven't heard anything. I just wanted

to say that you need to be careful around Mr. Rule. Asher, I mean."

"What are you talking about?" I ask as I push the door open again to leave.

"I wasn't around back in the day when he lived here, but I've heard stories. Please be careful around him."

Is there some kind of conspiracy among everyone who lives in this house against Asher Rule? Now even the staff doesn't want me around him?

"Like what? Is he a murderer or something?" I ask, itching to get going to meet him on that hill but genuinely curious what everyone's problem is with this guy.

"No, nothing like that. He's just been away for a long time, and when he left, it wasn't on the best of terms. Or so I hear."

"Well, people would say the same thing about me if I left today, now wouldn't they? I have to go. If you want to talk at lunch, I'll be happy to, but for now, I need to get going."

I let the door close on her, not interested in hearing any more gossip about Asher and why I shouldn't be talking to him. What could be the harm? There are cameras everywhere, so when I have to answer any questions Maddox asks about why I was talking to him, I can just say we happened to meet up in the same spot on the grounds.

Rushing across the lawn, I see the hill he must be talking about in the distance maybe five football fields away. I've never spent any time in this part of the property, mostly because there's a garden that's been allowed to go dormant back here between the house and the hill that's downright creepy. At one time, I imagine it must have been glorious with its benches and statues and fountains, but now it looks like a cemetery that's been left to decay. The concrete is chipped on all the surfaces, and weeds grow where water used to flow. It's far enough away from the house that I don't see it usually, but now as I walk toward it, I'm reminded why I never come back here.

Asher must have forgotten about it, or more likely, he remembers when it was beautiful and lush. That's why he didn't mention it in his directions to the hill he and my mother had such a wonderful time sledding on.

Ignoring the dead flowers and broken down statues all around me, I trudge through the garden and think of my mother laughing with every pass down the hill, her long brown hair flying behind her in the wind. I want to think of her that way, instead of the memory that usually fills my head when I think of her.

Sick, in a hospital bed set up in the downstairs of our house, gaunt with no hint of her lively personality in her dim blue eyes.

I shake my head as tears threaten to ruin this beautiful morning. I don't want to think of her like that anymore. Asher's story gives me the opportunity to remember her like she should be. Young, beautiful, and having fun, not broken and losing her fight against that mystery disease that stole her away from us right before our eyes.

Running through the back half of the dilapidated garden, I see Asher standing on the top of the hill in the distance. I wave my hand to let him know I'm coming and see him wave back. My feet get tangled up in the much taller grass than on the rest of the property and I nearly trip, but I catch myself and slow down so I don't twist an ankle or worse.

Other than that weird old garden, this really is a beautiful place. I've considered it a prison for much of my time here, but now as I look around at all the mature oak trees and patches of wildflowers that dot the grass back here, I have to admit it's quite pretty. When I come back here next time, I'll go the way Asher did so I can avoid that garden that makes my skin crawl so I can truly enjoy a nice walk to this hill.

"It's a pretty steep climb once you start up, so take your time. I don't see any cameras when you get to the top, so don't worry," he calls down to me as I begin my ascent to him.

"Okay! I'll be up in a minute."

In my excitement, I climb the hill far more quickly than I usually can since I'm not really in very good shape. My thighs feel the burn from overexertion halfway up, but I keep going, happy to live out the no pain, no gain mantra today.

I'm exhausted by the top, so I sit down in the grass to catch my breath. "This girl needs to work out more, for sure."

Asher stands behind me, and I glance back to see his black dress pants covered in brown burrs. Tilting my head, I smile up at him and point at his legs.

"Those things love to stick to anything, don't they? You're going to have to spend some time picking them off."

He looks down at where I'm pointing at for a split second but doesn't say a thing about all of them clinging to his pants. Returning his focus to the landscape in front of us, he looks up and sighs.

"The snow was coming down so hard that night. I knew Cate would be willing to come here with me, though. She wasn't afraid of anything," he says in a dreamy voice.

"I love the idea of her like that. That's how I want to always think of her. Fearless. That was her."

He nods, but I don't know if he's even listening to me. He looks like he's somewhere else or sometime else.

"Do you remember what she was wearing?" I ask, hoping to get those details to fill out the story in my mind's eye.

Asher doesn't answer for a minute, so I consider asking him the question again, but then his eyes light up and he looks down at me with a huge smile. "She had a red and white winter hat with a long thing that came off it. Not a tassel. What do they call those things? Whatever it was, it came all the way down her back and had a little ball at the bottom. A red poofy ball at the end of the thing that looked like a scarf attached to the hat."

I try to imagine her hat and come up with something that looks like a long stocking cap from pictures in old storybooks I've seen. I bet she looked so cute in that. It probably made her blue eyes sparkle.

"Why didn't you two wear shoes? Was it because they would make noise as you were walking through the house?"

He ignores my question and points down the hill to the bottom. "See how the hill just stops short there. She and I had to make sure we kept to the right of that area or we'd smash the sled to pieces and probably break our necks."

I follow his gaze to where he's looking and see what he described. "Was she good with a sled? Did she have her own?"

"She did. My parents always made sure to buy her whatever they bought us, but that night we went together on my sled. It was easier to get just one up here."

"Did she steer or did you?" I ask, trying to create the full picture of that night in my mind.

He doesn't hesitate to answer, as if he's replayed the event hundreds of times and he's sure of every tiny detail. "I steered. She sat behind me, her arms wrapped around my waist. She held on so tightly. I think she might have been afraid, but she didn't have to worry. I wasn't going to crash."

I want to ask why she'd be afraid since he just told me she wasn't afraid of anything, but I don't want to nit-pick. He isn't on the witness stand here, and it was over twenty years ago. I'm surprised he can remember all he does of that night with her.

"Did she scream? I bet she did," I say excitedly,

imagining them sailing down the hill in front of me, the two of them screaming and laughing all the way to the bottom.

"Right in my ear. I screamed too. It was so much fun."

I turn to my left to look back at him, but he's not there. Turning my head to the other side, I see him for a second and then something blocks my vision before hitting my cheek.

Then all I feel is pain shooting up into my eye and a sense of falling backwards.

CHAPTER TWENTY-TWO

*M*addox

I WOULDN'T HAVE BEEN WILLING TO TAKE THIS meeting with Delgado's surviving son at any time than during the day after the shit we've had to deal with lately from his father and brother. We've hit them in the past, and then they got us last month. We couldn't let that stand, so we hit them hard, taking out the head of the Delgado family and his son temporarily running things.

Of course, I expected them to retaliate when they regrouped, assuming they would. I hadn't expected to hear from Samuel, the younger Delgado son who never played a real part in the family business, this morning wanting a get-together.

Normally, I would have a few of our guys with me as back up, but I don't want my father to know what

I'm up to quite yet. I'm taking a chance here, but if it pans out, it'll all be worth it.

Ten o'clock in the morning in a shopping center parking lot isn't as risky as any number of meetings I've had in the past, so I should be okay. The bigger issue might be this is a waste of my time. Samuel never ran with his father or brother much, spending his time in school from what I hear. What he may know about anything that I'd be interested in remains to be seen.

This whole thing wouldn't be happening if he hadn't let me know it was about the ambush at the docks. He naturally plans to claim it wasn't all his family, of course, but it'll be names he offers after that will tell me how serious his information is.

I rotate my shoulder as I stand outside my car, wincing at the nip of pain that bites at me as I finish. That wasn't my first time getting shot and it certainly wasn't the worst I've had, but the fact that I'm still feeling pain tells me I'm getting too old to deal with that shit.

Too old at twenty-eight. I can't believe that thought just ran through my head. It wouldn't have a couple months ago. Hell, it wouldn't have six weeks ago.

As I silently blame Willow for my newfound opinion on my job, I watch a black BMW slowly roll toward me. It stops two parking spots away, and I reach back to make sure my gun is ready if and when I need it.

The door opens and I quickly look inside to see if the person driving is alone. He is. So far, so good. I've only seen Samuel Delgado once or twice, but he's the spitting image of his dead father, so when the man stands up out of the car, I know it's him.

Black slicked back hair and a killer tan, he looks the same as the last time I saw him. He's in a grey suit now instead of a Polo shirt and khakis, a sign he's left his schooldays behind him. I don't know if he's joined his father's business, but it sure as hell looks like it this morning.

Extending his hand to shake mine, he nods as if we're old friends, flashing me a perfect smile. "Maddox, it's been a long time."

"I was just thinking that myself," as I shake his hand. "You were still in college the last time we crossed paths."

Before I can say something about that night, he laughs. "How did that end up for you with that girl? She was beautiful, for sure."

Exactly the memory that flashed through my mind. "She was. I don't think we were together for more than two weeks before she was talking about marriage. Crazy talk back then for me."

He nods his agreement to that. "Definitely not what I was looking for with her. Always marriage with the beautiful ones. I would think they'd want to play the field a bit, but no. They jump right to marriage."

"I think it's that they know there's an expiration date on those looks of theirs. Got to lock down someone good early before everything begins to slide south," I joke.

As much as I wish our meeting could stay light, it

can't. His expression darkens even as we stand out in the warm summer sun, and he says, "Most in my family don't think I should have asked for this meeting, but things can't go on like they have between my family and yours. I'm not interested in dying for some fucking drugs, no matter how much money they're worth, and I told them we have to find a better way from this point on."

"I couldn't agree more. The shoot 'em up ways of our fathers' generation isn't going to get anyone what they want now. I'm all ears if you want to tell me what you've got in mind."

He takes off his sunglasses and slides them into the breast pocket of his suit so I can see his dark eyes and how serious he is about all of this. "We can work together and make money, or we can work against each other and see what happens. I'm a capitalist, so I say we see how we can work together."

"Sounds good."

"But you have a few problems I'm thinking might get in the way. First, your father, unlike mine, is still alive and at the head of your business. How are you going to convince him that what he thinks is the right way to do things is old-fashioned and out of style?"

I hate to admit it, but that's going to be the biggest problem I face in all of this. Samuel Delgado may not be someone I want to hang out with every night of the week, but he and I think along the same lines. Getting fucking killed for a few more bucks is no goddamned way to run your life or your business.

My father might not think the same way. To be

honest, I don't know if he does. He's set in his ways, but he likes the life he has, so maybe he might listen to reason instead of clinging to the ways he's relied on to run the Rule family for as long as I've been alive.

"He just seems to be stuck in the past sometimes. My father, like us, is a businessman before anything else. A capitalist who likes to make money and live to spend it. He might fight this at first, but he'll come around."

"Okay. I hope he does. That leads me to your second problem. Unlike me, you've got a family full of brothers. Is that something that's going to get in our way?"

I wave away that idea and smile, even as I think about Helix and his play to weasel his way to the top of my father's business. "Trust me. My brothers won't be an issue."

"Okay. The final problem I don't even think you know about yet. You've got a rat in your organization."

Instantly, the image of Captain and his overzealous attitude jumps into my head. Fucking asshole. I always had a feeling that over-the-top thing he has going on was hiding something. I just assumed it was that he was really a chicken shit.

"Do you have a name?" I ask and wait to hear it's that red-faced jackass.

I'm going to gut that fucker the next time I see him. No questions asked. Just get rid of him and his bullshit attitude.

"Yeah. I've got better than that. How does a note

in the bastard's own handwriting sound?" Samuel asks as pulls out a piece of paper from his suit coat pocket.

I take it from him and read the words, but they look like they're swimming across the page since I'm so angry I can barely see straight. Something about when we'd be at the docks, specifically me, and how to get at us. At the bottom the fucking traitor signed his name.

Asher Rule. My uncle who as of this moment has only minutes left in his fucking life.

"From what I gather, my father and brother didn't take this too seriously, but he followed up with a call promising he'd make sure you were there at the docks that night."

Fucking traitor to our family. No way my father will be able to hold me back from blowing his goddamned head off this time.

The memory of that night runs through my mind, and I can't help but think he somehow got to my father too since he was the one who sent me to the damn docks. Did he mean to send me to my death, or did his brother set him up just like he set me up?

I'll find that out once fucking Asher is dead.

"Thanks. I'm going to keep this note, if you don't mind," I say, barely able to keep my voice calm as I bite the words out.

"My pleasure, Maddox. Once you get your house in order, let's talk again. I think we can do good things working together instead of against one another."

I nod and force a smile. "I agree. I'll let you know

when this traitor is out of my hair and my father is brought into this century. Thanks, Samuel."

He gives me a pat on the shoulder and gets back into his car. For him, this meeting has gone as well as it could have, maybe even better than he expected. For me, I feel like my world is about to explode around me. My head throbs to the rhythm of my heartbeat, and all I can hear is what sounds like water in my ears.

But it's not me who's going to suffer now. It's Asher. I was willing to kill him for bothering with Willow. Now I'm twice as happy to put a bullet in that fucker's brain for being a traitor to our family and fucking with my wife.

Good riddance to bad rubbish, or however that saying goes.

I STORM THROUGH THE HOUSE ON MY WAY TO MY father's office, my need to strike out barely contained below the surface. The maid Emily makes the mistake of getting in my way in the hallway, and I nearly knock her over when I push her aside so I can walk past.

"Where's my father? Is he back yet?"

She nods, clutching some rag in her hand as she cowers against the wall. "He just returned, sir. He's in his office, I think."

"Good," I grunt out, not really as anything I want to say to her but merely the expression of my happiness that I won't have to go searching for him. I'm not in the mood to play hide-and-fucking-seek.

I find him sitting behind his desk, staring out the window. Normally, I wouldn't interrupt him when he's like this, but none of this is normal.

"We need to talk about Asher," I say as I reach into my suit jacket and pull out the note Samuel gave me. "I know you want to think he's due some respect or whatever the hell it is you think he's owed, but you aren't going to be able to save him this time."

"Why? What happened? I thought you were out working with Captain."

I thrust the note in front of his face in disgust. "Your loving brother sold us out. That fuck is the reason I got shot and Simon and Beck are fucking dead. It's right there in his own goddamned handwriting."

He reads what Asher wrote and sighs. "I can't believe this."

"Did you know about this? You sent the three of us down to those docks. Did you set your own goddamned son up?"

I barely get the words out before my father's shaking his head. "I would never do that to you, Maddox. I guess he found out about what happened with Delgado."

"How? He's been in the weeds for years, and now he suddenly reappears and knows who you're working with?" I ask, hating that I can't make heads nor tails of any of this.

My father blows the air out of his lungs slowly and sags against the back of his chair. "He contacted me a while back and said he wanted things to be right. I may have been a little loose with my tongue telling him things about the business. He's my brother. He wanted to mend our rift. So when he called me that day and asked to meet with me, I told him I'd be free that night because I was sending you to the docks and Captain to Delgado's. I never thought he'd ever do anything like this."

"Like trying to kill your oldest son?"

"He's never forgiven me for all that happened all those years ago. I thought he had, but he's never let it go."

"I don't give a shit what his problem is about whatever happened between you two and Willow's mother. That was the past. It was a lifetime ago. This is happening now. He sold us out a few weeks ago, not decades ago. He needs to pay for what he's done."

My father's face falls at those words. "He's my brother and your uncle. He's family, damnit. We don't kill family."

"We do now."

I don't give him a chance to talk me out of what I plan to do. Turning on my heels, I storm out of his office to go find the man responsible for my nearly dying on that dock, the man who knew what he'd done all the while I was threatening him just hours ago.

The library sits empty with only the book he'd been reading still on the floor as evidence he was ever in there. I race up the stairs and find his room empty. On my way back downstairs, I stop in the room I share with Willow to warn her she needs to stay there today since the last thing I need is to have to deal with her after I fucking kill Asher.

Our room is empty too. Where the hell is everyone in this house?

I take the stairs by twos and rush back to my father's office. The security chief from the front gate, a huge bald guy named Wilton, is standing in front of his desk pointing out toward the lawn and explaining something about the cameras around the estate.

"He's not in the house here. Where is he?" I ask my father, interrupting the bald behemoth.

The two men turn to look at me with horror in their expressions. What the hell is wrong with them now?

My father stands from behind his desk and puts his suit jacket on. "Wilton just told me about something strange he saw on the security tapes. Do you know why Willow would be back behind the old garden? Didn't you tell her to stay out of that area?"

"I don't know. Maybe. Who cares? So she wants to walk through dead bushes and old busted up statues. We have bigger problems right now."

For a second, the room falls silent and then my father winces. "Willow wasn't alone. Well, after she got past the old garden she wasn't."

He never gets to say Asher's name before I understand what's happened. I tear out of the office and run full speed throughout the house, throwing every door open and praying to God for Willow to be in one of those rooms.

But she's nowhere to be found.

I don't know if I'm more furious or terrified at what could be happening to her. If he lays a finger on her, I'll not only kill him for it.

I'll torture the motherfucker and enjoy every second of it.

CHAPTER TWENTY-THREE

illow

MY EYES SLOWLY OPEN TO SEE A ROOM I DON'T recognize in a place I'm sure I've never been before. Gone are the luxurious furnishings so common in the Rule home where I've lived for just over the past month.

This room reminds me of the inside of the home of an old woman who lived near us when I was growing up. Lots of white painted wood and knickknacks on the shelves in front of me make me wonder if I'm in Mrs. Golden's house again. Did my father somehow find a way to get me away from the estate?

My memory of today slowly unfurls in my mind, horrifying me with every detail that becomes apparent. It wasn't my father who brought me here. If only that had happened.

It was Asher.

But why?

I turn my head to search for him but see no one else nearby. The sun's still shining, so assuming I haven't been out cold for twenty-four hours, I can't be too far away from the house.

From Maddox.

From anyone who can help me.

My wrists are tied behind the chair I'm stuck in. I tug my arms to get free, but after an inch or so, I can't move them. The restraints are smooth, so I don't think they're rope, which would cut into my skin. Maybe a cord of some kind? Flexing my fingers, I try to reach the knot, but it's no use. My hands are too small.

Bending forward as far as I can, I see each of my ankles tied to a leg of the chair. I'm barefoot, which means Asher had to take my shoes off, and my legs are all scratched up. I let out a sigh of relief that he didn't take off my shorts or T-shirt. A shudder goes through me at the thought of that.

Why would he do this? I thought he liked talking to me about my mother. If he cared so much about her, why would he kidnap me?

"Are you awake? I thought you'd sleep the whole day away," he says behind me. A second later, he's standing in front of me, all smiles. "I was hoping you'd get up so we could talk."

"I'd like to get up, Asher. Please untie these restraints and let me go."

"Oh, I can't do that. I want to tell you all about your mother and me."

My frustration begins to unspool inside me, making control of my emotions next to impossible. As tears fill my eyes, I beg, "Please, Asher! I'm happy to listen to any story you want to tell me. Just let me out of this chair. I promise I won't leave. Honest."

He settles into a chair just like the one I'm in about six feet in front of me. His smile unnerves me, like he's not understanding that all of this that's happening right now isn't right. I want to scream, but I'm afraid what he'll do to me if I do.

Then again, I remember learning as a girl that if anyone ever tries to take you against your will, you should scream as loud as you can. If you can get their fingers near your mouth, you should bite harder than you've ever bitten anything before. And if you can cough or throw up, do it. Would-be attackers don't want to deal with a mess.

I try to work myself into vomiting, but there's nothing in my stomach. I skipped breakfast so I could meet with Asher this morning. There's irony there somewhere. I'm sure of it.

Maybe I can get him to come close so I can bite him. No, that won't work because I'm tied up. If I was free to run away, I'd bite his damn hand off if it got near my mouth.

That only leaves screaming. I have no idea where I am, so I don't know if anyone will hear me no matter how loud I get. Still, it doesn't matter. I need to scream just in case there's a single soul somewhere nearby who may hear me.

I tilt my head back and take a deep breath into my

lungs before letting out a sound a banshee would be proud of. I scream so loudly that Asher jumps up from his chair and begins to run around like a mad man.

"Stop! Stop yelling! Someone is going to hear you," he says frantically as he scurries back and forth across the room.

"Help! Someone help me! He's holding me here and he's going to kill me! Someone help me!"

Asher rushes toward me with rag from the table near the window. I smell the dirt and lemon furniture polish scent as soon as the fabric comes close to my nose. I can't let him put that in my mouth!

Shaking my head back and forth, I clamp my mouth shut, holding my lips tightly together as he attempts to stuff that filthy thing into my mouth. If I had any food in my stomach, the smell coming off that thing would absolutely make me puke.

He grabs my head and tries to stop me from moving, but I'm practically feral now. He won't do that without me putting up one hell of a fight.

"Just stop and you won't get hurt. I'll put that in your mouth so you can listen to what I have to say and not interrupt. That's it."

That's it? He sounds almost rational now as he tries to explain how in addition to kidnapping and restraining me, now he wants to gag me with some disgusting dust cloth.

I fight him as long as I can, and when he gets hold of my head and stops me from moving, I take advantage of his fingers coming close to my mouth as he tries to force that thing between my lips. I sink my teeth into his skin as hard I can, sure I'm going to bite the tip of his finger clear off in my utter terror.

Tearing his hand away as the tangy taste of his blood hits my tongue, he screams, "Fucking bitch! You bit me!"

"I'm not going to let you put that filthy rag into my mouth. I'll die from furniture polish poisoning!"

Expecting him to lunge at me, I'm surprised when he drops the cloth on the floor and calmly walks out of the room, as if any of this was just something he could brush off without a single word. I swivel my head around to see where he'll come from when he returns, and a minute later, he casually strolls back into the room holding what looks like a clean white washcloth in one hand and a piece of gauze in the other.

"Asher, please don't do this. You don't have to gag me. I won't scream again. I promise."

His dark eyes look so sad when he shows me his bloody finger. "I have to. You won't let me tell you my story, so I have to do this so I can."

I return to shaking my head desperately, but he gets the washcloth in this time. I try to push it out with my teeth and tongue, but I can't budge it. Immediately, my heart begins to race as I inhale and exhale out of my nose, my emotions spinning out of control.

Pleading with him, my words come out past the white cloth in a jumbled mess of muffled sounds that makes no sense. Over and over, I try to get his attention, but he's singularly focused on fixing his finger and then taking his seat again to tell me whatever this story is that he's so intent on sharing with me.

When he finally finishes attending to the bite I made in his forefinger, he takes a deep breath and smiles at me. "Now, let's get going on my story. It's important that you know what happened to explain why you're here."

I try to say that I'm there because he's crazy, but it comes out like how Charlie Brown's teacher sounds every time she says something to him. So I give up and try to calm myself. As much as I don't want this to be easy on Asher, hyperventilating and hurting myself isn't what I need to do.

What I need to do is find a way to get the hell out of here. As that doesn't seem like it can happen for the moment, I try to relax as he begins telling me this all-too-important story of his.

"I wish you could have seen your mother the way I knew her," he says in a dreamy, far away voice. "She was all I could think about from nearly the moment she came into my life. I don't know if I was capable of real love at that age, but eleven year old me loved her."

Even as he talks of loving her, his face is full of sadness. Frowning, he looks over at me and nods, like he knows I see that love or whatever he felt didn't make him happy like love should.

"She loved me too. She didn't know it, but she did. I know she loved me. I saw it every time we talked."

His eyes narrow in anger, and for a moment, I'm terrified that he's going to hurt me, but he just glares at me before continuing. "Stephen didn't believe she loved me. He was jealous. I saw from the moment she came to live with us he wanted her to be his little doll. She was too young for him. It was sick the way he looked at her sometimes. Sick. He was nearly eighteen and she was barely ten. My parents couldn't see it, but I could. It was right there in the open for anyone with eyes to see, and it made me sick. So I protected her."

I want to ask how he protected her, but I can't, so I wait and hope he explains what exactly he means. My father never mentioned anyone ever hurt her when she was a girl. She would have said something about that, wouldn't she?

Then again, she barely talked about her childhood, except to say her parents died in that accident when she was seven and she was a different person before she became an adult and met my father. Was that because something happened with Stephen that she couldn't bring herself to talk about, even to her husband?

"We were going to live together happily ever after. She was so excited about the ball. Her dress was the most beautiful one there. Pink with little ribbons around the neck. She was perfect, and she was mine. All mine."

I watch him as he shakes his head and wipes a tear away. He's crying. Why? After all these years, why does that make him sad?

God, I wish I could say something he could understand! I make a noise that I hope he understands means I want to hear more, but it's as if he's lost in his own little world of the past and can't even hear me. I can't wave my hands or stomp my feet to get his attention, so I have no choice but to wait until he finally feels he wants to continue the story of that night he took my mother to the Rule ball.

Asher shakes his head violently, bringing him back to the present. He runs his hand through his hair and takes another deep breath, letting it out in a rush.

"Stephen ruined everything. I should have known he would. He'd left the house for months before the ball. Off living his life like he never cared at all about her or me. But he came back that night and ruined everything for me."

For a moment, he stops, and then Asher says, "That's why you're here with me now. Payback. He took something from me, so I'm taking something from him. Well, not him because he has nothing now that every woman he's ever cared about is gone. Serves him right. I told him I'd make him pay for taking Cate away from me."

He continues to ramble on, focusing on Maddox's mother Victoria, and I can't help but wonder if he had a part in her death. Nobody has ever wanted to tell me exactly how she died. Is it possible he could have done something to her?

But he's been gone for years. So how could Asher have had any part in Victoria's passing?

All of this runs through my mind until Asher shakes his head again to clear his thoughts. "I can't think about that now. Today is to tell you what happened so you can know and you can understand how Stephen ruined everything."

Through the rag still stuck in my mouth, I try to ask him what he means, but he can't understand me. I'm not even sure he understands himself now. Something's snapped in him. I don't know when or why, but he's not the same person I've been speaking to since the ball.

"Cate and I had a beautiful night planned. It was going to be her first time, you know. She had saved herself for me. All for me," he says with pride, patting his hand over his heart. "I was the one who was going to have her for the first time. Stephen knew that."

My heart sinks as the reality of what he's about to say dawns on me. Did Maddox's father rape my mother? Is that what happened that night at the ball?

I can't stop the tears that fill my eyes at the very thought. They make Asher look like some horrible water-logged version of the monster he is, and I close my eyes so I don't have to look at him anymore.

"I had it all planned. We'd dance all night, and then afterward, we'd go up to that room no one ever used. I made sure it had been cleaned and looked perfect for us. If only I hadn't told Stephen about it first. I thought I could trust him. He's my brother, and he turned on me. He's the reason she ran away before she could give herself to me."

Through my tears, I see Asher put his head in his hands, and a second later, I hear him begin to sob. I can't understand most of what he says as he cries, but over and over one word comes out loud and clear.

Cate.

"She ran away from me that night, and then

Stephen told our father lies to get him to send me away too. I would never hurt her. I loved her. She was mine. She'd been mine since the moment she came to this house."

Asher drops his hands from his face and screams, "She was meant to give herself to me that night, but Stephen ruined it! He ruined all my plans because he was jealous. He wanted her for himself. I'd watched as he waited and waited for her to get old enough, but she was saving herself for me! Me! I was the one she wanted. Not him!"

Fear rushes through me at this change in him. He's no longer talking to me like I'm Willow or even anyone he even recognizes. I have no idea what he'll do next now that he's reliving that night and can't control his emotions.

My tears roll down my cheeks and onto the washcloth as my own fear and sadness mix together. He's going to spin out of control at any second, and then what will happen?

Suddenly, he screams, "You owe me! You took her away from me, and then you made Father cut me out of the will. You owe me, and I want what's due to me!"

Oh my God! He thinks I'm Stephen. He's going to kill me right here in this house God only knows where and this is where I'll die.

Alone. With a crazy man.

Why didn't I listen to Maddox? I should have listened when he told me never to speak to his uncle again. I should have listened.

CHAPTER TWENTY-FOUR

M addox

PACING UP AND DOWN THE HALLWAY, I IMPATIENTLY wait for my father and that giant security guy of his to figure out where Asher took Willow. For fifteen minutes, they've discussed every possible place they could be, Wilton radioing the other guys on the security team to check every square inch of the property as fast as they can.

And still nothing. No clue where she could be.

"I'm going to fucking kill him," I mumble as I pass the office door.

"Not now, Maddox," my father says in that tone of frustration I hear far too often. "I'm trying to figure out where they could be. If they aren't on the property, then where else could he go? He hasn't been back here in years. A hotel?"

Wilton immediately dismisses that idea with a shake of his enormous bald head. "We've checked all the local ones and nobody's seen him at any of them. He's got to be here hiding somewhere or someplace he knows he can hide out in and be safe."

My father hangs his head. "If he's not here, then where? It's not like there are a lot of homes around here."

I start off pacing down the hallway again when I hear him let out a yelp. "What? What's going on?" I ask as he comes toward me with Wilton following close behind.

"The house in Sherman. Your great-grandmother's house. It hasn't been used for years, but Asher would know about it. We need to check there before anywhere else."

"How far is it?"

"Half hour. Tops."

Heading down the hallway toward the front door, I try to keep my rage in check when I say to him, "Then he has thirty minutes more to live. And if he hurt one hair on her head, I'm going to chop him up into tiny fucking pieces with a goddamned wood chipper."

THE LITTLE WHITE HOUSE SET BACK FROM THE ROAD looks exactly like the kind of place a guy like Asher would take someone. Hidden just enough from the rest of the homes nearby, it looks like some old lady would live here. Vacant for more than twenty years, it's still livable because four times a year, the housekeeping staff at the estate comes over and gives the place a good dusting, according to my father.

I've never been here in my life, but given how small it is compared to the home I grew up in, I'm not surprised. The Rules don't like to admit any member of the family, including my mother, ever came from such modest beginnings. Great-grandmother or not, the woman who once lived here would have come to our house for any gatherings, not the other way around.

As far as I'm concerned, this will be the first and last time I see this place. All I want to do is get Willow out of here and get her the hell back to the house where she belongs.

"Don't hurt him unless you have to," my father whispers to Wilton before turning to look at me. "Understand?"

I shake my head, willing to let him know just how much I don't fucking understand this time. "No. Why the fuck should I treat him different than any other person who's crossed me? He's got my wife in there. He should consider himself lucky if I only kill him with one fucking shot. He deserves to have me torture him until I feel like I'm ready to let him die."

Out of the corner of my eye, I see Wilton glance over at me and nod. He gets it. Asher has broken the goddamned rules, including the big one not to fuck with a man's wife. Killing him is my right. My father doesn't understand that because he's letting family ties or some ridiculous memory of them as boys cloud his judgment.

ABBI COOK

And this time I'm not going to let him force me into doing something he wants instead of what I want.

Hearing me say no to him for possibly the first time in my life registers in his eyes getting wide, like he can't believe what I just said, but it only takes a second for that to fade away, leaving him scowling at me. If he wants this fight, he can have it.

But he won't win. Not this time.

"I won't have you killing my brother. He's your uncle. We don't kill family," he says sternly. As if that's going to be enough to stop me this time.

"No, you don't kill family. I haven't spent an hour with Asher without wishing I didn't have to. He's no one to me, and I warned him to stay away from Willow." I turn to point at the house behind us. "He's got my wife in there. You decided you wanted me to marry her, so now you get to reap what you sow. She's my wife, and that means I protect her. That's my fucking job. I warned him not to ever talk to her again. He didn't listen. I don't give a fuck who he is. He has to pay for what he's done."

Even as I say that, every part of my body aches at the thought of what he may have actually done to harm her. I never meant to be anyone's protective husband, but now that I am, I can't stop what I feel.

"I'm done talking. You can stay outside here with Wilton and discuss how you wish your brother didn't make the mistakes he's made doing this, or you can come in and help me get Willow the hell out of there. Either way, I don't fucking care. I'm going in."

They don't get a chance to answer before I start

266

marching toward the house. There's a front door and a side door, so since I don't know where he's got her, I choose the side door. Hopefully, that takes me through a kitchen or pantry and not into the room where he has her. I'd rather her not get caught up in what's about to happen.

I give the doorknob a jiggle and find the door unlocked. Surprised, I wonder for a moment if he's expecting me. Drawing my gun, I ease the door open with my foot, thankful when it opens wide without making even a single creaking noise.

Just as I hoped, the door led me into a room off the kitchen, some kind of mudroom or something. I stop dead at a sound I recognize all too well—the sound of someone crying through a gag.

Every inch of me goes on red alert, prepared to kill him and dice him up into tiny fucking pieces merely for gagging her. Behind me, my father and Wilton creep into the kitchen and spread out through the doorways that lead to two different rooms.

I hear Asher talking, but he's making no sense.

"You don't have to say anything. Just know that I never forgot you, Cate. I know what Stephen told you, but he lied. I would never hurt you. Never! I loved you. You were my Cate. My sledding partner. The person I could tell anything to. You were safe with me. Tell me you know that, though. Tell me you never doubted that and I can be happy."

The son of a bitch has lost his mind. He thinks he's kidnapped Willow's mother instead of her. I make my way toward the sound of his voice and stop in the doorway to the dining room. He's standing over her talking nonsense while she's staring up at him, tears streaming down her face as she sobs into a washcloth stuffed in her mouth.

Wilton or my father make a noise in the room next to this, and Asher turns his back to face that way. Seeing my chance to get Willow free, I run in and bash him in the back of his skull with the butt of my gun, sending him crashing to the ground and crying out in agony.

"It's okay, honey. I got you," I say, trying to keep my calm as I rip that fucking washcloth out of her mouth.

"He's crazy, Maddox! He thinks I'm your father one minute and then my mother the next. I thought he was going to kill me," she sobs as I get the restraints off her wrists and ankles.

I pick her up into my arms and spin around to see Asher just getting to his feet. In a flash, he grabs a candlestick off the dining room table, so I take aim and shoot a single bullet through the middle of his forehead. He collapses to the floor in a heap, dead.

Willow buries her head in my shoulder and cries, but I feel nothing but relief at that bastard's end. My father runs over to his brother and falls to his knees to take him in his arms, full of regret for whatever happened between them, I'm sure.

"I'm going to take Willow out of here," I say to Wilton standing in the doorway to the other room.

Cradling her in my arms, I walk out the way I came in, and when I take my first step out into the sun, Willow picks her head up to look at me. "I'm sorry I didn't listen to you, Maddox. You were right."

My anger at Asher for what he did begins to seep into my feelings for her, and I simply shake my head without saying a word. I don't want to get into that right now. She should have listened to me. Not only because it would have protected her from him but because I told her not to speak to him. The fact that she didn't and went against everything I said to her nearly got her fucking killed.

"I need to put you down to open the door," I say flatly when we get to the car, struggling to keep my emotions in check.

She nods and smiles at me in that sweet way I like, but I force myself to look away. I don't have control of anything I'm feeling now, good or bad, and I can't trust myself, even with her.

Fuck, especially with her.

I ease her into the backseat and close the door without saying a word. Since she's Willow, she can't stop herself from asking me a question or a hundred of them, so she sticks her head out the window and quietly asks, "Are you going to get in trouble for what happened in there?"

"No," I answer, shaking my head at how naïve she truly is. "We'll handle all of this and nobody will be the wiser. I doubt anyone will even know anything happened in there."

That makes tears well up in her eyes again, and she says, "I screamed as loud as I could hoping someone would hear me and come save me from him. That's why he put that washcloth in my mouth."

I look up and down the deserted road and shake my head again. "Nobody was hearing you scream."

"Please don't be mad at me, Maddox. I just wanted to hear him tell me stories about my mother. I didn't know he was a bad guy."

"But I did," I say, finally unable to hold back anymore. "I told you to stay away from him, and you went against what I said and did it anyway. You could have gotten yourself killed, Willow. If I didn't get here in time, who knows what he might have done. He was out of his fucking head. Do you think he would have stopped in time to figure out he shouldn't hurt you? Because if you do, you're as stupid as you are naïve."

I know what I'm saying is cruel, but I can't stop the words as they come tumbling out of my mouth on way too much fucking emotion. Nobody has ever made me feel as torn up as she has. I never wanted a goddamned wife to start with, and I fought caring anything for her. I don't know how she did it, but she got inside me, and just the thought of her being hurt by anyone, family or not, makes me so fucking crazy I don't know what to do.

She doesn't say another word and sits quietly in the back seat while we wait for Wilton and my father. I'm not sure what's waiting for me from him, but if he has any sense, he won't try anything with me after what happened inside that house.

A half hour later, the two of them walk out silently, Wilton's arms and shirt covered in dirt. I don't need to wonder what they did with Asher, and thankfully, Willow doesn't ask either. Maybe she isn't as naïve as I thought after all.

They don't say a word when they reach the car, so I slide into the backseat next to her and close my eyes. As the car begins to roll, I feel her rest her head against my shoulder.

Thank God I got there in time. I don't know what I would have done if I hadn't.

I don't know what to do with the emotions Willow brings out in me. My anger rises with every mile we travel back to the house, overwhelming everything else she makes me feel, and I come to the obvious conclusion I can't deny anymore.

I'm not the man for someone as soft as her.

CHAPTER TWENTY-FIVE

*W*illow

I PUSH AROUND THE FOOD ON MY PLATE, NOT really hungry like I haven't been for over a week. Each evening, I sit on my side of the long dining room table while Stephen sits at the head of the table more than six feet away. It's about as close as I imagine he feels like he wants to be to me since we eat in silence each time.

No one ever joins us, especially Maddox. Since we returned to the house nine days ago, he's been absent every day and doesn't come in until the middle of the night. I hear him when the bedroom door opens, and I feel the mattress move when he gets into bed, but he says nothing to me. I smell the liquor on him and what I've imagined is someone's perfume too, and then he falls asleep while I lie there staring up at the ceiling in the darkness, afraid to close my eyes and see the sight of Maddox shooting that bullet through Asher's forehead that rushes back into my mind every time I think I might be able to get even a few minutes of sleep.

Not that I've tried to say anything to him.

I don't know what words I can think of that will make things better. I know he's angry with me about what happened with Asher. He blames me for doing specifically what he told me not to do. I guess I could apologize again, but after the first few times that day got me no response from him, I just stopped.

I knew what would happen if he found out I went against his orders, and I did it anyway. Now I'm paying the price.

His silence is worse than any yelling. I've always been someone who thought being screamed at was horrible, but being ignored is so much worse. Now I know that.

"Are you feeling okay?" Stephen asks, surprising me out of my thoughts.

"Just not hungry, I guess."

He falls silent again, back into our usual dinner routine, and I push the roasted fingerling potatoes around my plate again. I wish I could eat. My stomach is always queasy lately, but I'd give anything to have a full meal.

"I'm sorry for what my brother did, Willow. I should have sent him away as soon as he came back here the night of the ball. I sensed he had an unhealthy attachment to you from that night on, but I didn't want to admit the truth."

As unusual as it is for Stephen to talk to me, my curiosity gets the better of me and I have to ask about what Asher said to me back at that house. "Why did he say that you ruined everything? He made it seem like you hurt my mother. Is that true? Did you hurt her?"

Sadness fills his expression as he slowly shakes his head. "I could never hurt her. I loved your mother. I told you. She was the sweetest person I've ever met in my life. I tried to protect her from my brother. I don't think he meant to hurt her either, but he had problems. Asher always had problems, even as a little boy. It's like he was born troubled. His problems would ebb and flow, and when they weren't so bad, we all told ourselves that things would be okay. But they were never really okay. He was never really okay."

"He said she ran away that night of the ball. Why? Did something happen to her?" I ask, my heart in my throat as I say those words.

Stephen nods sadly and looks away toward the windows where the July night is just falling. "He had this idea that they were going to live happily ever after. That was never going to happen. Very few Rules get happily ever afters, but especially Asher. I caught him in the bedroom with her that no one ever used. He had her pinned onto the bed and she was crying and begging for him not to do what he was doing. I pulled him off her, but I was too late. He'd already gone too far. She couldn't forgive him or me, and in truth, she shouldn't have. She ran away that night, and I never saw her again."

My heart hurts when I hear that, and I want to lash out or cry or something. I don't, though. He's already suffering from losing his brother and obviously still misses my mother, so what use would it be to pile more on top of him?

I still have one more question, though. "Was it merely a coincidence that you demanded me as payment for my father's debts?"

Again, Stephen shakes his head. "No. I didn't force him to incur those debts, but I knew he had a daughter with Cate. I was likely never going to get paid back, and I couldn't kill him, even though that's what a man in my position would usually do with someone like your father. So I decided I could take you and have you come to live here as my daughter-in-law. Maddox didn't want a wife, but you could have all the things I wished for your mother. It was selfish, but that's who I am, so that shouldn't surprise anyone."

"Why couldn't you kill my father if that's what you would usually do to someone in his situation?"

For the first time in so long I forgot what he looks like happy, Stephen smiles. "You don't kill people who mean the world to someone you love. Your mother may be gone, but the guilt would haunt me for the rest of my life if I killed your father, even if she didn't haunt me herself."

His kindness touches me, so I do what I've meant to do since that day out at the house. "I'm sorry for what happened to Asher. I don't think Maddox knows to do anything else when things like that happen. He's all emotion trapped inside a person who thinks he shouldn't feel anything."

I don't get a response to that, at least not a verbal one, but Stephen nods like he agrees with me on my assessment of Maddox. I'm not sure I'm right when I think of him that way, but it's the way I see him after all that's happened.

As I stand to leave the table, I wonder about Stephen's happily ever after. What happened to Victoria Rule? Looking at him now, I have a hard time thinking he could have been behind her death.

Or maybe it's that I just don't want to think about him like that anymore.

Like every night, I turn off the TV and stare up at the ceiling while my eyes grow accustomed to the darkness once again. The red numbers on the clock appear in my peripheral vision, and I turn my head to see it's a little after three a.m.

As usual, Maddox isn't home yet.

I'm so tired and want nothing but to sleep. My eyes feel so heavy. All I want to do is let them close, but if I do, I'll see that moment in time when Asher's life ceased to be. I can't see that again. The sight will haunt me for the rest of my life.

After all these nights fighting against sleep, I can't hold out anymore. My fear is overcome by sheer exhaustion, and I drift into nothingness.

. . .

I SIT UP IN PANIC, SWEAT RUNNING DOWN THE SIDES of my face and over my neck. Asher's face and that hole in his head is branded on my brain, and in the darkness of the room, I can't see anything else. I force my arms out in front of me to push that terrible vision away.

As I come back to life, I sense someone next to me in the bed. Beside me, Maddox sits watching me, his face highlighted by a stream of light coming through the window.

"You frightened me. Why didn't you say anything when you saw me awake?"

"I have nothing to say."

His words come out clipped, like he doesn't want to even utter that simple sentence. In the dim light that illuminates his face, I see nothing more than disdain for me.

The same expression I've seen on his face since that day he killed Asher.

"When did you get home?" I ask, not really caring about the answer but wanting so many others to questions I haven't dared to ask yet.

"I'm tired. I'm going to bed."

He strips out of his shirt and tosses it onto the floor in front of the bed but doesn't bother to even take his pants off before he lies down and turns his back to me. If the iciness in his voice didn't clue me into how he really feels, I certainly couldn't miss the meaning of that gesture.

The silence that grows between us is like a wall right down the middle of the bed we share, cutting me off from him with no chance to get around the barrier. I'm overwhelmed by the loneliness that surrounds me with him just inches away.

"I'd like to talk to you, Maddox," I whisper into the darkness and hope to hear something kind come back to me.

My wish isn't granted, though. "I'm not in the mood for talking, Willow. Good night."

"Please," I beg, desperate to end the isolation I feel.

He doesn't move to look at me or roll over when he says, "Not tonight. Go to sleep."

I've heard people say they can pinpoint the moment when something changes inside them right before they do something they never thought they were capable of. I never really believed that because I don't think people change who they fundamentally are.

I'm someone who's too kind. I've been told this and I know it myself. That's just who I am. I give too many chances, usually hurting myself when I do, but it's in my DNA to be good to people. Too good.

But at the moment when he refuses to even look at me, choosing to ignore my pleas for us to at least try to talk to one another after over a week, something snaps inside me and instantly I feel like I can't do this anymore. I'm still the same person I've always been—sweet little Willow—but now everything else inside me is different.

Swinging my legs off the bed, I begin walking toward the door, unsure where I'm headed or what I'll do but sure of one thing. I don't want to be in this room anymore tonight.

"Fine. Don't talk to me."

I open the door and hear Maddox behind me ask, "Where are you going? It's the middle of the night."

Braver than I've ever felt before, I spin around and snap, "Out! You know, the place you always go every night. So go to sleep, Maddox. I'm going out."

I don't wait around to see his expression, but I can't help but feel delight at the thought that it's one of shock. I've argued with him before and certainly tried to stand my ground, but even I know something's different about the way I just said that.

Like I don't need or want his permission anymore. As if I finally found my own voice in this world I've been thrust into, and it's a defiant one.

Hurrying down the stairs, to where I have no idea, I head down the dark hallway toward the living room. Maybe I'll sit there for a few minutes to figure out what I want to do next. Halfway there, I decide I don't want to stay inside right now and spin around to make my way toward the front door.

I fling the door open and take a deep breath of humid night air. The temperature hasn't dipped below seventy degrees tonight, so it's warm enough for me to walk outside in just my shorts and T-shirt. My feet are bare, but that's no problem. The perfectly manicured grass of the Rule estate wouldn't dare have any of those picky star-shaped weeds to cut up the soles of my feet.

As I march around the front yard just past the driveway, I love the coolness of the night dew on the grass hitting my skin. I wiggle my toes and smile before stopping just as the thought of my mother sledding barefoot that night comes back to me.

Bare feet.

Everything in this place is full of constraints on me, so being barefoot feels like an act of rebellion. I understand why she and Asher didn't wear shoes that night. It's foolish, but I get it.

In a world where everything you do is dictated by others, choosing to break even one tiny, unspoken rule feels more incredible than I could have ever imagined. But I've broken more than one of those rules tonight. In addition to my bare feet, there's my refusal to accept Maddox's silence.

He wants to not speak to me so much? Then let him have all the time in the world not to hear me talk.

I find myself walking toward the back of the property for the second time, but now I'm not searching for Asher or stories about my mother. Now I just want to sit on top of that hill and claim one spot on this entire damn estate as mine. One single place where I can be happy, and one day when I can, I'll escape here like my mother did.

"Willow, what the hell are you doing?" Maddox calls out, breaking the night's silence and interrupting my thoughts.

Without looking back, I answer, "I'm going out

like I told you I was. Go back to bed, Maddox. I don't need to talk to you anymore."

God, I like how that sounds!

I trudge my way back to that old garden that creeped me out the first time I saw it, but now in the moonlight, it has an almost mystical feel to it that enchants me tonight. This time, I march through it liking the bushes that I think could once again grow if someone paid attention to them. Maybe that's what I'll do tomorrow. I'll start cleaning up this little area to see if anything will bloom here again.

A statue of an angel with her wings unfurled stands at the edge of the garden. Although much of her is chipped, her smile remains undamaged. I smile up at her as I pass and say, "It's a good night, isn't it?"

Her smile doesn't fade when I step out of the garden, and neither does mine while I make my way toward the hill. I hear Maddox behind me mumbling about something, probably angry he has to walk through some old garden filled with dead things. He didn't have to follow me. He could be happily sleeping in bed right now. It's not like he has anything he wants to say to me tonight.

"Where are you going?" he asks with more than a hint of irritation in his voice.

It threatens to ruin my walk to the place I want to be my own, so I turn around and hold my hand up to stop him. "You should go back to bed, Maddox. I'm not really interested in talking to you anymore now, so just go."

His longer legs make staying ahead of him for

much longer impossible, and he catches up to me too quickly as I hike up the side of the hill. Still wearing his pants he wore out tonight and with his shirt hanging open since he didn't bother buttoning it when he came after me, he looks odd in this place.

I look down at his feet as I struggle to keep pace up the hill and let out a sigh. "There are no shoes allowed on this hill."

Maddox tries to stop me, grabbing my arm. "What's wrong with you?"

Yanking it from his hold, I snap at him, "Nothing's wrong with me! I wanted to talk to you and you didn't want to talk, so I left. Now you're here and it seems like you want to talk, but I've got nothing to say to you, so you should go back to bed."

He shakes his head like none of this makes sense to him, but it makes perfect sense to me. The time for talking is over.

I lose my footing and catch myself with my hand on the grassy ground before climbing the last few feet to the top. Unlike the last time when I had to rest, I feel like I could run a marathon right now. This is my place here. No one else seems to give a damn about this part of the estate, and the only other person who did is dead, so now it's mine.

Maddox reaches me a few seconds later and looks around like the spot disgusts him. "Do you mind telling me what we're doing here in the middle of the night?"

I can't help but stare up at him in confusion. Why did he say we? What we does he think there is between the two of us? We are married and we share a bed each night, but other than that, there is no we with us. There's Willow alone and Maddox alone, just the way he wants it.

"We're not doing anything here. I'm out for a walk. I have no idea what you're doing here at all. And as for the we you mentioned, that doesn't exist. You exist and I exist, but there is no we that exists between us."

"What the hell are you talking about, Willow? What is all of this?" he asks, still not getting it.

I spread my arms out wide and twirl around in the humid night air. When I stop, I'm finally ready to say what's on my mind at this moment. He wants to know what the hell I'm talking about? Well, now he gets to hear it.

"This is my spot, Maddox. I doubt you've ever come here in your entire life, so I'm claiming it. You're in my little piece of the estate, and you know what? You don't get to talk to me like I'm some useless piece of shit you couldn't care less about. Not here. I wanted to talk to you because I've spent the last week and a half lonely and sad after what happened with Asher, but you shut me out. You iced me out like you always do because you don't care about me. Fine. But that's not what's allowed here."

Stopping to take a breath, I point down at the ground and shake my head. "Right here, I won't be treated like that. So why don't you just go back to the house where I know you'll be happy to show me every chance you get that you never wanted to marry me and you don't even give a damn about me? I'll be back eventually, but for now, I'm going to stay here in this spot and find a shred of fucking happiness in this miserable place you and your family call a home."

While I speak, his eyes grow wide, but I can't blame him. Not that he's known me for long, but in the nearly two months we've been together, I've never spoken to him like that. I'm not even sure I thought I had it in me to speak like that to him or anyone else before this.

I do now, though.

CHAPTER TWENTY-SIX

illow

MADDOX AND I STAND FACING ONE ANOTHER, HIM staring down at me in what looks like utter confusion and me staring up at him in nothing less than pure defiance. Sweet old Willow would have tried to get him to see her point of view. Not this Willow. This Willow on top of this hill doesn't give a damn if he doesn't understand what she means.

And no matter if I'm trapped on this estate for years to come, I've never felt so free in my life.

Finally, after what seems like an eternity, he says, "I don't *not* care about you, Willow. And I never meant to treat you like a piece of shit."

"Do you hear yourself? You don't *not* care for me. You never *meant* to treat me like a piece of shit. Just be honest, if not with me then with yourself. Look at how you've been toward me since you took me out of that house and there's the truth of how you feel."

Maddox looks away toward the house and shakes his head. "You don't know how I feel. No one knows."

"Yeah, I'm sure. You're just an enigma. Stop trying to make it seem like you're walking around with deep feelings for me. There's no one here but me, Maddox. Your father and your brothers aren't here to impress. It's just me here, so forget the act. There are no hidden feelings inside you. There's just the truth. You never wanted to be shackled to me, and you don't care about me any more than you care about that dried up old garden down there."

"Stop. Whatever this is, stop it," he says quietly, still refusing to face me or the truth.

I move around him so we're face-to-face again and see he looks genuinely unhappy about what I'm saying. "You don't need to pretend for me. I'm nobody to you, Maddox."

His eyes flash pure anger at me. "You're my fucking wife. What do you mean you're nobody to me? I killed my uncle for you, Willow. I disobeyed a direct order from my father and killed his fucking brother. You're not nobody to me."

"You act like you don't kill people all the time," I say, dismissing his newfound claims of affection. "That gunshot wound in your shoulder didn't happen because you were in the wrong place at the wrong time, like someone held up a convenience store and you got caught in the middle of things. I'm not stupid, Maddox. I hear stuff. You shouldn't force me to stay at this house if that's where you're going to talk about business, or whatever you do. So you killed a guy. So what? You didn't do it for me. If you had, you would want to at least talk to me since then."

I stop for a moment and then add, "You did it because that's who you are."

"I did it because he took you from me. I did it because you're my wife and I had to protect you. I tried to do that by telling you not to go near him again, but you didn't listen. So I did what I had to so you didn't get hurt. You have no idea what I felt when I did that. No idea."

For the first time in so long, I see the man I'm married to might actually be more than that ice cold creature who sleeps next to me each night. I want to know what he felt. I want to know that he feels something.

"Then tell me. Show me you don't hate me. Make me understand why you've been out every night since we got back from that house. Why do you want to be with other women if you care about me, Maddox?"

"There's no one else."

He says that as if just the words leaving his mouth makes it the truth. Like I'm too stupid to know what's been going on.

"Fine. Nice talk. You should go back to the house because I'm going to stay here."

Turning my back on him, I stifle the feeling that I need to cry. I don't need to cry. I want to enjoy this night on my hill and think about my mother being here all those years ago.

"Don't turn your back on me. I answered your question."

I know I shouldn't take the bait, but I can't stop myself from spinning around and facing him again. Of all the things he's going to lie about, I'm not going to tolerate this lie anymore.

"No, you didn't! You lied. Do you think I can't figure out what you do every night? Stop treating me like I'm stupid. I know what you do and you know what you do, so just admit it!" I scream.

For a long moment, he says nothing. I wait for him to speak, probably to tell me I don't know what I'm talking about, as I get angrier by the moment. His lies are bad enough, but this one hurts me the most.

"I'm not lying. There is no one else," he says calmly, ratcheting up my rage even more.

Finally, I push my hands against his chest and scream, "Yes, there is! Stop lying! I can smell their perfume on your clothes. You go out every night and fuck other women, just like you did after we were first married. Remember you saying you were going to live your life just like you always did? I remember, Maddox. I remember, so stop lying!"

Something in his expression changes before my very eyes, and he grabs my shoulders. Holding me in front of him, he explodes. "There is no one else! Just you, Willow. Just you! Why can't you just believe me when I say that?"

Partly in shock at how he's acting right now, I answer more truthfully than I want to. "Because I needed someone after what happened with Asher and you're always gone. Why would you be gone if you weren't sleeping with other women?"

"I couldn't be around you, okay? I couldn't. At first, I was just fucking angry. You did exactly what I told you not to do and ended up in that house with him," he says, practically seething with every word.

As much as his rage frightens me, I keep pushing because I need him to tell me the truth. I need to know why after he saved me from Asher he turned his back on me.

"So now you can't ever forgive me? That's why you go out every night?"

Maddox levels his harsh gaze on me and frowns. "I go out every night because I can't handle what happens when I'm around you. I thought my uncle was crazy for being like he was all these years later. I mean, who the hell cares for someone that much for so long? But then when I thought you could be hurt inside that house, something exploded inside me. I've never felt anything like this. It's like I can't control how I feel."

"So you have to stay away from me because you feel something for me? Is that what you're saying?" I ask, searching his face for some hint of caring.

His hands leave my shoulders and cradle my face. "I killed him because he hurt you. You're my wife, Willow. I love you."

For a second, I wonder if any of this is real, but I touch his hands on me and know it is. Maddox is here with me at my spot on my hill telling me he loves me.

"You love me? When did that happen?"

"I don't know. The moment I found out he took you away from me. Or maybe the moment I saw you tied to that chair and gagged. I don't know. All I do know is I didn't think twice about killing him, and I'd do it again if I had to. You're mine, Willow. My wife. Mine to protect. Mine because I love you."

"I never thought I'd hear you say those words to me, especially after what happened. You're never home. Do you miss me when you're gone?"

Maddox hangs his head and lets out a heavy sigh. "I miss you and then I drink as much as I have to and snort whatever there is around to make me not feel anymore."

"Why can't you just be with me?"

He turns away from me, and instantly I miss his touch. "I don't know how to deal with these feelings. I've never felt anything like this. And after all I've done, I don't expect you—"

I wait for him to finish his sentence, but he falls silent. I know what he's thinking, though. Touching him on the arm, I gently turn him around to face me. He doesn't want to meet my gaze, but I step closer so he doesn't have a choice.

"You don't expect me to care about you? Is that what you were going to say? I do care about you, Maddox. You saved me from Asher. I know I didn't listen to what you told me to do, but you came anyway."

"How could I not rescue you from him? Even if he didn't mean to, he hurt you. I couldn't just let him take you like that."

"Because you love me."

He doesn't answer but nods. I take his hands in mine and bring them back up to cradle my face. "I know it hasn't been a marriage made in heaven, but how could I not love someone who cared enough to save me like you did?"

"I'm sorry for all the shit I've put you through, Willow. You didn't deserve any of it."

And then his lips touch mine, and for the first time, we kiss like two people who truly care for one another. I close my eyes and revel in how good he feels when I slide my hands under his shirt.

"Come back inside," he says sweetly. "Come home with me."

He takes my hand and I don't fight him now. As he guides me down the hill, I look back and smile. I'll come back here again after tonight. This place isn't just where I think of my mother being happy anymore.

Now it's a place where I found happiness.

MADDOX STOPS ON HIS SIDE OF THE BED CLOSER TO the door, so I continue on. We walked back in silence, hand in hand down the hill, through that old garden, and in the door at the back of the house. I didn't mind the quiet, though, since it wasn't a lonely silence like I usually have in this place.

He stops me, pulling me back to where he sits on the bed. "Stay here with me."

I glance over his head at my side of the bed just inches away and then down at him. "Okay."

Opening his legs, he makes a space for me in between them and tugs me closer to him. His hands slide over my hips and come to rest against my ass, creating need wherever they touch.

"There's no one but you, Willow. I swear."

"Promise?"

A slow smile lights up his face. "I promise. And no more going out every night."

I can't hide my surprise at that unsolicited pledge. "Really?"

Pulling me to him, he holds me close and begins to undress me. "Really. And one more thing."

He stops before sliding my shirt over my head, so I quickly wriggle out of it so I can hear what this one more thing could be. "What's that?"

With a chuckle, he hooks his thumbs on the top of my shorts and tugs them down my legs. "We can talk about it later."

I kick them away from my feet and push him back onto the bed before climbing on top of him. "Tell me now. I want to know what the one more thing is."

Smiling up at me, he slides his hands down my back to cup my ass as he lifts his hips off the bed. His hard cock presses against my belly, making me wish he'd tell me what he was going to say and stop talking, all at the same time.

"It's hard to think when a beautiful, naked woman is on top of you," he says with a sexy grin.

"Please, Maddox."

He stuffs his hand into my hair and pulls me down hard so our mouths crash against one another in a kiss so full of need and desire that I nearly forget what I was asking him for a second ago. This feels like everything I've ever wanted the two of us together to feel like.

What I've always wanted to feel.

When he breaks the kiss, he leans away from me and smiles. "As of tomorrow morning, you don't have to stay here on the estate all the time. You can come and go as you please."

"Are you serious?"

I can't believe what he's just said. I can leave here and go see my father and have a life away from this house?

"Yes, but if I sense that you're in any danger at all, that will have to stop. At least for a time until things get better."

What he means by danger and why I'd be in any of that doesn't matter at this moment. All that matters is he trusts me to leave and come back.

"Oh, Maddox! Thank you!"

I plant kisses over his cheeks and forehead before he pulls my mouth back to his and kisses me like I'm the most important thing in the world to him. His tongue slides over my lips, teasing my tongue with promises of what's to come.

Whatever it is, I want it all.

My hands roam over his body, tearing at his pants to get them off, as his hands travel over my skin, exciting me with each touch. He's the same beautiful man I married that day just a few weeks ago, hard and muscular under me. Now I just see him differently because of all we've been through and all I know about him.

I feel him kick away his pants, and then we're naked, nothing between us as we offer all we have to one another physically. He forces my legs open with his knee, spreading me wide so he can enter me. His cock slides through my wet pussy, and then a second later, he fills me completely.

He moans into my mouth before positioning his hands on my hips. Moving me up and down on his cock, he sets the pace as I ride him. The slightest hint of my control fades into nothingness as he sinks his fingertips into my flesh and pistons into me.

"Ride my cock, baby. Let me see you come apart as I fuck you, Willow," he moans in a voice that sounds like it's coming from deep inside him.

I want that more than I want my next breath at this moment. He feels so good inside me, stretching my body to take every incredible inch of his cock. I silently beg to come with every thrust of him inside me. I ride him with abandon, breaking free of his iron hold on my hips. He moves his hands to cup my breasts, pinching my tender flesh with each time he sinks into my needy pussy.

My release begins with a tiny twinge inside me and unravels through my entire body until it reaches the very spot where his cock hits with each thrust. He lifts his hips one final time, and then it's as if fireworks explode behind my eyes. I collapse on top of him, my body still writhing against his as I ride him through every wave of my orgasm.

As I come close to the end and feel the tremors of pure ecstasy begin to subside, his cock twitches and floods my body with everything inside him. I feel his heartbeat racing beneath my cheek pressed against his chest, and then he takes a deep breath in and lets it out as he wraps his arms around me.

"My Willow."

Against his skin, I whisper, "I love you, Maddox."

And just like that, the entire world changes. Our entire world changes.

EPILOGUE

M addox

I watch Willow from a distance as she tends to that little garden she's brought back from the dead. Every day this spring, she trudged back there with those tiny garden tools I would have bet wouldn't do a damn thing, and inch by inch, she cleared out the brush and debris left from years of neglect.

She said that she wanted to get it ready before the baby came, so no matter how tired she felt in those days right before he was born, she woke up early and headed out there right after breakfast making that little space new again. Wearing a maternity dress and an enormous yellow sun hat that practically obscured her entire face, she kissed me on her way out, her hands filled with those garden tools and gloves, and each time told me she was getting close.

I never knew if she meant to giving birth or what she called the unveiling of the new garden she so lovingly tended to day after day. By the time she was almost finished, I was excited for both.

Holding my son in my arms, I whisper to him, "Time to go get Mommy. We've got a big day ahead of us."

Willow stands near the new pink rose bush I know is her favorite part of the garden and smiles when she sees us coming toward her. "I just have to give the roses a little water and then I'll be done," she says as she tilts her watering can toward the ground.

I stop just outside of the wrought iron fence and lift the baby up to my shoulder when he starts to cry. "Somebody is gassy today. My father is going to love it if he burps through the whole christening," I joke.

She finishes her watering and sets the green plastic can on the ground before coming over to us. Walking behind me, she nuzzles Sebastian's little face in my shoulder. "Is my little man full of gas today? Who's Mommy's gassy little baby?" she asks in that sweet voice she uses only for him.

"Your father is just going to have to understand that his grandson is having an off day. That's all."

I smile down at her before planting a tiny kiss on her lips. "The garden looks great. If I'd never seen it in the condition it was in, I'd never know it was once all weeds."

"It just needed some tender loving care. A little attention and it bloomed just like I knew it would."

As she takes Sebastian from my arms, she kisses

me again. "I think my mother would be happy I did this. At least I hope she would."

Whether or not her mother would be happy about what she's done with this tiny patch of land I have no idea. All I do know is she made something ugly and unloved beautiful again. Not everyone can do that, and it has nothing to do with those tiny tools she insists on using.

Willow cares, and when she does, wonderful things happen.

"We better get inside and get ready. My father's already reminded me three times this morning what time the christening starts. I think he might be a little excited."

Willow chuckles at my understatement. "Well, it's a big day. Today the world gets to meet the next generation of Rules. You know how serious your father is about that stuff."

She nuzzles the baby's face and kisses his forehead. "But to me, he's just my little boy, isn't he? Mommy's little boy with the beautiful brown eyes, Sebastian. Ready to get dressed? You're the star of the show today, little man."

As we walk across the grass toward the house, my arm around her while she holds our son, I think back to the first time I saw him looking up at me with those dark eyes so similar to mine. I knew right then and there I didn't want his life to turn out like mine had, at least before Willow came here. Let him be like her instead of hard like me.

Or if that's not possible, at least I hope he never doubts how much I love him and his mother.

My father beams a smile that practically lights up the ballroom, happily thanking every guest as they walk through the door. I watch him and can't remember a time before this that he was ever this happy.

His mood today even beats the day I gave him the news that Willow had given birth to a son. The heir he so desperately thinks this family needs. He's not right about that, but I haven't bothered to tell him what's going to happen once he's gone. Better to let him think everything will go on as he has planned, with me at the head of the family business and my son waiting in the wings.

That's not my plan, though. He still clings to the way his father taught him, but that will change someday soon. Now that I have Willow and Sebastian, those old-fashioned ideas just don't work anymore.

Not in business and not with family.

Willow taps me on the forearm, rousing me out of my daydreams of our life in the future. "I think the grandfathers are the happiest people in this room. My father looks better than I've seen him look in ages, and I think your father's face may crack with all this smiling he's doing. I think he'd give you the moon if you asked for it today."

I smile and lean over to kiss her softly on the lips

as our son sleeps in her arms. "Unfortunately, I don't think I get any of the credit for his good mood. It's all you and Sebastian."

A pink blush colors her cheeks, and she looks up at me. "You were part of this, you know. That means you should get some of the credit."

"I was there for the fun part. You did all the work for the past nine months, and Sebastian here is the superstar in my father's eyes just for being him. In the pecking order, I think I'm the low man on the totem pole."

That sounds like I'm unhappy about something, but I'm not. Sebastian's birth has made my father happy because he feels like he can rest easy now. The future is set, in his mind.

For me, having Sebastian has made me happier than I ever thought possible. Months of worrying through Willow's pregnancy led to relief that I didn't lose the only woman I have ever loved and my firstborn son when the big day finally came.

I couldn't be unhappy now if I tried. What a difference just under twelve months can make.

"He's going to want us to get up on the dais so he can introduce Sebastian to everyone," Willow says in my ear.

"Probably. He does have that showman's flair to him. My father loves the presentation."

She smiles sweetly and nods. "I remember the last time I was up there in front of everyone. I was scared, confused, and unsure why all those people would care about me at all. I'm just happy Sebastian won't have to feel that today."

Her mention of the ball makes my mind flash back to those early days of us together. That she forgave me for all I did then still amazes me. I didn't deserve her forgiveness any more than I deserve to be this happy.

I never forget that fact either.

"So, does this happen with all christenings in this family, or only the firstborn son?" she asks before looking over toward where a crowd of people have begun to take their seats across the room from us.

I glance over at where my four brothers stand, knowing they're happy to have my father's attention off them for today. But their burden as the sons of Stephen Rule is merely different than mine, no less heavy.

Returning my focus to Willow and our son, I smile at how much effort has been put into making today the event of the season for my father. "Why? Are we having any more?" I ask with a chuckle, happy to oblige in the making of more babies if she wants to try for another child.

Or three or four.

Another blush covers her cheeks, making her more beautiful than ever. "I was just wondering. It seems like a lot of pomp and circumstance for a baby."

"Just one of the mysteries of the Rule family. Get used to it. You're one of us, and Sebastian is too, now."

"Well, I wouldn't be against the idea of a little girl," Willow says as the baby begins to stir. "Maybe a child that looks like I had any part in her DNA."

As she lifts Sebastian up, I can't deny he looks like me. With dark hair and brown eyes like mine, he's the spitting image of me and doesn't seem to have gotten anything from her. That may change in time, but it could be nice to have a little girl who looks just like her mother too.

"You let me know when you want to get started on the next one, and I'll be there with bells on."

"I bet you will be," she says with a giggle. "But what if it's another boy?"

"Then we'll just have to keep trying. I'm all in if you are."

I see my father walking toward us and take Willow's hand in mine. "I think it's show time. Ready?"

She squeezes my hand, and even though I sense she'd love to be anywhere but here as my father shows off his grandson, she gives me one of her soft smiles. "As long as it's the three of us, I'm good."

"No matter what happens, it's the three of us. Together."

I can't tell what the future may hold for us. I'm the same man I've always been, even if I'd willingly die to protect Willow and Sebastian. I'm a Rule, and that will never change.

But for this one afternoon in June, I'm just a proud father of the first son in the next generation of the Rule family and a man madly in love with the woman who saw that even a villain deserved love.

. . .

THE NEXT VILLAINS CLUB BOOK IS COMING! Preorder your copy of Take (Villains Club #2) and have it on release day! And be sure to sign up for Abbi's newsletter to make sure you don't miss anything, including new release giveaways!

ABOUT THE AUTHOR

Abbi Cook grew up wondering if she was different because she always wanted to know more about the villain than the hero in the stories she read. When she got older, she found there were others in the world like her and devoured their writing, loving every dark word. She's written her own tales for years, but in 2019 she decided it was time to take the next step and publish them. She's never looked back since that day.

Readers can find her at her website at abbicook.com, on FB and IG, and through email at abbicookauthor@gmail.com